TO WIN HIS WIFE

BRIDGER BROTHERS
BOOK ONE

KATE CONDIE

Copyright © 2023 by Kate Condie

Cover design 2023 by Wynter Designs

All rights reserved.

No part of this book may be reproduced in any form or by any electronic or mechanical means, including information storage and retrieval systems, without written permission from the author, except for the use of brief quotations in a book review.

PROLOGUE

They'd done it. Gotten married. There was little their parents could do now. Fenna clung to Will's hand, a giddy smile splitting her face. She wanted to laugh just thinking of it, but she kept her voice low as they traversed the forest. Normally, she would be frightened to be in the woods once the sun started its descent, but not with Will at her side.

She glanced at their hands, fingers interwoven. They hadn't any rings, but Will would remedy that soon enough. She glanced up at him, tall and handsome. Growing up, she never would have dreamed of a secret marriage to Will.

As an older son of the beloved Bridger family, he was always too busy with work or school to pay her much mind. As the daughter of the Bridgers' longest-standing employee, Fenna did the same until she'd turned sixteen and Will came home for the summer. Had she changed, or him? Just now she wanted to know, to be able to tell her children the reason their parents stopped being almost-siblings and became lovers.

"Will?"

He squeezed her hand and turned to her, that broad smile on his face. Surely that would have been reason enough for her to fall in love, but no, he'd had that smile all along.

"Was I much changed when you came home this summer?" Barely three months and she could no longer recall who she'd been before their romance had begun.

Will stopped and released her hand, sliding that arm around her waist and pulling her close to him. "You were a woman." Fenna might have sighed, but Will continued, "And you'd grown into those teeth."

Fenna scoffed and gave his shoulder a playful smack. She tried weakly to push out of his hold, but he doubled his grip, sliding his other hand up her neck, his thumb tracing her jaw and his fingers weaving into her hair. "But it was that Sunday when Greg Anderson was paying you too much attention that really changed things."

Fenna recalled the ride home from the chapel that Sunday. Will had interrogated her regarding Greg's intentions, had said he was too old for her, that he wasn't serious in his courtship. She was used to the Bridger boys coming to her defense, telling her which boys were scoundrels and which were appropriate. But Will's questions had held a different air.

"You were jealous." She lifted to her toes and kissed his chin.

He ducked his head, pressing his forehead to hers, the warmth of his breath heating her lips. "Why do you think I refused to go back to school without you?"

His jealousy made something well up in her, not just pride, but a sense of belonging. As long as she could remember, it had been only her and Pa, and she longed to belong to something bigger than one old man, even if he was the most dear papa any girl could ask for. To belong to the Bridgers by law rather than just in love. Will's jealousy settled a need inside her, gave her roots she didn't even know she'd been missing.

Fenna brought their lips together, his soft mouth reaching hers and the rough stubble of his jaw scratching her chin. That was life, smooth and prickly all in one. But Will was hers now and she would never be alone again. Wherever he went in this wide world, he'd take her right along with him.

They passed through the brush oak, staying on the path to save her skirts. As the sun dipped below the tree line, an eerie darkness spread through the once-cheery forest. A bit of her thrill dimmed at the prospect of arriving home and explaining to her Pa they'd gone against his wishes and married in secret. They'd have to do it again for Will's folks.

Mrs. Bridger was the closest thing to a mother Fenna had ever known. She had precious few memories of her ma — the few she had were hazed with uncertainty. Were they real images, or had she conjured them from Pa's stories? The fact was, she was equally anxious to tell either side about their rebellious decision.

A nicker further along the path made her heart leap into her throat. Will froze, and Fenna moved only to grip his arm with her free hand. He stepped in front of her, his arm winding behind him as she clung to it.

"Ho! Folks are about!" Will called into the forest. The last thing they needed was to be shot on accident by a hunter. It wouldn't be the first time a body had been hit by an inexperienced boy trying to prove his mettle.

"Will? That you?" Pa's voice was unmistakable. Fenna had barely managed to swallow before he spoke again. "Is Fenna with you?"

Will glanced back and sucked in a breath. There was no

use denying it now. He heaved a sigh and called back, "Yes, it's us."

He was met with a silence more foreboding than the fact that Pa suspected they were together. What else had he discovered?

Soon enough, Pa's horse, Red, rounded a corner and Pa came into view. Even in the darkness, Fenna could see the deep frown lines on his face, shadowed by his worn hat with its familiar drooping brim. He reined in Red and slid down from the saddle.

"Is it true?" He tossed the reins over a branch.

Fenna nodded, but it was Will who spoke. "We are married in the sight of God. Where I go, she goes."

Pa knocked the lantern from Will's hand and spat into the red dirt that nourished the hills. "You dare?"

Will straightened his back and, were it not for his admirable self-control, Fenna might think he was readying for a fight. "We tried telling you."

And Pa had rejected their plea as quickly as he'd just spat on the ground. Said Fenna was too young and Will had too much schooling ahead of him.

Will leaned closer to Fenna, but he couldn't block Fenna from her Pa's harsh glare as he ground out, "And I believe we told *you*."

Fenna stepped to the side and took Will's arm. "Pa, I'm old enough, and it's done. Can you just be happy for us?"

"Happy?" her father shouted, startling a bevy of pheasants from their nests. "Why would you even ask permission if you were going to ignore it? Such insolence, and from you?"

His words were as harsh as a slap. He'd said more than once how she'd impressed him with her good ways, not giving him half the trouble other children gave their parents, the Bridger boys included. She was his only family; he had no other children to take joy in, and it wouldn't do to disappoint him.

"I love him." The words, though they should have been shouted from the treetops, sank into the twiggy underbrush, weak and lifeless.

When a crack came from deeper in the woods, all three gazes snapped to the trees, searching for what, or who, had made the noise. Another sounded from the other side, and Will's head swiveled from one side to the other.

Fenna swallowed. Tramps sometimes frequented these woods, poaching the animals and selling their skins out of season. She'd never have come alone, but being with Will gave her what she feared was an unfounded sense of security.

"Who goes?" Pa's voice held a tremor that even Will probably didn't catch, but he wasn't Pa's blood, Pa's life. Hot tears turned her vision blurry. Tears. And on the day of her wedding, when she'd been so happy minutes before. But she'd betrayed her pa. She'd put him in a bad situation. If he was hurt because of her… She pressed her fists into her belly.

A voice came from far into the woods, deeper than that first crack. "Hands up, and we won't hurt ye."

Fenna squinted into the last remnants of daylight, trying to figure how many men were about. With the steps heard on both sides of them, she guessed there were at least three. Hopefully no more.

Will met her gaze, a broken twist to his features as he slowly lifted his hands to the darkening sky. Fenna mirrored his action, and to the side, her Pa did the same.

Two men with grizzled beards, wearing tattered clothes, stepped into view, holding old long-barreled rifles. Fenna knew a fair bit about guns, and these were as likely to backfire as they were to hit their target, but her small group was too close to try and run.

"Empty yer pockets," came that same voice from the third man they still couldn't see.

Will yelled back into the dark. "We ain't got anything. Just on our way back from a wedding."

The goons continued picking their way closer through the scrub brush. Fenna hoped they were picking up ticks with each step, enough to add scars to their bodies to match their marred honor.

"You got plenty," the one closest to her pa said. "For starters, you got a fine mount there."

Fenna glanced at Red, a gift from Mr. Bridger for Pa's fifteenth year as their employee. A generous gift, and one Pa was almost as proud of as he was of his own daughter—at least, he used to be proud of her.

"Stay back." Will's hand wrapped around Fenna's waist, and he shoved her behind him as he glared at the man on their side.

Pa stepped closer to Fenna, but the man nearest him said, "Stop, or I'll shoot."

Pa froze, agony in his gaze as he looked at her across the distance. She wasn't his to protect. Not anymore.

A whistle came from deeper in the woods. Some kind of call, a form of communication between these animals who held them at gunpoint.

In a swirl of hazy dark clothes, her pa lunged at the goon nearest him. Fenna reached for her pa, but instead of going forward, something pressed at her middle and she fell backward. She landed on her backside and before she could draw a breath, Will's full weight landed on top of her.

At once his weight lessened, and he turned. "Fenna—" A goon slammed the butt of his rifle into Will's head, knocking his words away. Will collapsed again, this time onto Fenna's knees, but he didn't get up. She twisted her body, cradling his head and calling his name, but his eyes were closed.

Blood issued from a gash in his forehead. Fenna's chest tightened, and each breath became difficult, shallow, almost gasping. Her hands hovered, unsure what to do. Will was the one who'd been to doctoring school. But she'd worked at his side all summer, helping with patients. She knew at least a little. She pulled the hem of her dress up and pressed it against the wound. She paused, caught between anger and terror as she looked at the man towering above them. She didn't have long to consider before her attention was drawn to a grunt from the other direction.

Pa was on the ground, a goon's foot in his gut.

"Stop it!" Fenna cried out, rising to her knees, one hand still applying pressure to Will's forehead.

"Don't worry," said the man nearest her. "We ain't plannin' to hurt *you*." His rotten sneer made Fenna shudder, but he'd stopped kicking at her pa. Though Pa's face was twisted in a grimace, his eyes were open, unlike Will's.

A groan issued from Will's lips and with fluttering eyes, he touched his fingers to the gash on his forehead. Fenna whimpered in relief, then reached under him to help him sit up.

A gargled yell came from her pa. Fenna turned to see him pull a knife from his belt, the blade she'd seen him use countless times to skin a rabbit or bleed a deer. Pa sliced at the man's legs, and the polished metal came away glistening with blood. Fenna's heart lifted and she turned back to Will, shaking him.

The goon who had hit Will jumped over Will's prostrate legs and swung the butt of his gun toward Pa, who was fierce as a lion, swinging his blade and grabbing for the man's gun. "Get her out of here!" he called. It wasn't until Will was stumbling to his feet and hauling Fenna up by her underarms that she realized Pa was talking about her.

Red still stood nearby, eyes wild at the commotion but

tethered to a tree. Fenna stumbled along, brambles pulling at her skirts as Will held her upright. Though her body moved one way, her heart was back with Pa. She turned, reaching toward him. He was on his feet now, that same cruel man parrying with him, trying to get close. But every time Pa's weathered hand swung at him, the man jumped back again. The fight was not an even one. The other man came at Pa from behind, kicking his legs. Pa fell to his knees.

Fenna stopped. "You'll kill him," she screamed. "Stop it. You can have everything!" Will had her by the waist now, and he hauled her onto Red's back. When her ribs hit the saddle, the air knocked out of her, cutting off her screams.

One of the men stepped to the side and pointed his rifle at Fenna's face. "Stop."

His words rolled over her, so cold and ruthless her heart nearly obeyed his command.

He moved closer with quick feet, probably aware his gun wasn't useful more than twenty yards away.

"Go!" Her father's shout was strong, though blood dripped from his mouth.

Will climbed up behind her and kicked Red's flanks.

"Pa!" Fenna cried out, reaching for him. Will's long arm held her tight as she bounced along. She writhed in his grip. "Will, stop! They'll kill him!"

But he only slapped Red's flanks with the end of the reins.

A shot rang out from behind them. Will curved his body around hers.

"Will!" she cried, unsure if the shot was meant for them or Pa. She clawed at Will's hands, desperate to be off this horse and back with her pa, keeping those heathens from kicking him to death.

"They'll kill him!" she cried again as the forest flew by, blurred by her tears. She writhed, trying to slide off the saddle. Her legs caught on a passing tree, yanking her to the ground. Bright spots appeared in her vision before everything went black.

Will sat slumped in the chair at Fenna's bedside. It had been three days since that awful night. Though he and his mama had tended her wounds, Fenna had yet to wake. In her concussed state, she had missed her father's burial, and though her face was serene in sleep, dark shadows tinged the skin underneath her eyes. If she didn't wake soon, Will feared she never would.

He closed his eyes, preferring to catch snippets of sleep in this chair rather than leave her. Mama's voice cut into his drowsy state, and he blinked himself into consciousness.

"Will, she's awake."

Ma sat on the edge of Fenna's bed, a bowl of broth resting in the space between the two women.

He blinked and bolted to his feet. He was awake. *She* was awake. A shuddering breath crawled up his throat. "Fenna." He stepped closer but her eyes grew wide and she cringed, the liquid in the bowl spilling onto the quilt. Will reached for it.

But Fenna cried out, "No!"

Will retracted his hand and whispered, "Fenna, are you hurt?"

The soft sound of his voice did nothing to soothe her. Instead, she balled her fists and pressed them to her eyes. She kicked at the quilt and the bowl clattered to the floor. "No, let me go. Let me go!" Her cries made no sense. Nobody was touching her.

Her voice was frightened, desperate. And he'd heard it all before. In an instant he was returned to that terrible night, the shot that ended her father's life ringing in his ears like it had happened only moments ago. Her pleas to let her go to her father.

"Will." Mama pressed at his arm and shoulder. "I think you better go."

"Me?" He took one last glance, and his heart crumbled as understanding settled on his heart, heavy as a yoke. She was afraid. Of him.

CHAPTER 1

2 years later

Fenna raced through the woods, branches whipping at her face, but she was moving too fast for them to pull at her clothes. Hair fell into her eyes and she slapped it away, staring ahead, painfully aware she was running for her life and if anything impeded her ability, she would certainly be caught by whatever was chasing her and swallowed up by the dark.

Dark.

She turned and it was only blackness behind her. Beneath her too.

She woke with a start, her hair in her face the same way it had been in the dream. A tender mark was raised on her cheek.

The faint light coming through the window told her it was too early to rise for the day, so she lay there, staring up at the black ceiling, willing herself not to remember that night.

This dream had been different from the others. For one, Will hadn't been there. This time she was alone. There also hadn't been any men chasing them, only a sense that something was trying to catch up to her.

Maybe it was her memories.

That night was nothing but a story to her, one that had been told so vividly, over and over again these last two years, that it almost seemed as if she could remember it. She could not though. Her doctor called it amnesia.

He could spout all the medical terminology he wished, but Fenna knew whatever had happened had frightened her so much that her mind was trying to protect her from it by forgetting. Perhaps that was what had scared Will away too. Less than a month after she forgot him, he left for his medical residency, only returning once or twice a year for holidays, and though his mother had given newly orphaned Fenna a room of her own in their house, it was easy enough to vacate when Will came to town.

She only wished her mind hadn't seen fit to lock away her memories from even before that night. The last few years of her life, her memories with her pa. There was no need to protect her from those, yet they too were gone.

And her memories of Will—gone too. Her mind was welcome to lose those. Her reaction to him those first few days and weeks after the head injury had been for the best. That unbidden fear had effectively chased Will away, sending him off to his medical residency where he belonged, not tending to a fiancée who no longer remembered falling in love with him and accepting his proposal of marriage.

Sure, she knew from his mother, Mam, that he wrote begging for news. But he'd kept his distance these two years. At least *his* life hadn't also been ruined that night. At least he could go on and learn to be a doctor himself, a dream Mam Bridger was sure to tell anyone who would listen.

One day, Will would write home telling Mam he'd found himself a new girl and Fenna would be freed from any lingering expectations. Until then, Fenna had only to keep her head down and be of use to the family who had so graciously taken her in.

Being needed was easy—with five boys still at home and a farm with too few workers, there was plenty to do. Plus, Mam enjoyed the female companionship. Fenna tried not to think what might happen once the Bridger sons started marrying. Perhaps Fenna would remain, or perhaps her usefulness would vanish. But there was no need to think on that now.

She readied for the day and made her way down to the larder to scoop oats for breakfast, then out to the pump to fill the pot. By the time she returned to the kitchen, Mam was there with her apron on and a smile. But her expression fell as she lifted a finger to Fenna's cheek. "What happened here?"

Fenna set the pot on the stove and waved Mam's attention away. "I got a bit unruly in my sleep."

Mam didn't drop her concerned expression. "Bad dreams again?"

The dreams had come often at the beginning. Now they were rare and changing. "Just one. I can't remember the last time I had one." A lie. She remembered each dream with a vividness that mocked her amnesia.

"Anything new?" As always, Mam was hopeful that Fenna would recall everything: her memories of her pa, and most of all, her love for Mam's second son Will.

"No." If anything, her dreams were moving away from the truth.

Mam nodded, but her mouth turned down. The change

was so subtle Mam probably didn't even notice, but Fenna was practiced in watching others' expressions, in learning just what was expected of her and adapting to meet their expectation.

Mam took the pot from Fenna's hands, setting it on the stovetop. "I'm glad we're both up early. I had hoped to find a chance to speak with you today; you know how it gets once the chores begin."

Fenna knew too well. Her forearms were as strong as Mam's with the effort of keeping up with the work.

"Take a seat." Mam gestured to the wooden bench that ran the length of the table.

Fenna glanced at the stove, curious as to what conversation was so serious that breakfast could wait. Soon the Bridger sons would thunder down the stairs as loud as a herd of wild horses and expect grub before their chores began.

She took the seat offered. Mam sat too and placed a gentle hand over Fenna's, the tender gesture only inflaming Fenna's suspicion.

"There's no easy way to tell you this, but I wanted you to know before word got out." Mam drew in a deep breath and as she let it out, she finished her statement. "We're moving west."

Fenna blinked, cold pulling her down and rooting her to the wooden seat. "West." She squeaked, then gulped away the thickness in her throat.

"I want you to come. *We* want you to come."

We meant Mam and Mr. Bridger, but all Fenna could think of was the flowers she'd put on her pa's grave on Sunday. She couldn't leave her pa. And everyone she knew was here. Except none of them mattered to her like the Bridgers did. Fenna shook her head, trying to clear away this new dream where she was alone in more than just a forest. Alone in wakefulness too.

"Of course, you don't have to. I'm sure you can continue to live here. Rent a place in town or stay with the Allens."

"When will you leave?"

Mam winced. "Very soon."

Fenna swallowed. She understood. She wasn't ignorant to the way folks were treating the Bridger family. Truly, it was a surprise they hadn't left sooner. A family who didn't own slaves wasn't welcome when politics was all anyone talked about these days, throwing out words like *Rebel*, *Confederate*, *Yankee*.

"Do your boys know?" They weren't 'boys' anymore, but The Bridger Boys had such a nice ring to it. Fenna would never call them anything else, no matter how old they grew. But… that was no longer right, was it? She might not know them much longer. She might never see them again if she decided to stay. And stay she must, for how could she leave everything behind?

Mam's hand traced the wood grain in the table, bringing Fenna's mind back to the kitchen. "Frank told them all yesterday." Mam stood, making her way to the stove to start the oats Fenna had abandoned.

Fenna's heart thumped in her chest at the consideration Mam was granting her now. Fenna hadn't known her own mama. Her pa had worked on this ranch as long as Fenna could remember. Mam Bridger was the closest thing to a mother Fenna had ever known, and now she was going west.

Without Fenna.

Everything in Fenna revolted at the idea of separating from Mam. If she stayed here, she would be able to visit her pa's grave, and depending on who bought the Bridgers' place, she might even be able to visit the house. But without Mam here to warm the kitchen, it would never be the same.

"I made too much soda bread. Couldn't sleep last night."

Mam's voice drifted up from the depths of Fenna's despair. "Will you run it to the Perkins?"

Fenna nodded, her face as numb as her insides. She understood the assignment. Get some fresh air. Think about it. But as she loaded up a basket and made for the exit, those lifelong insecurities rose up. Maybe Mam just wanted Fenna out of the house so they could have a *family* discussion about going west.

The truth throbbed, just like her head had ached after the accident. When she had awakened, she'd longed for the oblivion of sleep to take away her pain, both the pain in her head and her heart once she'd learned of her father's demise. Now that ache was starting again, and she couldn't blame death for it. Maybe it was loneliness that caused the pain and not death at all.

She threw back her shoulders. She'd adapted back then, so she could handle this new change. She truly did have a choice here: stay or go. If that dreadful night had taught her anything, it had taught her that she was hardy, and she could endure whatever came her way.

She imagined all the Bridgers gathered around the table this morning. The truth of what was coming would have soaked in. They'd all have opinions, concerns, and possibly even resistance.

All the brothers except Will, who was in Virginia.

Gone because of Fenna. Gone for a lie that she'd let continue. Gone because she had preyed on his kindness. Would she be the reason he remained separated from his family? There would be no visits for Christmas, not when they moved two thousand miles away.

"Is Will going too?" Fenna was forced to speak of the one topic she cautiously avoided with Mam.

Mam's hopeful face wilted. "We'll send him the news. I'll

be going to Harrisonburg to stay for a few weeks until I take the train and meet the men in Missouri. If he decides to come, he'll join me."

It was all planned. They would take the only family she had left, and they would leave her. She needed them, but that need was one-sided.

Mam's grip on Fenna's arm tightened. "The trail is dangerous, and Frank has asked me not to press you. But I want you to understand"—Mam squeezed her lips tight and her throat bobbed, her eyes shining with emotion—"I want you to come with all my heart."

Fenna nodded, though her mind felt like it was stuffed with cotton and no coherent thought was able to make its way to the front. It was nice to know Mam wanted her. That all the time she'd spent over the last two years to make herself indispensable meant that at the very least she would be missed. But the truth remained that she had a choice. A real daughter would not have a choice in the matter. She would join her family no matter the risk on the trail, unless she had a husband and a family of her own.

A husband. She glanced at the soda bread waiting to be taken next door to the Perkins. "I'll just... take the bread." Fenna stood on numb legs and lifted the basket from the counter. The moment she stepped through the door, she felt the wrongness of separating from Mam. She shook her head and shoulders, chasing away the odd feeling. She left Mam often enough. This was just an errand like any other day... except this wasn't any day.

The basket hung near her knees, banging against them with each step, but she didn't care. She couldn't stop thinking about Will. Would he join them going west? Had Fenna's deception separated him from his mother for the last two years, only for them to be separated forever? Again, she shook away the thought. Will was always going to leave for his residency. But Fenna's dishonesty, her contribution to him staying away so often, brought a metallic tang to her tongue.

The Bridgers had shared their home and she'd paid them back with deceit. She'd allowed them to believe she still could not look upon Will without having an episode. Had encouraged that belief by retreating to her friends' homes whenever he visited town.

If she joined them, and he did too, she would have to tell them the truth. How could she continue to avoid him within the confines of a wagon company? Her only hope was that by now he'd found a nice girl and had forgotten the girl Fenna had been, the girl he'd fallen in love with.

Or she could stay.

As she crested a hill, their neighbor's home rose in front of her. It was also sprawling, but unlike the Bridger home, its condition was pristine. The house had a fresh coat of paint and the lawn was trimmed. The cotton fields extending behind the house would provide ample income come harvest. Would she still be here then? Alone, with the Bridgers having abandoned the south for the west?

She'd barely started down the hill when Edward appeared out the back door of his house, looking up the hill. He lifted his hand in greeting and jogged up to meet her. His smile grew wider as he approached. "Is it true? The Bridgers are selling?" He caught her by the arms and dipped his head to read her face.

Something about his eagerness chafed at her. There was no point in lying—Edward's family would be among the first interested in buying, neighbors as they were. How had he heard when she had only just learned of the matter?

She sighed. "You heard correctly."

Edward whooped and turned, sliding Fenna's hand through the crook in his elbow.

His countenance brightened, for unlike her, he had no reason to miss the Bridgers. They were the town pariahs and growing ever worse as North Carolina attempted to cede from the union. "I'll buy it. They won't be expecting top dollar." He led them to his home at a quick pace. Fenna, with her shorter legs and heavy heart, struggled to keep up. Or perhaps it was that her mind was still in the Bridgers' kitchen, wondering what was being said around the breakfast table. Wishing it was her place to be included in the discussion.

It was a shock that the Bridgers had stayed this long. They should have moved last year, or even the year before that. Now she doubted they had a friend left who was willing to buy at a fair price.

As they made their way to Edward's home, she looked out at the rolling hills. She wasn't sure what she'd miss more: the Bridgers when they went west, or these rolling hills if she accepted Mam's offer and joined them.

Only, could she really stay back? Her closest friend was newly engaged. The family might have taken Fenna in, but she couldn't inconvenience them once Josie married and moved into a home of her own.

Her gaze swept across the lawn and up to Edward, standing tall at her side. More than once he'd expressed his hope for a marriage when he had a place of his own. Fenna had listened, content with the plan unfolding in some unknown future. She hadn't been ready then, but this new development meant she ought to figure out her heart soon. Would love come eventually? Was the risk of marrying a man she might never love more or less precarious than whatever waited on the trail?

She and Edward had seen much of one another for nearly a year. He was older and mature enough that when she'd told him why she wanted to keep their relationship a secret, he had agreed and hadn't felt the need to lay his claim on her for all to see. This had slowed the relationship down to a comfortable pace, a pace that was bound to be accelerated now.

Her insides clenched with a sick realization. Had her acceptance of his advances given Edward a false security? Even now, with the news of the Bridgers leaving confirmed, he didn't voice a fear of her joining the family. What had he to fear? Any person would choose a life of wealth at Edward's side rather than a life of toil and death on the trail to Oregon. If she stayed and Edward bought the Bridgers' land, she might even become mistress of the very house where she'd spent her childhood. The idea might have appealed to some, but it only turned her stomach.

Edward pulled her into his house, calling for his mama. Fenna smiled at Dottie, the African woman who held the door. "Afternoon."

"Afternoon, miss." She bobbed her head and closed the door behind them. The house was stuffy, and Edward called for an iced drink. A luxury few could afford, even among those who owned slaves.

Fenna glanced around the space, a new future teasing her. One of finery and ease.

Dottie moved through the room in near invisible silence. That finery and ease came from slavery, from the toil of another. Her insides revolted at the idea of having a woman like Dottie serving her. But it would be expected by almost all the families around here. If she stayed, she would have to make peace with it, and that was something Fenna wasn't sure she could overcome. Dottie disappeared through the doorway, but Fenna's awareness of the woman remained.

Edward offered her a seat at the table and Fenna took it heavily, running her sweaty palm along the fabric on the armrest.

Edward turned away and called again for his mama. She appeared at the bottom of the stairs with a wide smile for Fenna. "Ah, hello, darling. What did you bring me?"

As neighbors, Fenna was often sent to deliver one thing or borrow another. "Just a bit of soda bread, ma'am."

Fenna pushed the basket closer to Mrs. Perkins. Edward pulled a loaf from the basket and Dottie supplied a plate just in time. He cut into it, the slice tipping away from the rest, then falling flat onto the plate. Edward scooped it up and slathered it in butter, offering it to Fenna. She shook her head, her insides still in knots. All she saw when she looked at that slice was how alone it looked, cut away from the whole. It didn't matter that it now lay on a fancy dish.

He passed the piece to his mama. "Fenna has just confirmed the rumor. The Bridgers are pulling up stakes. They're going west."

Mrs. Perkins' hand froze before it reached the plate, her mouth making a small 'O'. "When?"

Edward set the plate down and turned to Fenna.

Fenna squirmed. "I'm not sure."

Mrs. Perkins edged closer. "Do they have family out west?" She turned her gaze to Edward. "Lord knows they have no business staying here, the *unionists*."

Fenna wasn't truly a Bridger, so it shouldn't have hurt so much to hear the family spoken about with such hatred. Yet she wanted to take Mam's gift of soda bread and turn tail for the Bridger home.

Edward's voice was deep, grounding. "It doesn't matter what they have out west, only that they are leaving. I want to buy it, Mama. We'd be neighbors." He squeezed Fenna's hand, and she understood his implication.

She looked at her palm, so small in his. Marriage. Was she ready to link herself to this man? She'd been ready before, with William, and she'd been only sixteen back then. Surely if she was ready then, she was ready now, even if she was a different person due to the loss of both her pa and her memories. Her situation was about to turn desperate, so that ought to count for something.

Fenna stood. "I really should be getting back. There is much planning to do, and Mrs. Bridger will need all the help I can offer her."

Unlike Edward, Mrs. Perkins had no reason to put her faith in Fenna. With narrowed eyes, she asked, "Are you going with them, dear?"

The pet name, so sugary sweet off Mrs. Perkins' tongue, held a bitter accusation. Edward stood and draped an arm across Fenna's shoulders, a gesture both familiar and somehow possessive. "She's not their daughter, Mama. We've been over this before."

Fenna couldn't tear her gaze from Mrs. Perkins, whose eyes had yet to return to their full, trusting size. *We've been over this before.* They'd talked about her, and in that conversation Edward had reassured his mama that Fenna wasn't a Bridger. Did his mother disapprove of their relationship? Was that why she, too, was content to keep it from the town?

Perhaps the Perkins' silence had nothing to do with not upsetting Mrs. Bridger and everything to do with embarrassment of her son cavorting with a penniless orphan.

Fenna swallowed the painful lump in her throat. With just one hour and one revelation, Fenna's whole future was in question. Did she stay here, where she was a beloved orphan to the town? Marry Edward and possibly live on the very plantation she'd spent most of her life serving? Or did she go west with the only mother she'd ever known? If she did go west, what of William? What if he decided his medical residency was complete? Surely he would join the family out west? If she was forced to face him, perhaps she could find the courage to demand answers about that night, answers that might be as painful as they were terrifying. Answers she was finally strong enough to receive.

CHAPTER 2

William stepped through the wide doorway of his aunt and uncle's house, his home for the last two years. Both his body and his mind were heavy and ragged from a day spent working at the clinic. But when his aunt met him at the door, he mustered a smile. "You're up late."

"Dr. McFarland is taking advantage, letting you work such late hours."

"You know I enjoy it." Working was the only thing that allowed his mind to be fully engrossed, unable to wander home to Fenna.

Aunt Harriet held out a letter. "From your pa." She nodded at the stiff parchment. "Your family is going west."

William felt like his heart stopped, an impossibility, yet his hand lifted to press against his chest to be sure the organ was still thumping away in there. He took the letter with shaking fingers. "Is Fenna joining them?"

Aunt Harriet tsked and huffed, a combination all too familiar to Will. She hated how he'd thwarted her many attempts to match him with one of the nice girls she knew. "William, you cannot wait for her forever."

Two years wasn't even close to forever. And avoiding other women had been rather easy, as he'd used those years to throw himself into becoming the best student Dr. McFarland had ever taught. The only difficult part had been missing Fenna and the knowledge that she might never come back to him. But one thing a doctor was capable of was placing errant thoughts in a compartment of his mind and ignoring them for extended periods of time.

William tore the seal and pulled out the paper inside, moving closer to the sconce on the wall so he could read by its light.

William,

We hope you are well and have learned all you can from Dr. McFarland and are ready to join us. We are selling the house and moving West. Will you come?

The air left William's chest, ruffling the paper in his hands. He scanned the rest of the page for Fenna's name and saw nothing.

His aunt was still standing before him. "Will you go?"

There was more to the letter, but he wanted to read it in private. "I don't... there's still much for me to learn from McFarland."

Once again, his aunt made the noise that meant William was disappointing her. "There will always be more to learn. Even Dr. McFarland makes mistakes. You cannot work for him forever. He's paying you so little; you'll never be able to support a family."

A family. William thought of Fenna. If she wasn't going, it didn't matter whether his education with McFarland was complete. He would have to move back to North Carolina to be near Fenna. He would no longer have his mama close to her, funneling him information, to know when she was healed enough to allow suitors.

He met his aunt's gaze. "Perhaps now is exactly when I should be learning all this, before I have a family to provide for." He held the letter aloft. "Thank you for waiting up." He leaned closer and kissed her forehead.

With long legs, he took the stairs two at a time and entered the sanctuary of his room. Once more, he opened the paper and read every word, hoping for even a hint of news regarding Fenna. The letter was in his pa's hand, and Pa wasn't one to write about Fenna. How he wished for a letter from just Mama, updating him on Fenna's happiness.

Aunt Harriet was right. Two years was a long time to wait for a girl who he was no longer engaged to.

But it was little time to wait for his wife.

Their situation was unprecedented, and who was he to say how long a woman needed to grieve the loss of her father and her memories? When she was ready to be courted, and could bear the sight of him, Will would be the first one on the doorstep. He kicked off his shoes and laid down on the bed, the letter still in his hand.

West.

As children, he and his brothers often played cowboys and Indians. His elder brother, Ben, would be thrilled to go. Not so much for the adventure, but for the challenge. He always did love being tried.

If Ben had been the one to marry Fenna, he would have stayed and fought for Fenna's memory. Told her she was no longer in charge of her own life, but a wife and his responsibility. When it came to that, Ben would never have married her in secret. He would have told the world they were marrying, and they could all eat their socks if they didn't like it. He would never have left for Virginia with only Mama knowing the truth, relying on correspondence to assure him of Fenna's safety and happiness.

Judging by the vague contents of this letter, Will guessed his mama had kept her word and not told a soul, not even Pa, about Will and Fenna's wedding. Unlike many women he knew, Mama was as tight as a vise when it came to secrets. He glanced around the room, half expecting to find a second letter from her on his bedside table. She would have known how worried William would be about this letter, how he would need to know Fenna's choice before making one of his own.

His eyes scanned the room that had become his over these last years. Going west or not, he would leave here. It was comfortable, and his aunt and uncle had been more than hospitable, but he had no desire to stay. Will was tired of hiding the truth. His fingers itched to write back and tell them he would go where Fenna went. He highly doubted that would be here, where he could continue his education. His options would be west if that was her plan, or back south if it wasn't. Like examining a patient from the wrong side of the physician's table, everything that lay before him was the same and yet totally different.

He closed his eyes and tried to picture Fenna's reaction to this impending journey. Was she scared? She was loyal to his family, but such a large move would make her hesitate. Joining them meant she'd leave behind her father's grave and all the other folks who loved her. The journey west was not an easy one. A railroad had been started, but it only reached Missouri. New graves still lined the trail to Oregon. Once they made it, if they made it, they would still have to carve out a life in the harsh landscape that was the west.

The persecution back home must be worse than Mama had described. It had finally grown into something they could no longer live with. Perhaps that was why his brothers had yet to marry; they could not find one family with enough kind feelings to allow their daughter to marry a Bridger boy.

With a small smile, William remembered the days before his own wedding. Fenna crying in his arms when both her pa and William's parents forbade the marriage. They had all agreed an engagement would be sufficient until Fenna was older and William had finished his schooling. The young are never patient, and the adults who suggest it are fools. William had been twenty-four and his bearing mature enough to pass for older. When he had approached a pastor in a neighboring town, the reverend had given his assent and, mere days later, Fenna and William had made their way across the county and to his chapel.

One of the best adventures of his life, and he was the only person who still remembered it. He glanced at the drawer of his desk, picturing the stack of papers under which hid his marriage certificate. The only proof of that day. That and his word. Fenna wouldn't believe his word, wouldn't even try to look upon him, so scarred was she by the way her body had reacted to a memory she still couldn't recall. He hadn't forgotten her initial reaction to him, how it had gotten worse every time he tried to see her, until she'd begun shaking if she even heard his voice from afar.

He couldn't blame her for avoiding him these past two years, but the period for grace was over. If she didn't remember anything by now, chances were she wasn't going to remember anything. He was no longer risking her health by seeing her. Possibly her discomfort, but surely by now she had made her peace with that night. He had to either force her to look at him or grant her an annulment without the gift of one more day with her.

In his mama's last letter to him, she'd mentioned that Fenna still wouldn't speak of him, not with Mama, not with any of them. Mama had been diligent to write whenever a memory of Fenna's returned, but he knew better than most that the mind is something physicians knew little about. It followed its own whims; logic and learning were no match.

As much as he tried not to take it personally, he couldn't understand why her mind had chosen to target him as the culprit for that night, leaving only brief flashes of horror. Thinking of it now made his blood run cold. The brutality of those men, the coarse things they'd promised to do to Fenna, and William's own desperation to get her away before they carried them out.

Will scanned the letter again and turned it over, hoping to find anything more. He was rewarded with a brief note in Mama's hand.

Fenna is joining us.

CHAPTER 3

The day after he received his parents' letter, he found himself in Dr. Louis McFarland's office. Though the two had grown close these last few years, William still shifted uncomfortably in his seat the same way he'd done that first day when McFarland had agreed to be his mentor and teacher.

McFarland's hair was gray but still thick. Though he was older, he was a fine-looking man and, as a widower, he had more than one patient with her cap set on him. William's own cousin was one of them. Five years ago, this might have been a scandal, but though she was the same age as Will, Molly was on the verge of spinsterhood. The doctor, however, had yet to give any of the women his attention, focusing instead on his practice and his pupil, William.

He looked at William now. "West, you say?"

Willam nodded, swallowing the lump in his throat. He was scared and he didn't know why. Was it that Fenna and his mama would be joining them in Harrisonburg for a few weeks before boarding a train for Missouri? Was it that he'd now told someone outside the family of his choice and that made it seem more real? Or was it the idea of going west at all, with its dangers? What if he didn't survive the journey? What if Fenna didn't? What if he wasn't learned enough to go off on his own? A wagon train consisted of at least one hundred people. There would be any number of maladies along the journey. What if William wasn't prepared to treat them?

"Is it money you want? A practice of your own? I can provide you with both."

William jerked out his reverie. "I…" He shook away his shock. "I must go where my family is going."

McFarland narrowed his eyes, running a hand over his neatly trimmed beard. "You have been away from your family for years. Why not start a family of your own right here? I know I haven't been paying you much, and surely that is at least part of why you refuse to court any of the fine ladies in town." He stopped, drawing a breath as though settling himself.

William had the familiar feeling of playing cards with his brothers, of searching his opponent for a tell of some sort. McFarland was watching him in the same manner.

"I've been thinking of this for some time. I would like to open another clinic in the south side of the city, in my name, with you as its director."

William blinked. This should have been an honor. It was certainly validating, knowing McFarland would allow William to work unsupervised under his name. If things were different, William might jump at this chance.

"I'm flattered, really—"

"Since you've come, we've been able to take on more patients than ever. Without you, I will have to turn away countless folks in need."

William thought of the way McFarland had started

raising his prices so their services were too expensive for the poorer citizens. If Will had a clinic of his own, he'd also have the leverage to keep prices reasonable. He could help so many.

Will traced his thumb along the curved pad of each finger. This offer should have been presented long before now, at least as something for William to look forward to. Not many men had the reasons William had to stay single, stay focused, and work his every day away until his mind was too tired to stay awake. Or to think of Fenna.

"I'm sorry to upset your office. I understand all too well how my leaving will affect your schedule. I will be here for a few more weeks, allowing my mother to see her sister before we depart. We can search for a replacement during that time."

McFarland pinned him with a stare. "Your cousin may never marry. If you won't stay for yourself, will you stay for her?"

William's brows lowered. Molly was perfectly healthy. She had no need of William's care.

"I've been considering taking a new wife," McFarland continued. "Of course, if we move forward with the second clinic, I'll be far too busy for courting. But with our families combined through marriage, I might consider putting your name up on the new practice. McFarland and Bridger." He passed his hand along the air, as though picturing their names carved into the sign above the building.

William didn't even try to conceal his shock. "You're intending to make Molly an offer?"

McFarland's jaw ticked. "Not exactly."

Bile rose in William's throat. "Are you saying if I stay, you'll put my name on the practice and make Molly an offer?"

McFarland only lifted an eyebrow.

In that moment, William hated this man. The man who had taken advantage of William's hard work, who had withheld a promotion until William was about to leave, who hadn't considered Molly, sweet Molly, for a wife until it would benefit his business.

William stood. "I won't take any more of your time. We should get back to *your* patients."

He said the word with more venom than expected. He'd never felt bitter at McFarland for the past years, but now he felt hard pressed to be grateful.

He went home earlier than usual, hoping to speak with Molly before dinner. The last thing he wanted was for her to learn of the proposal and expect Will to make the sacrifice for her future. She had rejected more proposals than any other girl he knew, and yet he had a sick feeling she might accept McFarland's.

As expected, he found her in the sitting room, her feet tucked under her and a book in her hands. Molly raised her eyes at his entrance, and they lit with her smile. "Mama says you've decided to start an adventure."

William nodded and sat next to her. "Any chance you want to come along?"

She laughed and looked into her book again. William knew he had little time before she was through talking and would stop listening in favor of reading. She wasn't shy about preferring the company of books to people, written words to spoken ones.

"I wanted to speak with you about McFarland."

She looked up again and *almost* closed her book. He'd finally touched a topic she was interested in. The thing was, McFarland didn't return her interest as a person, only as a pawn. But how to tell her without making her feel as low as the rug beneath his feet?

"You cannot marry him."

Molly narrowed her eyes in that same way her mother did. "I didn't realize I had the option." She closed her book, though her thumb remained between the pages, holding her place. "Has he spoken to you of his intentions?" She narrowed her eyes and cocked her head an inch. "Has he spoken to Pa?"

William shook his head. "No." It was a partial truth, and it would have to do.

Molly's brows rose, challenging him. "No, and yet you are here now, speaking to me of his nonexistent intentions. Telling me not to accept them." Will shifted and her eyes followed every movement. "You have worked with him for all this time. You respect him."

William winced at her accusation. "I have learned much, professionally, but as a man he is not to be admired."

Molly laughed, opening her book once more. "Men will never understand the things a woman admires in a man."

Will shifted closer, knowing he was losing her attention. "Molly, he cares only for money. You deserve love and affection. He will not give anything that does not benefit him."

Molly's eyes stayed on the page. "And who is to say giving me his love and affection will not benefit him?"

William ground his teeth together. Molly was too quick witted to get to anything but the heart of the matter. "He tried to use marriage to you to encourage me to stay and work for him permanently."

Molly's mouth twisted into a smile. "How very medieval. Did he also pledge his shield to my father? Or perhaps he offered a few fatted pigs."

"Molly, this is not some story in a book. You are not a princess to be bargained for." He wished he could ensure Molly understood her worth, how much she could bring to a marriage. Perhaps then she would have accepted an offer from one of the men who had wanted her for who she was.

"I know I am not a princess, which is good because I can't stand the knights, all brawn and no brain. Dr. McFarland is well learned. None of the men who have offered for me have been my match in intellect. The doctor is."

"He is not your match in heart."

The two cousins stared at one another, neither surrendering to the other's point.

"Come west. Have an adventure like the ones in your books. Those knights with so few brains have children that need teaching."

His aunt walked into the room and a shocked smile graced her features. "William, you are home early."

Molly returned her gaze to her book once more. "He has come to spend time with me. He will miss me greatly when he goes."

"It is time for supper. Wash up." His aunt turned again and left them alone.

"I *will* miss you. I've never had a sister before." His mind pulled memories of Fenna, always part of his childhood. He had almost had a sister, but she'd been so much more, and now she couldn't bear to look at him. He pushed away the hurt, and as usual it relocated to a dull ache at the back of his head.

"I'll consider it."

William's gaze snapped to Molly, whose face was still as ever, only her eyes moving along the lines of her story. Not for the first time, he wanted to yank the book from her hands and toss it across the room. Such an action would be unforgivable, so instead he stood and made for the door. Before he stepped through, he cast over his shoulder, "I think you'd surprise yourself. You're capable of much more than reading in that chair and marrying a man for his money."

As he walked away, Molly shouted through the doorway, "I'd marry him for his mind! There's no shame in that."

She was right. It wasn't the worst reason to marry someone. But it was the man's heart that worried William.

CHAPTER 4

Fenna followed Mam off the train, her worn boots scuffing onto the cobbled platform. Her feet froze, but a bump from the person behind told her this was not the place to stop. She took another step, one step farther from home. To their left was a group of soldiers, but they didn't wear the gray uniforms the girls at home swooned for. This was Virginia and these soldiers wore the deep blue of the union army.

She took another step.

She'd never been this far from home, and her journey wasn't done yet. It had barely begun. Every step she took from this point forward would make that statement truer. She was tempted to step backward, just to see what it felt like, but the throng of folks with suitcases bumping against their shins made her squeeze closer to Mam. She was the most important person left in Fenna's life.

Edward came to her mind, but as much as she wanted to, she could not pretend she loved him. Nor could she live in a household that owned slaves. Perhaps she wasn't ready for marriage, or perhaps his mother had mattered more than she would admit. Whatever it was, their courtship would remain a secret that now nobody would learn about. Just in time too. As the crowd pressed and jostled her, she knew she'd have to be strong if she was going to continue to pretend she could not look upon Will.

A call for Eliza Bridger drew Fenna's gaze. A smartly dressed woman who must be Mam's sister, Harriet, was waving with one hand while the other held the arm of a bulldog of a man. Mam tugged Fenna along until the two sisters embraced, while Fenna smiled awkwardly at the man.

Harriet Marx released Mam, then took Fenna by the shoulders, giving her the chance to note Harriet's smooth braids that covered her ears and swooped into what was surely a beautiful knot in the back.

"You are quite the beauty," Harriet said. "It's too bad I didn't have any sons. I see why Will is so devoted." She chucked Fenna's chin and took the smaller suitcase from Fenna's hands.

Fenna's cheeks colored, but not at the compliment. Will was devoted? She cut a look at Mam, but she had her head against Harriet's and the pair were whispering like the worst gossips in town.

Mam's hair was tied into a simple knot, small compared to the complex thing weaving Harriet's hair. Fenna would have to offer to help Mam with her hair tomorrow. Or perhaps this family had hired help to do those things.

One look at Harriet's fashionably cut clothing told Fenna that life had taken these two sisters to very different corners on the dance floor of life. Fenna appraised the woman with calculated interest. This might have been her life had she stayed behind with Edward. She supposed money wasn't a reason to marry a man, but it sure did make things easier. And Edward had treated her well. She shook her shoulders. Pa would have wanted more for her. He would have wanted love. She needed to remember that if she was going to make it through the trials ahead of them. Besides, there was no going back now. Even if she wanted to, Edward wouldn't bring himself so low as to accept a woman who had spurned him.

Harriet took her husband's arm once again and they led the way out of the train station to a well-kept coach. Once they were all settled inside, Harriet turned her attention to Fenna once more. "I have a daughter still at home, a bit older than you. You will share her room. William sleeps down the hall." She glanced at Mam with a lifted eyebrow. "You're sure about this?"

Mam smoothed the fabric on her lap. "We aren't staying. I don't mind what folks think." She stopped adjusting her skirts, her gaze flashing to Harriet's. "Do *you* mind?"

Harriet cocked her head with feigned nonchalance. "More than one girl has her sights set on your boy. Perhaps if we pass Fenna off as his sister..."

The Marxes were worried about Fenna staying in the house with Will. Such scandal. Fenna faced the window, doubting for the hundredth time today if she'd made the right choice in coming along.

Mam patted Fenna's leg. "It would barely be a lie. She's as much a daughter to me as I'll ever get."

The words were kind and accepting, but they only served to remind Fenna how she was hurting Mam with her refusal to re-engage with Will. Even if she could remember their courtship, she wasn't sure she would have still wanted him. He was as unknown to her as a story in a book she hadn't even read. Even if she had read it, it wasn't as though a woman could fall in love with a man on a page.

She glared out the window. If so many girls were set on him, why hadn't he married already? He'd be settled down by now and she could go west without a thought for him or how any of the Bridgers might feel about her being part of their family in a different way than they had planned. *Devoted*. Mrs. Marx's word bounced around her head with each jostle of the carriage.

If Fenna had taken the time, she might have wondered about this before now. The Bridger boys were all strong and handsome. Even as despised as they were, it had become quite a tradition for the girls back home to give their first kiss to a Bridger boy. In secret, of course, where nobody could accuse them of being traitors to the cause. One of the younger brothers, Sam, was all too willing to feed this tradition. Fenna smiled softly. Mam was right. She felt like a daughter, just as she felt like those boys were her brothers.

Except she wasn't. And they weren't.

Harriet nudged Fenna. "I bet you're excited to see William. It's been three months since he's been home."

Fenna turned away from the window and faced Harriet, a forced smile fixed to her face. Last Christmas, when William had returned home, she'd gone to stay with a friend for the two weeks. She allowed them all to think it was fear of another traumatic episode that drove her away. What they didn't know was she *could* look at him.

Last year he'd come home for a holiday, and during the Sunday service, she'd found herself hidden from his view but able to stare at him for the entirety of the sermon. No matter how she squinted and tried, she couldn't recall anything. Courtship. Attack. Nothing. He remained as familiar and distant as Ben, the eldest Bridger brother, had been. Too old to be her playmate through childhood and too busy to pay her any mind.

Mam gave a short chuckle. "She doesn't miss him any more than she misses any of my boys. They all tease her to no end and take advantage of her kindness if they can.

Sammy even asked her to take a few of his socks to darn on the train. I had to pull them from her bag myself."

Fenna gave a genuine smile at that. Sam always did get his way, and it seemed nobody minded the doing of it.

The carriage bounced along the streets of the bustling city, but the windows were too small to enjoy the scenery, and Fenna kept her eyes down, hoping to get no more scrutiny from Harriet.

The woman cleared her voice. "You truly think it will only take two weeks to sell everything?"

"Oh, Frank is anxious to get to Missouri. Says we want to be there early to make sure we've got everything we need before we depart."

Harriet shook her head. "You should have been able to sell everything down there. This war… it's pulling brothers apart."

Silence fell in the cab, the quiet of mourning, and anger, and regret. What they had to regret, Fenna didn't know. But when a person feels helpless, it always gets them thinking how they could have done differently along the way.

Finally, they pulled to a stop and Fenna stepped out of the coach to find a home with a wide porch that stretched across the front and wrapped around one side. Mr. Marx and his driver unloaded the luggage as Fenna followed the women up the walk and onto the porch. It had a bench hanging from chains, the wood oiled and glossy. Nothing like the disrepair they'd left behind.

Her mind flashed to William, to the women that Mrs. Marx mentioned were hoping to catch his eye. Were any of them so bold as to come here for a visit and rock on that swing, holding his hand?

Though she knew she could look at him without recourse, the thought of seeing him again had ricocheted around her all day. The waiting was the worst part. She wasn't ready to tell the truth, but the image of him lingered in her mind. That day in the chapel, the sunlight had caught his hair, showing traces of gold in his mostly dark locks. His hair was the same color as his mother's, and it had a wave that came out when it was humid. He was a catch, there was no denying it. All the Bridger brothers were, and here, without being the town pariah, Will was sure to have many women doing their best to draw his dark gaze.

They entered the home and the swing disappeared from sight, but it still took up too much space in Fenna's mind. They'd been engaged. Enough folks had told her that, and she would have believed it if Mam had been the only one to say so. But it was strange…if she'd loved the man, she felt no sadness at the thought of him courting another. She felt less even than she'd felt when the girls back home chased after the other Bridger brothers, for those girls Fenna knew. She'd always felt the need to determine their intentions and whether they were good enough for a Bridger. Even now, she regretted letting Ben get so carried away in his affection for Jane Connor, only to hear she'd broken his poor heart.

Ben, Alex, Nate, Sam, and Chet—they all felt like brothers to her. William… he felt like a stranger and worse, a sort of devil. One who had survived the worst night of her life and lived to remember it. She resented him for his ability to remember what she could not and, worse, she couldn't shake the surety that he had benefited from her memory loss in some way. Like he'd done something she never would have forgiven him for if she could only remember it.

The staircase before them was wide with a curling handrail on one side. It was so like the Bridgers' handrail that Fenna touched it, a sharp pang of homesickness nearly doubling her over.

A young woman floated down the stairs, a wide smile on her face. "You must be Fenna. I'm Molly."

Her tone was an exact mirror of her mother's and Fenna smiled, offering her hand for a greeting. The two young ladies shook, and Molly pulled Fenna in close. "I know we'll be fast friends. Will has told me plenty about you."

Will. They all loved him, and Fenna ought to at least feign tolerance. "I fear you have the advantage."

Molly grinned. "I'll show you our room."

She turned and marched up the stairs again.

With one last glance at Mam, who gave her an encouraging nod, Fenna climbed the stairs behind Molly, her heart in her throat as she trailed her free hand along that rail. She cleared away her homesickness and lifted her eyes to the natural light that brightened the second floor.

Harriet had said William's room was in the same hall. Was he there now? Though she felt sure she could endure seeing him much closer than she had that Sabbath day, she hadn't yet decided if she wanted to continue to feign an inability to look upon him. Or if she better fess up sooner rather than later. Mam had been patient with Fenna's inconvenience and Molly may think they were to be friends, but when it came to sides, everyone in this house was firmly on William's. Once they knew her secret, she'd be surrounded by matchmakers.

CHAPTER 5

The sun had long set when Will decided he must stop working for the night. Mama had arrived today and was waiting for him at home. If she'd been the only one, he might have taken the day and picked her up from the train station himself. But it wasn't just her. It was Fenna too.

As much as his heart ached to see her, he couldn't deny she was still afraid of him. He hadn't looked into her eyes for over two years. Any sightings had been her profile, and even those were rare. When he came home, she made arrangements to be away. If he saw her at church, she was sitting across the chapel, her bonnet covering most of her face. And now he would sit across the table from her and... what? Would she close her eyes? How was this supposed to work? How were they to travel two thousand miles and keep away from one another?

He'd waited long enough. As a physician, he knew the further they got from the incident, the less likely she was to regain what was lost. Similarly, enough time had passed so that pressing her beyond her comfort would not damage her memory. There was no need to be gentle, not anymore. Perhaps he'd been a bit afraid of confronting her. Of giving her the chance to decide one way or another what to do about this marriage.

Selfishly, he grieved for himself, for his unrequited love. He should grieve for her, for the last year of memories with her pa being wiped away, and for what? The money in their pockets?

He shook his head as he placed a brown glass bottle back in the cabinet and closed the door. The gas lamp flickered and he gave it a bit more wick. As he stared at the dancing flame, he recalled that night, the lantern he'd been holding, knocked from his hands by her pa in his anger. Righteous anger, for he'd only been trying to protect his daughter.

Perhaps if his lantern had been lit, the tramps would have known there were three victims instead of one and they might have passed over them and chosen easier prey. Or perhaps if there had been no lanterns at all they might not have seen Fenna, might not have known what a beauty she was, nor desired her for their own pleasure.

But no, they chose them, and Will had been foolish enough not to carry his gun on their outing to the church. His reverence only earned him the loss of that which he held most dear. She wasn't dead, but she was gone all the same.

A glance around the clinic told him all was put together. He turned the wick down again and darkness blanketed him. The streets weren't empty. He wasn't the only one late for dinner. Perhaps the family had eaten already and he could take his meal alone. But this was only one night of many, and Mama was bound to be angry with his delay.

She should understand. Of anyone, she should understand. Yet she was still his mother, and she deserved his attention. A small part of him knew that her bringing Fenna along was the best favor anyone had ever given him. It was a second chance—or at least it wasn't the snuffing out of his chance to win her love once more.

The clinic wasn't far from his aunt and uncle's home, and he reached the steps before his heart was ready. He stopped at the door, steadying his breathing and straightening his clothes. He pressed inside, his chest filled with anxiety. It ran about his torso like a racehorse around a track, all thundering hooves and torn up earth. Their servant, Smith, took Will's hat and coat but Will kept hold of his medicine bag, a habit Dr. McFarland had ingrained in him from the start. *A doctor is never without his bag.*

It also housed powerful remedies that could be poisonous if administered wrong. He could easily picture Molly with an anatomy book in one hand, administering remedies without even lifting her eyes to look at the patient.

Quick footsteps sounded and soon his mama rounded the corner. She wore a wide smile and a pale floral dress he recognized. He pulled her in for a tight hug, astounded that though he'd never thought about it before, she smelled every bit the way she always had. Like home.

He released her and leaned close to whisper. "How is Fenna? Are you sure about this? I can sleep at the clinic."

Mama gave a slight shake of her head. "No need to sleep there. Let's give her a chance. You two will be traveling together for the next several months. She needs to find some peace when it comes to you." She glanced around and leaned closer, her whisper growing softer. "We may as well know one way or the other."

Will whipped his head left and right, ensuring they were truly alone. Just because nobody was in sight didn't mean Mama's words went unheard. The last thing he needed was Fenna finding out before he was ready. He had many reasons for keeping his marriage to Fenna a secret, one of which was the scandal that accompanied divorce.

The mere thought made him wince. He hoped it didn't come to that. His heart would never recover from that final, killing blow. But if it did come to that, if he couldn't make Fenna fall in love with him again... they must be careful. Keep the secret a little longer. As much as he adored his aunt and uncle, they could be busybodies, and no secret remained so in this town. He didn't so much care for himself, but Fenna had dealt with enough hardship over the years. She didn't need one more reason for folks to look down on her. Even though Fenna too would be leaving this place and the people behind, he couldn't stand the thought of his aunt and uncle sharing this story for years to come. The gossip they did share at the table was nothing compared to the drama of Will and Fenna's story.

"We'll know. There's no need to rush it." He stepped closer to the dining room, but a door on his other side opened. His uncle stepped out of his office.

"Will, may I speak with you for a moment?"

Will glanced at Mama, who nodded her approval. With one more look at the dining room door, Will turned away and followed his uncle into his office. He'd waited years for Fenna. He could wait a few more moments.

Not more than two steps into the office, he saw McFarland seated inside.

"Sir," Will said, glancing between McFarland and Uncle Sven.

"Have a seat." His uncle gestured to the seat next to McFarland's. Then Uncle Sven took his seat on the other side of the desk.

Uncle Sven cleared his throat. "Dr. McFarland here has made us an offer."

Will's gaze shot to McFarland, who gave a small nod.

"Yes, he spoke to me about it." Will clenched his jaw at McFarland's audacity.

"That's not the whole of it." McFarland uncrossed and recrossed his legs.

Will had the strange sensation that the doctor was nervous, which caused an anxious flutter in Will's chest.

Uncle Sven spoke, drawing Will's gaze. "He's considering linking our two families."

Will shot a look to McFarland, but the man had eyes only for Uncle Sven, so Will returned his attention there as well. This was the whole of it. McFarland had already tried to unite their families. He stared at his uncle, waiting for whatever revelation McFarland had come to deliver.

"He had plans for you and a clinic, but your intention to leave jeopardizes that plan."

Will nodded. He knew all of this.

"Losing you would cause considerable stress on McFarland. So much stress that courting a future wife would be impossible."

Will remained silent, waiting for more information.

"Dr. McFarland wishes to see us united. You can take on more patients at the new clinic, and Molly would understand if McFarland were less than attentive in the weeks leading up to their wedding."

Wedding? "Molly has accepted a proposal?" His attention shot to McFarland. "You two are engaged?"

In staying late at the clinic, he'd obviously missed more than Ma and Fenna's arrival.

"Well, no." McFarland smoothed his hair. "You see, this offer is contingent upon you staying."

The understanding, though he'd been presented with it before, chafed like a loose knot in a hem. He only wished for it to be as clear to his uncle. "You'll only marry Molly if I stay."

"Well…" Uncle Sven shifted in his seat. As well he should.

From Will's vantage point, it looked like these men were discussing Molly like she was business.

McFarland, however, wasn't too ashamed to speak. "I wouldn't put it so crassly, but yes. Any marriage of mine, to anyone, would be contingent upon you staying."

"You don't love her."

"Love her." McFarland gave a soft chuckle and shared a knowing look with Uncle Sven. "At my age, marriage isn't so much about love as it's about convenience. Molly will make a fine mother to my children. As you said, she'll be tolerant of my working hours. And I thought an offer to your dear cousin would please you."

Please me. Will swallowed the anger rising up his throat, trying to choke him.

He took that energy and stood. "I'm sorry, but as I said the last time we spoke, I am going west with my family."

Before anyone had a chance to say anything more, Will exited the office. Furious at the underhanded way McFarland had come here, pretending like Will hadn't already rejected that very offer. Fuming, he marched right into the dining room.

He was met with several startled glances, but the one that meant the most was Fenna's. In his anger, he'd only thought about his original destination: the dining room. He had forgotten just who was in there.

Here she was. Fenna was looking at him. Without fear, without sadness. Just wide-eyed, the same way everyone else was.

That was until she blinked and turned her face to the table, showing him her cheek, that same profile she'd done any time he had seen her these past years. The instinctive angle that meant she wasn't seeing him. But just now he wondered how practiced it really was. How long had she been able to look at him without fear and trembling?

CHAPTER 6

Fenna excused herself and made her way up to Molly's room. Her heart was hammering in her chest. She'd looked *right* at him. What happened to her plans of feigning the inability? Now Mam would be vying for opportunities to throw them together. She'd seen Mam play her hand at matchmaking, and Fenna was less than thrilled at the prospect of being on the other end of that hobby.

Except Mam hadn't seen Fenna look at Will. Fenna could imagine the joyful cry that would have emitted from Mam's lips. No, Fenna was sure she hadn't seen. But Will had, that was for certain. If she could talk to him, let him know that... what? She didn't want to be matched with him? For all she knew, he didn't want to be matched either. Just because Harriet had *said* Will was devoted didn't mean he truly was. If Fenna's relationship with Edward Perkins was any indicator, the mothers didn't always know as much as they thought. Perhaps Will was merely devoted to his work. He'd certainly come home late enough.

She dressed down and tucked herself into Molly's downy bed, but it was too early for sleep to come. She lay there, staring up at the texture on the ceiling until she heard steps on the stairs. Fenna shifted deeper into the covers and rolled onto her side, away from the door.

The creak of the door sounded, then the click of it closing once more. More than once today, Fenna had caught Molly looking at her in such a peculiar way. No doubt she wondered what was so great about Fenna that the Bridgers took her on in this way. Fenna didn't blame Molly. Fenna often wondered about it herself. Was it her father's years of devotion? Was it that Mam didn't have a daughter of her own? Was it her previous engagement to Will? Was it the fact that her and Will's actions were the reason Fenna was an orphan?

Any of them could be the reason. Fenna wanted only to ensure she didn't do anything to be exiled from their family, even if that meant faking the need to stay far away from Will. Just because he had loved her once didn't mean he would love this new version of her. She'd seen couples, even engaged ones, decide the match wasn't right and separate. Fenna couldn't afford the risk of engaging with Will once again, only for him to decide he didn't love this new version of her. No, her best chance was to make herself as useful as possible with Mam, make herself indispensable, and hope Will's presence wouldn't jeopardize everything she'd built over the last two years.

Eventually, Molly tucked into bed next to Fenna and settled in for sleep. Fenna did her best to regulate her own breathing, not just for Molly's sake, but because the longer she lay here thinking about how Will could ruin everything she built, the more certain she was that she needed to speak with him. Soon. Tonight.

Mam didn't know Fenna was capable of looking at Will. Fenna had planned to hold her trump card until the right moment, but earlier, at the table, she'd shown Will her card, and she had no choice now but to beg him to follow her lead.

Once Molly's breathing turned deep and Fenna was sure she was asleep, Fenna slid out from under the covers and tiptoed from the room. She closed the door softly behind her and crept along the hallway to the door she knew belonged to Will. Molly had gestured toward it earlier in the day. But then, Will hadn't been on the other side. She stood there, chewing her lip and curling her toes against the cold wood floors.

With a slow breath, she tapped softly on the door. As she waited, she considered the scandal such an approach would cause. A woman alone in a bedroom with a bachelor in the late hours.

Outside of society, there was no reason to fear Will. If anything, the last time she'd been alone with him, he'd saved her life. Or so everyone said. Yet something in her pulled at her courage, like forget-me-not seeds clinging to the hem of her skirt.

The door opened and sucked wisps of her hair forward. She blinked and looked up at Will's darkened form, backlit by the lantern behind him.

"Fenna." He breathed her name like it was the first flow of spring water in a dry creek bed. Fenna wanted to lie down in it, to feel the cold awaken her skin. She'd lived with the murky unknown for so long, and Will had every answer she'd been too scared to ask.

She glanced into the room behind him, at a desk on which two lanterns stood, casting their light over a paper. "I wanted to speak to you."

His throat bobbed, the only reply to her request. Then, finally, he stepped to the side and allowed her entrance.

She stepped over the threshold, knowing full well this behavior was the very reason Mam and Mrs. Marx wanted to pretend Fenna was a sister. Once all were abed, there was no accounting for what the young people did.

Will stayed at the door. "Shall I leave this open?"

"No." She stayed standing, uncomfortable with the very situation she'd hoped to be granted. She glanced at the desk once more, a quill and open pot standing just to the side. "Are you writing a letter?"

Will clicked the door shut and took two long strides to the desk. He laid a wide palm over the paper, then squeezed his fingers together, crumpling it.

Fenna fixed her gaze on the paper as he balled it smaller in his palm. "I can look at you." It was obvious, but just now she didn't know what else to say.

"Did you know before you came?" His tone was terse, guarded.

Fenna's gaze met his, and his eyes didn't hold the softness she expected. Mrs. Marx was wrong—he'd not been waiting for her. A man in love would have... she didn't know. Embraced her. Or at the least offered her a seat. The hope that he wasn't as enamored as the mothers thought granted her a sliver of courage.

"I did."

The wind left Will and he collapsed into the desk chair, the hinges squeaking with his returned weight. The lantern light caught his hair, illuminating that same gold she remembered.

"How long?" He leaned his elbow on the armrest and pressed his fingers into his temple.

Fenna chewed her cheek, debated lying. But the way his face twisted, she couldn't bear it. If she was going to ask him to lie for her, she should at least do him the courtesy of giving him all the truth. "Last Christmas."

Will squeezed his eyes tight. "Four months."

Oh. Fenna gulped and he must have heard, for he looked up. "The Christmas before."

He lifted his head off his hand and stared at her with such intensity, she scratched at the flannel collar of her nightgown.

"Do you remember me?"

"No, no." Fenna's chest loosened just a bit at a truth that would coincide with what he already suspected. "Not that much. I just noticed you at church, and I didn't have an... episode. So I looked again just to be sure and..." She shrugged. "I was fine."

"Why didn't you tell me or my mother?"

"I never minded staying with the Allens when you were in town. I didn't think it mattered. It's not as though I remember our courtship."

"Engagement." His voice was harder. She surveyed his face, but in the scant light, she couldn't tell if he was scowling.

"Yes, well. I didn't remember that either, so I figured it was all the same."

"Is that why you came?"

Fenna couldn't help but give a soft laugh. "Because I wasn't afraid to look at you? The Oregon Trail isn't something to choose on a whim. I hope I would have gone either way. But it is nice to know I won't have an episode in front of your aunt and uncle."

"The doctors, they said it could be harmful to press you to remember. Said it might send your brain into forgetting more."

Fenna nodded. "I know." As soon as he'd left, Will had sent specialists to his parents' house to meet with Fenna. She'd also spent plenty of time with their town doctor and Will's first mentor. She knew the things they knew about amnesia. She also knew how little they truly understood.

"If I'd have known—"

"What? You would have abandoned your schooling? Will, I hope I'm not being cruel by saying this, but our engagement is like another life to me, one I don't remember. Even if you had been there, nothing would be different now."

Will scoffed and Fenna's temper rose. "Molly said she's surprised you're even leaving now, so attached are you to your mentor. Do you not agree that nothing would be different?"

"It is not another life for me."

Fenna felt herself shrink. Not at his bluntness, but at her own callousness. "I'm sorry." She glanced at the door. She'd hardly thought about the fact that this man used to love her. He remembered everything she didn't. She might be safe from physical harm, but the real danger was the prospect of him falling back in love with her. "I'll go."

"Is that why you came? To tell me you could look at me? I discovered it at dinner. You needn't have come at this hour."

"I hoped, well, I wanted to keep it from your mother. Just a bit longer. I believe once we are on the trail..."

"Keep it..." His brows lowered. "You are asking me to lie for you?"

Fenna winced at his base reduction of the facts.

"Why?"

"She still harbors hope for us."

"And you'd like to crush that hope?"

"Stop it." Fenna's voice was firm. "I have no wish to hurt her. That's the very reason I want to prevent her from false hope."

"False hope." He echoed her words, but she couldn't read his tone, nor his expression, so she waited.

"How long?" He sucked his tooth. "How long do you wish for me to lie to my mother?"

He was phrasing it all wrong. "You disagree."

"Yes, I disagree." He stood and Fenna took a step backward, hitting the back of her legs against his bed.

She stepped to the side, nearer the door. "I should go."

"No." He put out a hand. With closed eyes, he drew in a slow breath. "I've had enough conspiracy tonight. My uncle… Never mind that. I wouldn't have wished to lie to my mother in any case, and I don't understand your reasoning." He stepped to the side and gestured to his vacated seat. "Please, sit and explain."

Fenna took wary steps toward the chair, unsure what there was left to explain.

They shifted, trading spots in the small space until he sat on the bed, his hands clasped as he leaned forward and rested both elbows on his knees. "You think if she knows, she'll hope for us to reunite."

"Yes." Fenna took her seat. The lantern was behind her now, and she enjoyed the ease of knowing he couldn't see her so easily. In contrast, she could see every line on his face. The shadow of his stubble and even the light scar that cut above his eyebrow. She couldn't remember when he'd gotten it, but it must have been there for a long time because it was familiar.

"And you think such an occurrence is impossible."

"Yes." She answered, but too quickly. After she spoke, she realized if he was asking her this, it meant he didn't believe the same himself.

"You wish for me to keep away from you."

"Well…" This made it sound like she was afraid of him, which she no longer was. "I don't mind being near. I just don't want your mother to get ideas."

Will nodded, his gaze fixed to a spot on the floor near her feet.

With his focus elsewhere, Fenna was able to study him once more. His shirt collar was open, exposing a wedge of bare chest. He had the same broad shoulders as his brothers, but the rest of him, down to his fingers, was slim and spoke to a nimbleness that must be useful as a physician. He was quite handsome. Once again, she wondered why he didn't have a girl of his own. If he did, there would be no need to fake anything. Mam would latch onto this new prospect. The idea, once started, blossomed wide like a magnolia, spreading far enough to cover every other thought. She needed to find Will a wife.

"How about a deal?"

Fenna's attention returned to Will's face. "A deal?"

"Yes. I'll agree to your scheme, with one condition."

She narrowed her eyes, listening.

"You come here, and we do this every night."

She gestured between them. "This? Talking?"

"Yes."

She chewed her lip. It was innocent enough, but she knew there had to be more. "Why?"

"Your memory. We lost precious time waiting for you to get it back. Spending time with me might coax it to the forefront of your mind."

Fenna folded into herself. Her shoulders curled and she even lifted her bare toes off the floor for a moment before realizing it would be inappropriate to tuck her knees to her chest.

"Remember?" She breathed, her fear forcing her voice into a whisper. How many nights had she tried to stay awake because she feared a dream might bring back everything she'd forgotten? At first, she'd missed those memories, but the more she learned about that awful night, the more certain she was that her mind was protecting her from the gruesome memory of her father's death. She did not want her memories back.

"I can't guarantee anything. How long has it been since

you have discovered a new memory?" Will's face lit with animation as he spoke. Did he see how Fenna cowered, or did the lantern at her back prevent it?

"Over a year."

Will's face fell. Fenna knew the improbability of getting her memories back. So used was she to the idea that she feared what their sudden return might do to her progress. She'd finally made peace with who she was now. The people around her accepted her differences, even if they made her inferior to the Fenna she'd been before the accident. So sure was she that she wouldn't regain any memories that she nodded. A little time each night was an easy trade for Will's cooperation. "How long?"

"Half an hour."

She stood and held out her hand. "You have a deal."

He stood too and took her hand in his. But he didn't shake it. Rather, he turned it so the back of her hand was facing up, then dipped forward and brushed his lips across the back of it.

Before she had time to react, he'd released her, and to his credit he wasn't smiling when he raised his face once more. "Until tomorrow."

Fenna made her way to the door, but paused. "You must stay away from me during the day. We cannot risk Mam discovering the truth."

The corner of Will's mouth hitched. "I forgot you call her that." He nodded. "I'll do my best to not come upon you unexpectedly."

Fenna nodded and stepped through the door, shutting it quietly behind her. He'd agreed to her terms, yet her stomach roiled at the deal she'd just made. Was a kiss on the hand going to be the extent of their physical contact? Or was he going to use these nights as an opportunity to rekindle their old love?

As she crept back into Molly's room, she soothed her worries by focusing on her plan to get Will married. She could likely get Molly on board. Once he understood Fenna wasn't going to remember him, it would be easy to get him to move on. It would be like a tug-of-war, both her and Will vying for their wants to be fulfilled. But once Will realized the ground beneath his hopes was soggy, he would cave soon enough. She just had to wait him out.

CHAPTER 7

If his mind hadn't been full of Fenna, he might have spent more time worrying over his remaining time at the clinic with McFarland. As it was, when he arrived that morning, Will was informed McFarland would be seeing most of the patients today. McFarland spent the entirety of the day grumbling about how he'd have to get used to it now since Will was abandoning him.

At first, Will didn't mind the lighter workload, as it gave him more time to think of Fenna in his room. To think of the feel of her hand in his, her skin beneath his lips. His time away from home had made her presence feel like a dream. But last night, she'd been very real.

The only downside was that being idle meant the day dragged on. If Fenna weren't at the house, he might have left early, but he'd promised to avoid her as much as possible. That didn't mean he needed to avoid his mama.

He sent a missive home asking Smith to prepare the coach, and he followed shortly after to ask his mother if she wanted to take a ride.

Once the pair were settled into the coach, Will relaxed.

His first encounter avoiding Fenna had been a success. But even so, he wasn't sure how they would avoid one another on the trail. Fenna would have to be willing to give up her ploy by then. That meant he had two weeks of late nights to make her fall in love with him.

He took his mama's hand as the carriage bounced through the streets. "Tell me about home. How bad was it?"

Mama heaved a sigh and watched out the small window as she replied. "Not so bad. At least, not unbearable. Folks were kind enough at church and you know we've always been too busy for the socials." She turned to Will. "It was Ben who finally made up your father's mind. He wanted to marry Jane Connor and her parents would never have approved."

Will's heart twisted. This wasn't new. There had been plenty of girls interested in one of the Bridger brothers, who never pursued more than coy glances. All of them knew there was no future with a Bridger, and not just because they were one of the poorest landowner families in the county.

The ache came not from the fact that Ben hadn't been good enough for Jane, it came from the fact that for Pa to finally pull up stakes on land that had been in his family for generations, it meant he thought there was no future for them now, or ever. It meant he'd experienced persecution greater than he'd revealed to any, save perhaps Mama.

"How did Ben take it?"

Ma frowned. "You know your brother. He took it with a glare and a grunt."

Will smirked. He missed his brothers dearly. The camaraderie and working hard at their side. It was something he knew he would never replace. In fact, as frightening and dangerous as the trail west was, Will couldn't think of it without a level of excitement. They would all be able to get their own plot next to one another.

Property like that didn't even exist in their hometown.

Not anymore. The original families who settled the area were long gone, married away or moved. Some remained, but no longer were there wide swaths of family-owned land. Not like what they would build when they reached Oregon. One hundred and sixty acres each with the Land Act. All of it on lush soil.

He and Ma caught up for the rest of the drive. As soon as they turned onto his aunt and uncle's street, Will turned to Ma. "I have a favor to ask."

Mama's eyes glittered. "Fenna?"

Will shook his head. He recalled her in his room last night, her hair in a long braid down her back, asking him to keep her secret. "Not Fenna. Molly. I need to speak with her. But I assume Fenna and Molly are one another's companions. Might you take Fenna into the yard for a bit while I speak with Molly?"

Ma gave him a long look. "What is your plan with Fenna? When are you going to tell her?"

"I have a plan. Hopefully by the time we are on the trail, she will be able to look at me again. She fell in love with me once."

Ma let her head fall to one side. "She's a different woman. She lost her father. She's harder, quieter." Ma gave a sorrowful shake of her head. "Fenna is not the youthful girl you courted before."

Will nodded, his throat going tight at the very real possibility that she would never love him again. "I can grant her an annulment. The marriage was never consummated."

Ma's eyes flew to him, and at first Will thought he'd scandalized his own mother. But then she spoke. "You cannot tell her that. She'll take it for sure. You two belong with one another. Why else would you both still be single?"

Will gave Ma a curious look. "Ma, neither of us is single."

"Yes, well, not technically. But Fenna didn't *know* she was married. And she had no interest in any of the suitors, some of whom were quite eligible."

That fact had baffled Will too. Over the years, he'd fully expected to receive a letter from his mother with news that Fenna was being courted. In the event of such a letter, he had planned to rush home and tell Fenna of their nuptials, then she would finally know the truth. Until then, he intended to be patient and allow her to heal. Except two years had passed without her so much as giving any hint to Ma that she was growing interested in making a family of her own.

He shook his head at Fenna's revelation last night. Over one year of wasted patience. He'd given her space when she hadn't even needed it.

But a word from Ma sprang up in his mind. *Eligible*.

"Which suitors did she decline?"

Ma made a dramatic roll of her eyes. "You don't want to hear that." She straightened and turned to Will. "Did you know the Perkinses bought the property?"

Will knew the family well. Edward was Ben's age, but still close enough to Fenna's age to take interest. "Was Edward one of the suitors?"

Ma nodded. "I was sure to watch her on that one. You know I'm always sending Fenna back and forth with one thing or another. The last thing I wanted was to be sending her to the wolves."

Will nodded, calmed. He hated to think of the Perkinses living in his home, but not as much as he would hate to think of Fenna receiving love notes from Edward.

The carriage stopped and Will touched his ma's arm. "You'll take Fenna somewhere?"

"Are you sure? Perhaps we can have her look at you, just once."

"In front of Molly and Aunt Harriet?" His stomach should have lurched at the pretense, but all his words did to him was to make him think of what would come tonight when everyone was abed.

Ma pursed her lips. "No, you're right. It won't do. What if she has another episode?"

"Exactly." His chest constricted at the omission of truth. She'd been his only confidant for two years, and now he was lying.

Ma nodded. "I'll go now. Give me a few minutes before you come inside."

The driver handed Ma down from the carriage, and Will signaled he would be staying inside.

The door clicked closed, and Will leaned his head against the cushioned backrest. What if Ma was right? What if Fenna was too different and he couldn't make her fall back in love with him? What if he was no longer the type of man she wanted? What if she wanted someone rich like Perkins? What if she refused suitors because she didn't want to marry at all?

Questions spun in his head until he thought enough time had passed and he could go speak with Molly.

He climbed from the coach and made his way up the walk. When he entered, he cleared his throat to alert those inside of his presence. The last thing he wanted was to surprise Fenna and ruin her ruse. As much as he didn't want to lie to his ma, he had grown attached to the deal they'd made. A daily half hour alone with Fenna was more than he could have hoped for.

Will strode to the sitting room and entered to find Molly curled up in a chair, a book on her knees.

"Good afternoon, Will." She looked up and he was startled by her attention. When Molly had a book in her hands, her company entered a silent battle between fiction and reality.

"Are you well?"

"Yes." Molly set the book aside and removed her spectacles. "Your mother just took Fenna on a walk."

"I had hoped to ask if you had given any more thought to going west." The visit from McFarland last night had unnerved him. It was only a matter of time before a man, even as obtuse a one as McFarland, discovered what a gem Molly was. He would want her for a wife even if Will left.

"A bit."

"And?"

Molly gave a soft chuckle. "And that's all."

Will pegged her with a suspicious eye. "You've done no research?"

"In a day?" Molly's tone was disbelieving, but Will didn't buy it. In the rare event that Molly didn't understand a subject, she never left it alone for even hours before widening her understanding on the topic.

Will remained silent, waiting for the truth to leak out.

Finally, Molly huffed. "I've done a fair bit." She shifted closer in her seat and lowered her voice. "Did you know one in ten travelers on the Oregon Trail die?" She leveled Will with a hard stare. "As a physician, you should know those odds are reckless. *You* should not even go."

"I'm going." Will's retort was immediate. He'd wasted enough time giving Fenna fruitless space. He was not going to lose another single moment with her.

Molly's expression changed from horrified to amused, and she lifted the side of her mouth into a half smile. "What happened between you and Fenna?"

This was not the first time Molly had inquired about Will's broken engagement. It was only Aunt Harriet's fear of the scandal that had prevented Molly from pestering him more often. Over the years she'd desisted, but he should have realized Fenna's appearance would dredge it all up again.

"There was—"

"*An accident.* So you've said. But Fenna is healthy, capable of walking two thousand miles. I do not understand."

Will bristled. His reasons were all for naught, and he'd barely acknowledged that fact to himself. He wasn't about to speak it aloud to Molly. "You have no need to understand."

Molly lifted her chin. "So I don't. And *you* have no need to understand my reasons for staying here while you embark on a suicide trail."

Will stood, irritation welling inside him. "I'll not press you to go. I only worry what your life would be like if you stayed." He gestured to her. "But I see my concern was wasted. If you're smart and refuse McFarland, this will be your life forever."

He whirled from the room, collecting his coat and hat from the stand before exiting the front door.

The coach was gone, so he bounded down the steps, intent on the clinic, his sanctuary. Only it wasn't a sanctuary anymore. Not with McFarland, who surely resented Will's rejection. Now it was a hostel, a place to endure for a short time before his next adventure began. He wasn't ready to quit his learning, but his aunt was correct. Practice was the only way to get better, and on the trail, even a doctor as inexperienced as he was better than nothing.

Molly's numbers on deaths along the Oregon trail was staggering, but he tried to look at it from the perspective of a doctor. There would be many to help, and those he lost would be a mere side effect of the trail and not a reflection upon him. He would be the only one who knew which ones had been lost due to his ignorance. And as he had learned early in his schooling, mistakes are part of a doctor's education. Better than any lecture or lab was the truth that a doctor never forgot the ones he should have saved. He blinked hard at a memory of Fenna, her face a mask of fear as she looked at him.

CHAPTER 8

That night, Fenna found herself once again in her nightgown, lying in bed and waiting for Molly's breathing to slow. But it didn't, and Fenna felt herself drifting off.

"Can't sleep?" she whispered to avoid falling to sleep herself.

A breathy laugh came from Molly. "No." She turned so she was facing Fenna. "Will..."

Fenna still wasn't used to Will's name being so casually used. Mam had always been so cautious, so gentle when she had to mention Will in Fenna's presence.

"He spoke to me of a marriage proposal from Doctor McFarland."

Fenna blinked, then turned to face Molly. "The man who is Will's mentor and teacher?" Fenna hadn't met the man, but she had always imagined him as elderly, perhaps with age spots covering a balding head.

"Yes. He's a widower and brilliant."

"Isn't he a bit old for you?"

Molly shook her head. "Older yes, but he's young for how learned he is. His eldest daughter is just ten."

"Oh." Fenna replied. That was younger than she'd thought, so long as he didn't marry too old to begin with. "Are you going to accept?"

"No." Molly's tone was thoughtful, and Fenna waited for whatever Molly seemed to be working out in her mind. "It's just... The way he offered, like it was a favor to me. I wonder if the rest of the men think that too."

Fenna's blood grew hot. She knew well what it was to be pitied among her peers. "You are beautiful and so smart. Your parents have raised you as a woman of class. Any man would be lucky to have you."

"Thank you."

"I didn't mean it as flattery. I think you've got things wrong."

"I've turned down thirteen proposals. An unlucky number, but I fear that is the number I am stuck with, as they seem to have stopped."

"Until recently?"

Molly scoffed. "That wasn't a proposal, that was a barter."

"If you're not considering the marriage, what is keeping you awake?"

"Will suggested I come along. To Oregon."

Fenna froze, her breathing stopped for a second. "You should." Imagining Molly on the trail alongside Fenna was as easy as if she'd lived it all before.

Molly sighed. "It would be a fresh start, but it would also be a guillotine on my marriage prospects."

"Guillotine?"

"It's what the French used to decapitate their prisoners. There's a wooden block and above it hangs a large blade the length of a man's shoulders, held up only by a rope—"

"Yes, I see." Fenna swallowed, trying not to picture the image Molly had so casually painted. "You can marry in Oregon. In fact, I've heard the farther west, the more men there are to every woman. You'll have your fourteenth proposal before we even reach Oregon."

Molly gave a soft laugh. "If I cannot find a suitable man here, I won't find one there." She shook her head. "But I might be content not marrying if it meant I still made my own way in life. Outside my parents' home."

"You want to get away from them?" Fenna tried to keep the annoyance from her voice. Harriet and Sven seemed like ideal parents. Kind, attentive, alive.

Molly clicked her tongue. "It's not easy to explain. My sisters all married young. They have their own families. I want that, but not by marrying any man in a suit who comes along. I want someone who challenges me."

Silence settled in the darkened room.

Molly's words were softer. "What do you want in a husband?"

Fenna stared at the scant moonlight that filtered in the windows, casting rectangles on the wall. "The last time I tried, it didn't work out so well for me."

Molly laughed softly. "I can promise you the next time you get engaged, you will not lose your memory."

Fenna smiled along with Molly. "It's not just that. I was so young, and our parents didn't approve."

"Aunt Eliza didn't approve of you marrying her son? I would think there was nothing she wanted more."

"It wasn't me, but our ages. Will still had his internship to do. She didn't want him throwing away his future."

"He wouldn't have been."

"Right. But I could never say so now. She regrets opposing the marriage. Has said so. If we'd been married, we wouldn't have been out that night. Wouldn't have been attacked. My pa would still be with us."

"And you wouldn't be here now."

Fenna considered this, how much of her life would be different. "Perhaps I would." Fenna smiled at the memory of her pa's devotion to the Bridger family. "My pa would have gone west with them."

"Truly?" Molly's voice was incredulous. Then she laughed outright. "Well, then you might be in this house, but you'd be in the bed next door with Will."

Fenna's heart clenched. It was a wonder that Molly, a maid herself, could speak of such relations so casually.

"Sorry," Molly said, but the laughter in her voice said she wasn't sorry in the least. "I do wonder though: why not try again with Will?"

Fenna chewed her cheek, unsure why it mattered to tell this lie to Molly. She might even have noticed that night at supper how Fenna had been sure not to look at Will. The difference was Mam believed it for herself. Fenna just hadn't corrected her. To Molly, this would be an outright lie. But if she was asking Will to lie to his mama, Fenna ought to be willing to feed Molly the same lie.

"When I first woke after the accident, I saw Will and had... an episode."

Molly was silent for a beat, then asked, "Like a fit of madness?"

Fenna shrugged. "I guess. I hardly remember it. Like my mind is doing its best to forget that as well."

"And this happened because you saw Will?"

Fenna nodded.

"How do you know you wouldn't have had it anyway? With anyone?"

"I had no reaction to Mam or any of Will's brothers. We

tried once more, and it happened again." Fenna did recall the second episode. How she'd pressed her heels into the bed, trying to put more distance between herself and Will. Shadowy images had filled her vision, blocking out the daylight that had streamed into the bedroom. A familiar fear had ratcheted up her heartbeat. She remembered well the inexplicable desire to shout and scream, to beat her fists against him.

"I'm sorry."

Such a simple phrase, and one she'd heard numerous times. But for the first time, Fenna didn't feel like the person saying it was sorry for the loss of hers and Will's love, but for Fenna alone. Tears pricked her eyes and she rolled onto her back.

"Thank you," she whispered, her throat thick with the urge to cry.

The silence stretched as memories tried to surface the way they did, rising just to the top but refusing to break with the waves. Eventually, Molly's breathing grew slower and deeper. Fenna lay there after Molly had fallen asleep, that dark memory her only companion. Would she be able to fall asleep, or would it run around her mind like it had done so many times before? Begging to be played out again. Begging her to remember.

She slid from the bed, same as the night before, and exited the room. With a soft tap, she rapped on Will's door. It opened almost immediately. Will leaned out and scanned the hallway. Then he stepped to the side, and Fenna stepped into the room, her hip brushing against him as she passed.

He closed the door and whispered. "What took you so long?"

Fenna wrung her hands, the memory still taking up too much of her mind. "Molly wanted to talk."

"About what?"

Fenna pushed the memory away. It would come back anyhow, she knew. "About McFarland's proposal."

Will took a step closer. "She's not going to accept, is she?"

Something in her heart relaxed at Will's protectiveness over his cousin. It was sweet, something she'd not been able to see—or remember—about him. "I don't think so, but it has her considering her future." Will's movement had brought them too close. Fenna took a step back.

Will's gaze flicked between her and the space she'd created. "Are you scared of me?"

Fenna took a seat in the chair and glanced pointedly at the bed for Will to take his seat. He did.

Fenna put out her hands, the movement punctuated with a sigh, "I've been thinking about this."

"Me too. I could hardly focus on my work—"

Fenna put up a hand. "I think we need a few rules."

"Rules?" Will's brows clashed together.

"Someone could walk in at any moment."

"They would knock first."

"And what? I would hide behind the door?"

Will's gaze flicked to the corner behind the door. "Not a bad idea."

Fenna straightened her back and lifted her chin. "No touching. We should stay on opposite sides of the room."

Will sucked his tooth, surveying her that same way he'd done the night before. "Okay." He folded his hands in his lap, giving the impression of an obedient schoolboy. Fenna had to duck her head to suppress a smile.

Will's deep voice filled the room. "Why did you decide to come west?"

The question nearly took all the air from her chest. She glanced back up at him and he lifted an eyebrow.

"Do I have to answer?"

Will chuckled softly. "No."

"Why are *you* going west?"

He shrugged. "That's easy. My family is going."

Fenna cocked her head. "You haven't lived with your family for two years."

"My residency is complete."

"Is it luck that your residency happened to wrap up the same month your parents decided to move west?"

He opened his mouth, but nothing came out. She had him.

"I guess I might have been done before now. But by staying I became a greater physician."

"And now you've learned everything?"

"Hardly." Will's expression darkened. "But it takes a lifetime to learn everything."

"And you changed your mind about spending that lifetime here?"

Will's shoulders drooped, and she had the impression that he was disappointed in her. "I was never going to spend my life here. I was always going to come home, and you know as well as I do there was no future for anyone in my family in Mecklenberg County."

Fenna gestured to herself. "You found one once. Who's to say you wouldn't find it again?"

Will's gaze hardened. "What we had was special. I'll never find anything like it again."

Fenna's stomach flipped and her gaze darted away from the sincerity in his face. Her focus shifted around the dark room. It had all the personality of a rented room. Or perhaps this was who Will was and she just didn't remember. "How do we know when I've served my time?"

"There's a clock on the desk." He gestured behind her, and she turned to see a small wooden clock with a brass face. Unlike the room, this space did look inhabited, from the ink stains on the wooden desktop to the book that lay face down. Probably something medical. But at the least it was his, and he'd been reading it recently enough to keep his place.

"Will you be able to stand another twenty-three minutes?" he asked.

Fenna lifted her chin, refusing to cave to his goading. "I'm tougher than I look."

"I know." His response was so immediate, it was like he'd anticipated her words. "How was your day? Are you enjoying your time with Molly?"

Fenna smiled, her worries eased at the change in topic. "Yes. Your cousin is a dear."

Will laughed. "You must have taken more of a liking to reading then."

Fenna made a face. "Not enough to keep up with her. I don't know how she does it." She stopped, Will's words clicking in her mind. *More of a liking*. Did he know she didn't have a love for the hobby?

"Plenty of practice. What did you do instead?"

"Well, I did a bit of embroidery, then your mama rescued me and we took a walk around the neighborhood. It is a beautiful area you've been living in."

"But it isn't home."

Fenna searched his face, trying to determine whether his comment was for her benefit or his. She couldn't quite tell. "Do you miss it? Home."

Will's eyes lifted to the ceiling, as though he was imagining something far off. "I miss the fields, the openness, and that giant willow."

"Your pa had to cut it down last winter."

"I know."

Of course, he knew. He'd been home for Christmas. It was easy to forget that Will had been home, so detached was she from his visits.

"So, it was two Christmases ago that you learned you could look at me?"

Fenna nodded.

"How?"

"At church. I saw you on accident." Fenna smiled at the memory. "I thought you were Ben at first. A moment later, I realized I was looking at you and with no consequence, no reaction."

Will smirked. "And so you kept looking?"

Fenna's mind was still in that chapel, in that memory. "No. I was afraid if I looked too long, I would remember."

Will's smirk died. "You don't want to remember?"

"My father's death? Hardly."

"Fenna, you didn't see him die." His voice was low, filled with reverence.

Fenna swallowed, her throat thick with emotion. "Sometimes I have these flashes. Not quite a memory, but not completely forgotten either."

Will's gaze narrowed and he leaned forward. "What do you see?"

Fenna shifted, feeling like she was being examined by a doctor, which in truth she was. She drew a cleansing breath, pretending that Will was merely a doctor and this his office. "I see darkness, but I feel more." She shook her head and met his gaze, expecting him to laugh at her apparent ability to *see* things that are actually *felt*.

But his expression was earnest. "Memories are created using all five of your senses. Taste, touch, smell, sound, and sight."

Fenna closed her eyes, her brows drawing tight at the effort. But the memory had been hailed moments before she'd come here, and it was still lingering near the front of her mind. "I'm frightened." Though her heart was beating normally, she could almost feel its thumping in that long-ago moment. "There's something to the darkness." She opened her eyes and walked over to look out the window. "Like those branches outside. You know they are there, you can see some of them, but you know there are others out in the dark, beyond the ones seen. And stretching past the frame of the window. There's so much more I can't see, can't remember."

When she turned, Will was looking at her with an expression of such agony. He stood and took a step toward her. But she stepped backward, her shoulder hitting the window.

She put a hand out. "No touching."

He froze, his hands limp at his sides. "I'm sorry, Fenna. I cannot pretend to understand what it is like to be a stranger to your own past."

Fenna sighed and glanced at the clock. "What time did I come in?"

"I think the half hour is up."

It wasn't. She knew that well, but Will's voice was thick, as though her revelation was enough for one night. She remembered too well the way the Bridger family had treated her after the accident. She wasn't afraid of any of *them*, yet they'd spoken softly, touched her gently and been unwilling to ask for her help with any of the tasks she was more than capable of performing.

As she exited the room, her steps slowed with the heaviness of a horrible realization. When she'd been unable to share company with Will after the accident, she'd taken that healing time from him as well. Though her own wounds had long scabbed over, he was still hurting. She clutched her hands in her dressing gown. Perhaps she should be content to allow him a moment to touch her gently, to treat her the way the rest of his family had. And yet, she wasn't that girl anymore. Far from it. She wasn't planning to go back, not for Will. Not for anyone.

When she went west, the folks she met might learn of her

amnesia, but it would be an interesting tidbit and not something that deserved petting or comforting. They all left their pasts behind. Those courageous and innovative enough to go west focused on the future. The past was east, and Fenna wasn't going back.

CHAPTER 9

Will spent the next week visiting apothecaries. Each of them had their own ideas as to what ailment was most prevalent on the Oregon trail: cholera, smallpox, dysentery, blood poisoning. One even suggested burn ointment for lightning strikes. Will bought a jar, because even though he didn't think such an occurrence would truly happen, burns from fires were bound to be common.

Much to Aunt Harriet's dismay, Mama and Fenna had used the backyard to learn how to cook over an open flame. He heard the updates at dinner and was assured it was quite a change from the way they usually cooked.

As he considered the possible maladies that would follow them west, he fretted over the fact that most of them were incurable. He made his way home with the unsettling inspiration to bring as much laudanum and alcohol as he could afford. Even so, he worried over his ability to replenish his supply along the trail. Those with ailments near the end of the journey would suffer without medication to ease the pain.

When he arrived back at his aunt and uncle's home, he was not only late for supper, but he'd missed a large chunk of a conversation between Molly and her father.

Molly was leaning forward, her face red with emotion. "I have my own plans for marriage."

Uncle Sven's gaze met hers, fire for fire. "Oh? And what is that?"

"I'm going west with the Bridgers."

Ma sat up straighter in her seat and mouthed to Aunt Harriet, "I didn't know."

Will didn't dare take another step into the room, but Molly must have already seen him because she pointed in his direction. "Will isn't staying. Even if he were, I'd not accept Dr. McFarland's neanderthal proposal."

"Neader— Molls, you cannot possibly—"

"Don't *Molls* me. He doesn't love me and, as I understand, there is no proposal without Will's commitment."

Uncle Sven's shoulders lifted and lowered with a calming breath. He glanced at Will. "Welcome to the circus."

Will took his seat, noting how Fenna kept her gaze down. He hated it. Hated how it made her look cowed and weak. Broken. When she was none of those things.

Uncle Sven cleared his throat and took a drink, his eyes glued to Molly. "You mentioned plans for marriage. How is going west a plan for marriage?"

"There are twenty men for every woman, and that's in the city."

"You'll find a man in Oregon?"

"I'm bound to. You and Mama both know I've a reputation here. I will get no more true offers. McFarland's proposal only proves that theory."

"You've had your share of proposals. True proposals. And you denied every one of them."

84

Molly had the sense to look ashamed. "I was young and foolish. I see my error, only it's too late to remedy it."

Aunt Harriet interjected. "If you go to Oregon, we may never see you again."

"Nonsense. The rails will get there." She turned to her father. "Pa, just last month you invested in railway stock."

Aunt Harriet wasn't done though. "It does me no good to see you married far away. I wouldn't know your husband. I wouldn't see your children born. We can afford to keep you. There is no need to go west for a husband. Are you really so unhappy here?" Her voice was pained.

Molly laid a hand over her mother's. "I want to marry."

Even to Will's untrained ear, he heard the lie as it sprang from Molly's mouth. That girl wanted to get married as much as a cat wanted a bath. But desperation must have been clouding his aunt and uncle's vision, because both their faces softened. "Let us try and make an arrangement with McFarland."

"No." Molly was firm. "I will not marry a man who tried for an arrangement in such a way."

"Molly," Ma cut in, capturing Will's attention. Of course, she too would have an opinion in this matter. "The trail west is dangerous. We are only going because that is our only hope for a better life." She looked around. "You have a wonderful life here."

"Auntie Eliza, will I be such a burden to you?" Molly's eyes were wide with concern.

Mama's face softened. "Of course not."

Molly's concern vanished like magician's smoke. The girl was an excellent actress. "You see? I will be no trouble on the trail. I'm reading a book, a trail guide, written by the most prestigious mountain man the west has ever seen. I know the risks and I also know the reward." She took her pa's hand.

"Please, let me have a future outside the mess I've made here in Harrisonburg."

Uncle Sven glanced at his wife with an unreadable expression. "We will discuss it."

Molly smiled and, with her pa's hand still in hers, she turned her attention to Will. "On another topic, Mother says she's finally convinced you to attend your last dance. The girls will be thrilled."

Will cut a glance at Fenna, who was, as usual, not looking at him. Did she care that other women took interest in him? Probably not. What did it matter to her? She probably thought of him as much as any of his brothers. "Yes, I am going to accompany my mother."

Molly's eyes danced as she turned to Ma. "I hope you do not wish him to stay by your side. With his elusive behavior these past years, Will has all the ladies curious about why he refuses to court any of them. They understand, of course, that he is still a student and unable to provide a living, but being young and poor has never dissuaded the men from flirting and trying their hand at a stolen kiss."

"Molly." Aunt Harriet's voice was stern.

Molly tucked her lips, uncharacteristically apologetic. She must truly be unsure of their answer and so meant to feign utter obedience to convince them to let her go west. As though a few days of good behavior meant she was changed.

Ma smiled up at Will. "I would never expect Will to spend the evening by my side when there are so many young prospects." Her eyes darted meaningfully toward Fenna.

As intent as Fenna was to continue her ruse, Mama wasn't going to wait much longer. As far as Fenna knew, Mama was only hoping for an engagement, and if that was all they truly were to one another, Fenna's plan might work. But they were much more, and with only one week until they departed for Independence, Will knew he should be able to push Mama's hopes off for just a bit longer.

When at last all were abed, Fenna sat at his desk chair and he found himself confiding in her. His fears for the trail, his hopelessness of curing anything along the way. His confidences came not because he needed release, but because she was pulling away. She'd done it before the accident and, back then, it had been his vulnerability that brought her back. She was different now, but he hoped it would still work.

The guarded way she'd been speaking to him since that night when she'd told him of the vision of darkness—how he'd wanted to hold her, to press his mouth to her hair. He hated that through all his schooling, he had yet to discover a cure for her memory. He would help countless folks on the trail, yet he could do nothing for the woman he loved.

"Can you buy those medicines anywhere?"

Will nodded. "Laudanum and alcohol, yes. But I have no idea of the state of the apothecaries in Independence. I'm going to fill a crate with as many tinctures as I can and take them with us on the train."

"One more week. Are you ready to leave this behind?" She glanced around the room as though this was home. It had only begun to resemble home the moment she started filling this space with herself, her thoughts, her scent, her sighs.

"More than ready."

"Your aunt is thrilled to have you for one dance before we depart."

Will controlled his grumble. "Yes."

That brought a smile to Fenna's face, and a tiny ember burned brighter in his chest. Not until he'd seen her look at him without fear did he allow himself to hope he might also see her smile. Now he found it was something he'd be hard pressed to live without.

"Do you think we should reveal the truth to her?"

His heart lurched at the prospect of quitting these late-night meetings. And for what? A few shared glances over the supper table? He could deny his mother her wish to be escorted to the dance. Uncle Sven could accompany both women.

"I can take a separate carriage, stay away."

Fenna tilted her chin. "Will, you cannot guarantee our paths will not cross. We will both be dancing with others, moving around the space."

The thought of Fenna in another man's arms was like a needle to his heart, to imagine being unable to twirl her in his own arms and instead watching from across the room as she gifted that smile to another.

"You're right. Perhaps we can break the façade just before the dance."

Fenna rested her chin on the heel of her hand, her lips pursed in thought. "Perhaps a day before. Give her time to process the information. Who knows how she'll react."

Will smiled to think of his mother, usually calm and collected, having such a fit that the household's plans would be ruined.

"The morning of?"

Fenna nodded. "That works."

"We work well together." He winked.

His flirtation didn't have the effect he hoped for. She straightened her relaxed posture and glanced at the clock. He only had five more minutes, and he was determined not to leave on a negative note.

"I'm glad we will be able to face one another once we start on the trail. I'll need an assistant, and I thought you might be interested in the position."

Fenna cut him a suspicious look.

Will laughed. "You did it before."

"I did?"

"Nobody told you?"

"I was your assistant?"

Will chuckled. "I was barely learned enough to *need* an assistant, but you accompanied me on many visits. Ma said you continued while I was away."

Fenna blinked a few times, as though digesting this information. "I am often called to bandage or stitch a wound, but I only thought that was because your ma hates the sight of blood."

"She was giving you the chance to continue a thing you used to love."

She mouthed the word *love*. Her eyes got that glassy look like she was trying to remember the past.

Before she got frustrated with it, Will spoke again. "Mama will be too busy with my brothers and the wagons, and I thought you or Molly might want the job. It'll get you away from laundry and cooking. Chet can be Mother's helper in that regard. And I fear Molly would start spouting death statistics and frighten my patients."

Fenna huffed a quiet laugh. He would be especially grateful to be able to talk with her in more than whispers and stifled laughter. To hear her laugh out in the open again would be a balm to his heart. And if they were going to tell his mother the day of the dance, that balm would be here before he knew it.

CHAPTER 10

Fenna couldn't stop thinking about Will's revelation. She'd helped him back when they were engaged. A familiar uneasy feeling crawled around her gut, and it took a bit for her to identify what it was.

It was the feeling of not knowing who she was.

She'd felt it often enough just after her accident, but as the months and years went by, she'd begun to believe she was finally finding some idea of who she truly was, without anyone expecting anything different from her.

Just after her accident, her friends would say things like, "Remember when," only to drift off, biting their lips at their misstep. Other times they would forget altogether and completely relay a story she'd totally forgotten. It was like being told about a gathering she wasn't invited to attend. She tried to understand, to wave it away, but she'd often felt in competition with her old self. Which Fenna was superior? If the old one was better, how could new Fenna even begin to know what it would take to live up to that version of herself again?

"Time's up." Will's voice drew her out of her reverie.

She stood, a yawn overtaking her. These late nights were going to start wearing on her if she wasn't careful. Perhaps tomorrow she would sneak away for a nap while Molly was reading.

She set her hand on the doorknob, but turned back to Will before leaving. "Rule number two. No talking about the time I don't remember."

Will's face went slack. "Why?"

"I've heard enough of it over the years. It won't bring the memories back."

She opened the door and slipped out before he could formulate an argument. He was sure to have some medical explanation as to why she should participate in conversations about the past. But leaving North Carolina had granted her freedom from the expectations of everyone who surrounded her. Only now did she realize that Will hadn't had the chance to overcome his expectations. And, just like him treating her like a porcelain patient, it was her turn to be gentle, to be understanding while he processed his own loss.

Rather than get her nap the next day, Fenna found herself in the backyard of the Marx home standing over a cauldron. Cooking over an open fire was a sight more difficult than the coal oven they'd used back home. Before now, the only thing they had practiced cooking over an open fire was soap, and that was only because it didn't matter if it burned.

Finally, Mrs. Marx came out and said that was enough for today. The way she glanced around made Fenna suspect Mrs. Marx was more afraid of the smell than the need for Mam and Fenna to take a break.

When they got inside, Fenna found she was wrong. A break was not in order. Mrs. Marx scooted both ladies up the stairs and into Molly's room. The bed was covered with silks and satins and Molly's upper half was buried in the wardrobe, her arms scooping aside gowns like she was a mole making its burrow.

Mrs. Marx turned to Fenna. "Molly won't have much need for these when she goes west, so we thought to tailor a few to fit you. If you find one you like well enough, we can have it done first and you can wear it to the dance this week."

Fenna looked over the many dresses, more than she'd had in her lifetime. And they were surplus. She surveyed the visible half of Molly, unsure whether this pampered daughter was truly going to make it all the way to Oregon.

Mrs. Marx strode over and pulled a sage green one from the pile. She held it up to Fenna's chin. "You'll look gorgeous in this one."

Fenna gave a tight smile, feeling too much like a doll being dressed up in clothes that belonged to her owner.

"Mama." Molly stood, nothing in her hands to show what it was she'd been looking for. "Let her look. In fact"—she closed the wardrobe doors and ushered Mam and Mrs. Marx from the room—"let her have some time alone. We'll get you when she's chosen her favorites."

Molly clicked the door closed, and though Mam and Mrs. Marx hadn't been making a ruckus of any sort, a quiet seemed to settle over the room.

Molly huffed and shook her head. "You don't mind if I stay, do you?" She crawled into the bed and plucked a book from the side table.

Fenna shook her head. "Of course not. This is your room."

"Well, it's yours too, so long as you're staying here."

"So, your mother has agreed to you going west?"

Molly smiled into the pages of her book. "I think she's

asking me to purge my dresses as a test to see if I'm willing to give up luxuries for the west."

"And?" Fenna sat on the bed, careful to find a small section that wasn't covered by the full skirt of a dress.

Molly chuckled. "And I'm not sure she knows me at all." She glanced up and looked pointedly at the dresses. "Are you going to try anything on, or just let them wrinkle?"

Fenna stood and surveyed the gowns. They were not only fine, but vibrant, as though made for the very purpose of catching every man's eye. That fact made Fenna withdraw her hand. They were too much. She was meant to divert Will's attention to another woman, not draw it further to herself. "They're so… elaborate."

"If you hate them, you can say so. I'm sure I can find someone who wants them."

"I didn't mean—"

Molly spoke again without taking her eyes from the book. "Try the sage my mother chose. She has an eye for color. Also, the midnight blue one will compliment your eyes."

Fenna lifted the sage dress and scanned the bed but didn't see a dark blue one.

She started on the buttons of her blouse. "My eyes aren't dark blue."

Molly chuckled. "I never said that."

Fenna worked the buttons on her blouse and slid it from her shoulders. She was working on the buttons of her skirt when she heard the thump of Molly's book closing. Molly climbed off the bed and strode toward Fenna, reaching out and gripping the sleeve of Fenna's shift between her fingers. Fenna had embroidered a bold pink cosmos there.

Fenna moved out of Molly's grasp, stepping quickly into the sage dress and pulling it over her shoulders.

"I would never have guessed your shift was so embroidered. Doesn't it bother you under your corset?"

Fenna colored. In her excitement over the beautiful gowns, she'd forgotten to be mindful of hiding her elaborately embroidered undergarments. She'd survived a whole week, only to have revealed her secret now. She chewed her lip, unsure how to explain her obsession with embroidery.

Mam was the only person who knew, and her initial reaction was enough to ensure Fenna kept it hidden. "I dislike wearing my embellishments on the outside."

Molly gestured for Fenna to turn around. At the back, her only needlework was along the hem of her shift. "That explains a lot. Your clothing is rather bland. I daresay my mother has been itching for a chance to get you into some finery. She cannot stand to see a woman's potential being wasted."

Women paid gads to have their clothing embroidered so intricately. It did Fenna no favors to put on airs and give Mam the impression that she wanted more than she already had. "I like to think of it as survival."

"So does Mother." Molly finished buttoning the back of the dress and gripped Fenna by the shoulders, leading her over to the wardrobe and opening the doors so Fenna could see her reflection in the inner mirror.

The green of the dress made Fenna's golden hair look richer, the browns deeper, the blondes lighter.

Molly looked over Fenna's shoulder and nodded. "This is a type of survival too. It's as old as time itself."

"What?"

"A woman wanting to catch the eyes of the best of men to care for her and her young. We still see it in the animal kingdom today." Molly pinched the extra fabric on the waist and shoulders. "It won't need much tailoring. Just a small amount at the top. The midnight one is off shoulder, and I doubt it will need any alterations. Our waists are almost the same."

Fenna nearly laughed. She'd lost weight since deciding to go to Oregon. At first at the prospect of seeing Will, and now at what a bore each meal was, trying to keep her eyes down all the time. "I'm not looking to catch anyone's eye."

Molly returned to Fenna's back and started undoing the buttons. "That's because you've already claimed the best man."

Fenna swallowed and watched Molly's reflection. Part of her wanted to argue. The other part wanted to pretend she hadn't heard.

Molly turned and sifted through the dresses, pulling out a dark blue silk that caught the light in a way that looked like the milky way smeared across the night sky.

She held it out as Fenna stepped in. Then Molly stepped back, allowing Fenna to adjust it only to find that this was the one Molly meant didn't cover the shoulders. It merely cut a horizontal line just under her collar bone and wrapped just under the curve of each shoulder.

"Stunning," Molly said, stepping up behind Fenna. Rather than do the buttons, Molly just gripped the back, holding it together while Fenna surveyed the look in the mirror. It would draw attention all right. But perhaps, just for one night, she could be bold. She would be leaving this town and all its inhabitants behind. She could feel beautiful once more, just for a few hours.

She raised her elbows and the material cut into the flesh below her shoulders. "I can barely lift my arms. How am I supposed to dance in this?"

Molly smirked, letting go of the back. "The designer's goal is to draw the eye. He doesn't much care what you do next."

Fenna smiled as she stepped out of the dress and hung it in the wardrobe to prevent wrinkles.

Molly passed her another gown and sat back as Fenna

tried it on. "You know," Molly said from behind her, "I woke up last night and you were gone."

Fenna's breath froze, her movements stalling. She glanced at Molly in the mirror. Molly was watching her with a coy expression.

"I heard voices in Will's room."

"We were only talking."

Molly's grin stretched. "So it *was* you."

Fenna silently cursed herself for giving in so easily.

"You can look at him just fine."

"It's a rather new discovery."

"And so you're spending your nights with him?"

"Not in the way you are insinuating. Just for half an hour after the house is asleep."

"Why not in the sitting room when the sun is out and there are witnesses?" Molly's voice held laughter, and she lifted a brow. Her mouth quirked in such a way that said she didn't necessarily disapprove of Fenna's late-night actions.

Fenna turned and faced Molly. "Eliza doesn't know. If she did, she'd... well, she'd try to match us again."

"I don't see the problem. You loved him once."

"I was a different girl then."

Molly tilted her chin up, looking at Fenna in a new direction. "Are you sure?"

Fenna remembered last night with Will. The desperate desire to be loved for who she was, not for who someone thought she could be, nor for who they remembered her being in the past. "I've spent enough time expected to be someone else. I'm not going to let Mam's dreams run away with her."

"So you'll just keep your eyes down for the rest of your life?"

"No. Just until Will finds another wife."

Molly laughed outright. "Fenna, he's been waiting for you

for two years. You're here now. What makes you think he's suddenly going to stop now that you're within reach?"

"I'm not within reach. I'm different. Everyone says so. If anything, talking to him will force him to realize it too. I'm not the girl he proposed to."

"Is that what you two do during your late night rendezvous? *Talk?*"

She said the word with such sarcasm Fenna wanted to waltz out the bedroom door, but she was still in her shift. "No, we talk about our lives. We say nothing of the past. Only the now and what's to come. He's worried about being a lone doctor. Worried about the ailments we will face on the trail, both as a physician and as a mortal."

"And do you tell him that you hide your beauty beneath your clothes? Or does he see that for himself?"

Fenna gasped at her wicked words. "I *never*."

Molly raised both brows. "Just wanted to see if you would confirm another suspicion."

As scandalized as she was, Fenna couldn't help but laugh. "If I was doing anything like that, why would we hide it from Mam? Why not tell the world and agree to marry one another once again?" Her chest tightened at the casual jest. Fenna shook her head. "No, not even Will would even understand who I am now. He'll continue holding on to whatever we had before. My best bet is to get him married off, and to do that, I must make it clear that I am not intending to engage with him ever again."

"Ever?"

"Never."

Molly studied her for a moment, then her smile turned sinister. "In that case, I have another dress I want you to try. You will be irresistible at the dance. Will will have no choice but to admit that you are considering other suitors. So many, in fact, that it will be a rebuff to know he's not counted among them."

Molly went back into her closet and sifted through the dresses that had not been intended as gifts for Fenna.

"I don't want to offend him," Fenna said, stretching her neck, curious as to what Molly was searching for.

"Darling, if he doesn't see it written in fire, he's never going to give up on you."

She turned and pulled out a pink dress. As Fenna saw it in its entirety, she understood why it had been left back in the closet. It was a deep rose color and had enough flounces that the material alone could have been used to make three other dresses. The neckline was embellished with ruffles and lace, but the waist was unadorned and would cut a flattering figure.

It was like a sparkling jewel one had to hold in their hands to admire properly. Fenna tucked her hands behind her and stepped back. "I couldn't. You should wear that."

"I should." She tucked the dress against her shoulders and looked down the length with a grin. "I could show McFarland what he's been missing all this time. But I think your purposes are more important."

Fenna sat on the bed. "Will you help me find Will a wife?"

Molly took a seat next to her and drew a deep breath. "Are you sure?"

"I'm sure." And she was. To enter any type of relationship with Will would undo all the work she'd done over the years. Work to become loved, or at least appreciated, for who she was, not for the potential she had to be a lawful member of this family.

Mam loved Fenna as a daughter despite her inability to love her sons as husbands. Fenna had worked to make herself indispensable at Mam's side. She'd been a daughter just as Mam had been a mother. She wasn't going to throw all of that away on the chance that Will would like this new version of Fenna as much as he'd liked the old version. And what if *she* could never love *him*? There were too many unknowns, and Fenna had been taught never to gamble.

She knew too well how much a risk could cost. In time, he would see they were no longer a match. Until then, Fenna would do her best to make it crystal clear that she was the one uninterested in him, starting with forcing herself to wear embellishments on the outside for the first time in two years.

Rather than try to keep her head down, she was going to take a chance and hope it worked to undo the damage she'd done to Will. That, finally, he would be allowed to move on. And after that, she would be allowed to as well.

CHAPTER 11

When the morning of the dance came, Fenna whispered her lines, practicing how she was going to tell Mam about her ability to see Will. The most frightening part wasn't the unveiling of the truth, but whatever Mam's reaction was going to be.

Even though Fenna had informed Molly what would transpire this morning, when Molly played her part and begged her mother to leave early to accompany Molly on an errand in town, Fenna's heart picked up so much that she wanted to catch Molly's perfectly pressed sleeve and tell her she didn't need to leave, because Fenna wasn't telling Mam anything.

Why couldn't she and Will just continue to see each other in private? Mam would find out eventually. Fenna wasn't an actress, and she doubted even the most skilled of thespians would continue a charade like this forever. But just now, as she watched Molly and Harriet's retreating forms, she longed for whatever delay she could conjure.

Mam worried her lip as she stared after the two women. Then she turned toward Fenna. "I do worry a bit about her coming along." She smiled and her shoulders relaxed. "But you two do get along so well." Mam's head fell to the side and her smile turned sad. "I wish you had a sister."

Fenna tried to smile. She'd be happy with a sibling of either gender. She even missed her pa's horse, Red. He was about the only true family Fenna had left.

She straightened her back, letting courage build up in her stiffened spine. "I—there's been a development."

Mam straightened her neck and her expression turned from sad to curious.

Fenna huffed, her fear suddenly feeling too heavy to bear any longer. "With Will. I can look at him without any reaction."

Mam's mouth made a small "o" and she blinked several times before saying, "You can? When?"

"I looked at him last night, and I was just fine." Skating the truth a little, but it was nothing compared to the subterfuge she and Will had performed for over a week.

Mam placed both hands on Fenna's arm and squeezed. "Oh, Fenna. I'm so glad. Do you know what this means?"

Fenna placed her palms flat on the table. Now was the difficult part—settling Mam's dreams. "All it means is that I'll be a sight more comfortable on the trail west."

Mam sat back in her seat, bumping against the backrest. She squinted at Fenna. "You didn't remember anything? Didn't *feel* anything?"

Fenna recalled her time in Will's room. She'd felt something, to be sure. Respect, attraction, a growing level of comfort, but mostly she felt uncertainty, doubt, and a shred of that old feeling she'd gotten when someone knew more about her than she did. She shook her head. "I was just focusing on the part about me not crying uncontrollably."

Mam gave a soft chuckle and rose from her seat, reaching her arms out wide. Fenna stood and embraced her. Mam petted Fenna's hair. "Of course. That will come in time. You don't know how happy this makes me."

Fenna pulled back and both women took their seats once more. "Mam, I want you to know that this doesn't mean I will be taking up any sort of relationship with Will. The girl who fell in love with him is gone. We both know I'm not her."

Mam lifted a shoulder, but she couldn't keep the quirk from her lips. Joy was practically rolling off her. "I'm not the same girl I was when I married Frank. That doesn't mean he loves me any less."

Fenna drew in a calming breath. Mam wasn't listening. Just like Will, Fenna would have to show her indifference, even if it meant disappointing her. Again.

Smith came in and took their empty plates. When he left, Fenna said, "I must say, I was worried about the dance. Molly is intent on me going and wearing a dress of hers. Now I won't have to hide in the corner."

Mam's eyes turned softer. "You were never meant for the corner. I wish you hadn't had to hide yourself all these years."

Fenna smiled, but inside she was recalling that day she'd shown her first embroidered gown to Mam. She struggled to remember exactly how Mam had reacted, but the message Fenna took away was clear. *You are too pretty like that, and I don't like it.*

Back home, Fenna managed to forget about Will most of the time, but here he was the sun and the whole household revolved around him. With Will on her mind, she wondered if that wasn't the reason Mam hadn't liked her dress, because she might draw attention from another man. It was no secret that Mam did her best to keep Fenna away from any interested suitors. Most of the county knew, even if Mam thought she was being discreet.

If hiding her hobby granted Mam comfort when it came to Fenna, it was worth it. Mam was everything, and if Fenna insisted on sticking herself to the Bridger family like a stitched-on flower, she ought to do her best to ensure they had no reason to cut the strings and allow her to unravel.

The idea still stuck in her, as deep as a burr in the sole of her boots. *Go unnoticed. Be unremarkable.*

Mam's voice came, interrupting her thoughts. "We need to tell Will."

Fenna remembered her rehearsed line. "I sent a note to the clinic earlier."

Mam scoffed. "He must not have gotten it, or he would be here now."

Fenna wrung her hands under the table. They hadn't anticipated the devotion Mam would have expected Will to show at such a revelation. After all, he'd seen her look at him that first night and it had been *her* who approached *him* after Molly fell asleep. "I, uh, told him not to return, just to keep working. Your sister is so intent on him finishing his work and joining us at the dance, you know."

Mam's brows smoothed a miniscule amount. "Harriet has been rather insistent. But, Fenna, it's *you*. Will has—" She narrowed her eyes at Fenna. "Well, I'm sure once he gets it, he'll be right over."

Fenna nodded, letting Mam think whatever eased her concern.

That evening, Molly and Fenna readied in Molly's room. Occasionally, they would hear loud laughter from Harriet's room and know the sisters were having a grand time.

Molly stood behind Fenna, arranging her curls to frame her face before braiding the rest of her hair back. "You should see the dress Mama and I got today. I've never seen anything so drab. And the material." Molly grimaced. "You must work your magic and make it beautiful." Molly slipped the embroidered ruffle of Fenna's shift between her fingers and slid her thumb over the deep blue flower.

"I'll be happy to."

"You should do your own too."

Fenna met Molly's gaze in the mirror, and she could see the calculation in Molly's eyes. "I don't wear my embellishments on the outside."

"I know."

"So I have no need to decorate my dresses."

"You should."

Fenna felt a flush creep up her neck as hot irritation flooded her mind. She tried to tamp it down. She was literally sitting in Molly's chair, letting Molly fix her hair, and about to put on Molly's dress. There was no reason she should feel anything but deepest gratitude for this woman.

And yet.

"It isn't your fault." Molly's voice was gentle.

Just as quickly as it burned, her blood cooled. She couldn't stop her eyes from flashing to Molly again. "What do you mean?"

"I mean, whatever happened to make you think you should not be beautiful, it isn't your fault."

Eased that Molly didn't know as much as it seemed, Fenna let her shoulders relax. "I don't think anything is my fault. It's just…it isn't righteous to be vain."

Molly clutched at her chest and gave an exaggerated moan. "Such cruel words when you've seen my closet. I fear vanity is a vice of mine."

Fenna chuckled.

"In my defense, my mother nourished it. I was taught the things a woman is allowed to excel in. So long as I performed where she wished, I was allowed to spend my free time with my own interests."

"Books."

"Yes, books. I swear if I have a daughter, she'll not be forced to learn French. The only time I ever use it is when I am with Mama's stuffy friends. And some of them don't even know it themselves. New money." She waved a dismissive hand.

Fenna ignored the barb and watched Molly with the same intensity, hoping to read her expression when Fenna asked her question. "A daughter? You might want to be married to have a daughter."

Molly's finger froze on Fenna's braid. Her throat bobbed. "Of course. I said *if* I have one."

"Does that mean your argument about marriage out west might be just a little bit true?"

Molly's eyes cut to the closed door and back to Fenna's reflection. She lowered her voice. "There is little chance I'll meet a man out west who will take my interest."

"Of course." Fenna suppressed a laugh.

"But what I said was true. The rails will get there. And when they do…" Molly scoffed. "It won't be for years, so it really doesn't matter. I'm old now. By the time the rails get there, I'll be good for nothing except being a stepmother."

"You'd be a wonderful stepmother."

Molly smiled and focused on Fenna's hair once more. But Fenna saw the flush that colored Molly's high cheekbones.

Fenna thought of the time they'd spent in the library. "So long as the children know how to devour books."

Molly's smile grew.

As she finished Fenna's hair, Fenna considered what the marriage prospects would be like out west. She doubted there would be many widowers; more bachelors. Fenna wouldn't mind a man with a few children. She'd always wanted a big family, but she knew better than most that little in life could be planned.

Perhaps she would never marry. She could be auntie to all the Bridger children. Devote her life to them the way her pa had done when he was alive. First, she would need to get them all married. And who better to start with than Will? Once he was married, there would be no disappointing Mam with her unwillingness to marry him.

Molly and Fenna helped one another dress and soon a call came from downstairs. Mr. Marx informed them the carriage was ready. Fenna stood, and the idea of Mr. Marx seeing her so dressed—of anyone seeing her—made her knees wobble, so she sat down once more.

Molly came and stood at Fenna's knees. She held out both of her gloved hands. "Come now. You are the one who wanted to show Will he's out of your mind."

Fenna swallowed through her thick throat. She glanced at the table for a glass of water. Molly reached it and passed it to Fenna, who drank it carefully, though a spill might not be the worst idea just now. "It isn't Will I am thinking of."

Molly crouched down, her full skirts billowing and then slowly deflating. She met Fenna's downcast gaze with her own inquiring one.

Fenna set the glass on the vanity. "Everyone will look at me."

Molly laughed. "So sure? You really are prone to vanity."

Fenna gave a shaky laugh and Molly stood once more, holding out one hand. The click of heels on the wooden stairs told Fenna that Mam and Harriet were heading down.

Molly's voice was soft, holding none of the jest from before. "No harm will come to you or anyone else just because you look beautiful."

Instead of comforting, these words brought tears to Fenna's eyes. Her vision blurred and Molly crouched down again. "Oh no. I said the wrong thing."

Fenna sniffed back her tears and fanned her face, hoping her eyes weren't already red or puffy.

Molly passed her a handkerchief. "Or maybe I said the

exact right thing. I can't quite decide. Either way, this isn't what I intended. Shall I ask them to come back for us?"

Fenna sniffed again, deeper this time in a most unladylike way. "Of course not." She stood and took Molly's hand with a firm grip, using her other hand to fan away the tears.

Molly eyed their hands and smiled up at Fenna. "You've got more backbone than I gave you credit for."

Fenna feigned a glare at the backhanded compliment. Though Molly was anything but sugary sweet, Fenna had grown to enjoy the idea that she would always know where she stood with Molly.

The pair held hands as they made their way down the stairs. Will waited at the bottom, his hair combed neater than she'd ever seen it. His waistcoat was a silky green that matched the leafy embellishments on Fenna's gown. She darted a glance at Molly, wondering if she'd planned this, but the woman had eyes only for her cousin.

"Will, you are looking quite handsome."

She reached out and he handed her down the last several stairs. She passed him right out the door.

Fenna swallowed. She hadn't expected their first public meeting to feel so... intense. She couldn't tell if Mam's eyes were on them from where she stood outside, but the feeling that all eyes were on her was unnerving.

Will offered her an upturned palm, and she took his hand in hers, grateful for the gloved barrier between their flesh.

He nestled her hand in the crook of his elbow and led her out the door. "I got an earful from my mama. She didn't approve of my ignoring your note."

"I never sent a note."

He laughed, but Fenna cut him off. "Shh, we are supposed to be strangers."

He quieted, but said, "Ah, but you have never been a stranger to me. Mama knows that."

They approached the carriage and the conversation halted as they climbed in. Only two seats were left on the same side. Fenna's gaze darted to Mam, who was grinning as she looked out the opposite window with forced casualness.

And it had begun, the very matchmaking Fenna had feared. She supposed it was always going to happen. At least Will had agreed to her ruse for a bit. Once they were on the trail, everyone would be too busy for romance. Perhaps there was just a small piece of sweetness to the mortality of the Oregon trail. Surely nobody would expect romance to bloom among such sorrow.

CHAPTER 12

Will handed both Mama and Fenna down from the carriage and each of them took an arm. He couldn't keep his eyes off Fenna, and he knew the moment they stepped out of the carriage no other single man would be able to do so either.

As they entered the brightly lit home, Will got his first decent look at her dress. It was a deep pink that made her cheeks look brighter, her lips redder. His gaze swept across her bare shoulders and down her figure. He'd never seen her in this dress before, and it pained him to really consider how much life she'd lived without him these past years.

He longed to remove his waistcoat and drape it over her bare shoulders. But short of covering her face, he knew even that would do little to solve his problem. He was going to have to cope with the churning in his gut and deal with the idea that it was only going to get worse as the night wore on.

They joined the Marxes in a circle of friends and Will received a hearty welcome from those who had longed for him to attend events such as this.

He introduced his mama and begrudgingly introduced

Fenna as "a dear family friend" as he tightened his arm on her hand.

Mama's eyes darted to him, but he only raised his brows. Up until now, he'd been content to allow them to lie about Fenna being his sister, but he meant to court his wife this night.

Molly broke away from her parents and came to Fenna's side, whispering something in her ear. Fenna's hold on his arm loosened, and only then did he realize she'd been gripping it so tightly. He'd been holding on himself, and even as she slipped her hand off his arm completely, he was comforted by the fact that she'd clung to him for the duration of whatever storm had roiled inside her mind.

Molly touched Will's arm. "I want to introduce Fenna around just a bit. She doesn't want to listen to this drab talk."

Will glanced at the parents and found they were speaking of the war. He'd not heard a word of their conversation before now. When he turned back, Fenna and Molly were making their way through the crowd, Fenna's blush skirts the last part of her to disappear.

Will swallowed and he stretched his neck, catching the occasional glimpse of Fenna's golden hair.

Of all the stuffy things his aunt and uncle did, these dances were the stuffiest. The sole purpose was to dress up their children of marrying age and come to judge each contestant. The adults gossiped while their children played cat and mouse. Molly had explained the rules early on, and Will had been quick to make his excuses to be absent.

Mrs. Weathers, a buxom woman, waved to Will and started in his direction. "William." She glazed meaningfully at Mama. "I heard your mother was in town."

Mama turned at the mention and took Will's arm once again.

"My, she is pretty enough to be out there with our girls, catching all the men's eyes."

Mama gave her a demure smile.

Will's smile tightened. "Mrs. Weathers, this is my mother, Eliza Bridger."

Rather than a handshake, Mrs. Weathers sidled up so her shoulder brushed Mama's as they faced the dance floor. "Pleased to meet you. I heard you have a girl here too."

"Fenna."

"Oh, what a beautiful name."

Mama's smile was tight, too, and Will wondered if she was trying to figure a way out of Will's inconvenient honesty.

"Will you point her out to me?"

Will could have done so in an instant, so glued was his attention to her.

"There she is," Mama said as Fenna and Molly rounded the far side of the room.

What were they even doing? They hadn't once stopped to talk with anyone. Rather than introducing her, Molly was parading Fenna for everyone to see. His blood turned hot as realization hit. That was precisely what Molly was doing. Fenna was going to have men lined up to dance with her as soon as the music began. And Will was helpless, all the way over here on the other side of the room.

"Oh, she is a beauty," Mrs. Weathers said. "Are you settled on going west? I have a son up at the university. He'll be needing a wife soon."

"We are decided. Besides Will, I have five other sons who need to make a living."

"Six sons? Hmm." Mrs. Weathers lips were pursed, as though Mama had missed a question on a test. "That's too bad. I hear tell there are no women out west. Men are ordering brides from the east and taking whomever they can get. That's no way to build a family if you ask me. But I suppose if they are desperate enough…You best get yours married before they get too far from civilization."

Mama's grip on Will's arm tightened. "That's mighty good advice."

Abigail Weathers appeared then, and her mama pushed her toward Will as the musicians started a quiet melody. "William, why don't you take Abigail for a turn while your mama and I gossip a bit?"

Will suppressed a desperate sigh at being so far from Fenna when the music started. He had hoped for their turn around the room to bring them a bit closer before the musicians began. Nevertheless, he offered his arm to Abigail, who turned and with a dry voice said, "Thank you, Mother."

As they walked onto the floor, he remembered why he didn't come to these. It was impossible to spend an entire evening without a companion, and even if Fenna didn't want his faithfulness, he was going to give it.

"I thought you hated these," Abigail said as they turned and joined hands.

Will reluctantly removed his gaze from the dancers and abandoned his attempts to locate Fenna. He met Abigail's eyes. "I am very busy, trying to learn all I can from Dr. McFarland before I leave."

"It's true then? You're going west."

The music started in earnest and they moved their feet to the steps. Will nodded his head and used it as an excuse to find Fenna, but her golden hair was nowhere in sight.

"I know more than a few ladies who will be crushed to hear this news."

Will looked back at Abigail. She was one of the few young ladies who didn't pressure him. She was smart and sensible and possessed enough pride not to chase after a man who showed no interest.

"You know I have given none of them cause to pursue me."

Abigail threw her head back and laughed. When it died down, she wiped away a tear, a bit dramatic if Will had anything to say about it. He found no humor in what he'd just said. "You know nothing of women."

Will bristled. He didn't know *nothing*. But perhaps, being raised with only brothers, he had missed out on a few lessons.

"Until you are married, you give them cause to pursue you. Your refusal to become a rake when many of them would allow it only adds to your allure."

A golden head caught Will's eye—Fenna in the arms of James Marshall. Will stiffened and he held Abigail as far away as he wished James would do with Fenna. But, strangely, James didn't alter his position in the least.

"It's rather stuffy in here."

Abigail laughed, but tightened her hold on his hand. "Perhaps a fiancée would solve your problem."

"Perhaps," Will said absentmindedly.

"Who is that girl? The one you haven't taken your eyes off of all night."

Will's focus snapped back to Abigail. His mouth worked, but he couldn't make himself speak the lie.

"Some are saying she is your sister, but I remember you saying you have five brothers, all of whom I am very much looking forward to meeting."

"Abigail, we are all going west."

"It's not as though you've signed a contract."

"Committing to my mama is near the same."

Abigail smiled. "A man who respects his mama." She gave a wistful sigh.

The song ended and Will led her off the floor. "Your mama is suggesting they marry before we go. Perhaps our mothers have already arranged for you to marry my younger brother, Sam. You'd like him."

Abigail smirked. "Would I? Does he look like you and adore his mama?"

Will heard the flirt in the comment, but he answered nonetheless. "Yes, quite."

"Then that's an investment I might take up without inspecting the property first."

They parted ways, each of them reaching their mothers' sides. Mama met Will's gaze. She wasn't enjoying her conversation.

"Mrs. Weathers, Abigail," Will said, "it was a pleasure. I have many more folks to introduce my mama to, so we will be on our way."

The two mothers exchanged their goodbyes and Will was off, scanning the crowd for Fenna.

"You're obvious, you know." Mama patted his arm. "A head above most men here and swiveling it round like a stool at the soda shop."

Will started to argue, but just then that same swiveling gaze snagged on Fenna's hair. Soon her face was in sight as she made her way through the other guests. But before she reached them, she and Molly stopped, and they were led back onto the dance floor.

Will ground his teeth. Molly had always been somewhat popular with the gentlemen, most of them inclined to look upon a beautiful woman whom they didn't have to worry about taking anything they said as a promise of marriage. In fact, Molly's aloofness with the men in this town had earned her more than a few male friends, and he suspected she was using those connections to ensure Fenna had a partner for every dance this entire evening.

"Excuse me, Mother." Will broke away from his mama's side and found a quiet nook where he would be undisturbed until Fenna was released from Rich McAllister's hold.

As soon as the pair exited the dance area, Will broke away from the wall and marched straight for Fenna. She broke her hold with Rich and, with wide eyes, looked up to find Will standing before her.

"Fenna." Will held out a hand.

Fenna shot a worried glance at Molly, of all people, before cautiously taking Will's hand. If Rich hadn't been standing there, looking expectantly at Will, he might never have found the words.

Finally, Will asked, "Will you dance with me?"

Fenna nodded and Will swept her away from Rich's perusing eyes.

"You don't want to get too close to Rich McAllister." Will placed one hand on Fenna's waist, wishing he could slide it lower, slide it so low that everyone watching would know Fenna and he had an arrangement.

"He was kind, and he's Molly's friend."

Will took a steadying breath through his nose, but it only served to draw in Fenna's scent, the same one she left in his room every night. Different from the way she'd smelled before. Then she'd been flowers and sunshine. Now she was cotton and soap. With every change in her, he wondered if this was who she would have become if nothing had gone awry that night. People changed, and perhaps she would have always been exactly who she was in this moment. It didn't matter either way. She was his wife, and he still wanted every bit of her.

He twirled her fast enough that she had to grip his shoulder, and he nearly purred at the feel of her fingers clutching him. He longed to spin her such that she would wrap her arms around his neck in earnest and bury her face in his shoulder the way she used to do.

But she would never do that if he didn't stand out among all the men Molly was introducing her to. Will had always been adamant about keeping his secret, but just now he wished Molly had been privy to it. Was it too late to pull his cousin into the alcove and tell her everything? Get her working on his side instead of in the interests of every bachelor in this room?

"Molly said there are more than a few women here who are dying to dance with you."

"Did she?"

"Which one are you most interested in?"

Will's jaw clamped shut. This was absurd. He'd heard enough scheming women in his life to know her words for what they were. "I don't need your help to pair me with a woman."

Fenna laughed. "I was curious. You know, I've advised your other brothers over the years. I have a fair idea what a Bridger man wants in a wife."

"Do you?" He tried to keep his voice light.

Fenna only scrunched her nose in a mock-glare.

"I'll play. Tell me what we want?"

"Well …" Her lips pursed in the cutest look of concentration Will had ever seen. He looked away, because if he didn't, he feared he would do something unforgivable. Kiss her, or tell her they were married, or refuse to release her for the entirety of the evening.

He'd only just gotten her comfortable with him. Even after seeing her look at him the first time, she wouldn't have been comfortable enough to dance in his arms like she was doing now. No, she was like a stray cat. He had to earn her trust and affection slowly, or else risk her running away before he could catch her in his arms.

"For starters, you want a sensible girl, but not so sensible that she cannot see your dreams."

Will nodded. "That seems like a reasonable want. Probably not unique to a Bridger."

"You want a woman who is against slavery."

"Perhaps that was unique back home, but here that's the majority of the folks at this party."

"She can't be spoiled, especially now that you're going west. You'll need someone with grit." She shot him a look. "Did you know Jane Connor refused Ben?"

Will considered this for a moment. "I can't say I blame her. I wasn't even sure you would."

"She didn't break things off because Ben was going west." Fenna glanced over her shoulder and leaned closer. "I think that is part of the reason your pa was so intent on going. He knew there weren't enough options for you boys in Charlotte. Your mama wants grandbabies. She's waited long enough. Both you and Ben should have wives by now. The twins could also be there if they weren't so reliant upon one another."

The more time Will spent lying to her, the harder it was. It took all his willpower not to tell her he already was married. His hands automatically pulled her closer. Her eyes grew wide, and it took everything inside him to loosen his hold and take a half step back, allowing the proper distance, not for the sake of the onlookers, but for Fenna. He could see that stray feline in her eyes, and he wasn't going to scare her away, not when he'd just gotten her back. "How did Ben take the rejection?"

"I might speak Bridger, but that man is a vise. That might be the reason Jane left. Perhaps she was searching for something that showed Ben truly loved her. I don't think it was in him to give it to her."

Ben wasn't the only Bridger who had that flaw. She wouldn't remember, but Fenna had once threatened to leave Will, saying she wasn't sure of his intentions. Said there were plenty of men who wanted to court her. That was the night he had proposed on a whim, without her father's permission. "Sometimes I wish I were a bit more like Ben."

Fenna made a face. "Why?"

"He's tougher, has a heart for adventure."

"You left your family and went to school here in Virginia. You cannot say he is the only brother to seek adventure."

"That decision was calculated. Once Ben sets his mind to something, he follows it through to failure if that's the way it's going."

"Do you think going west will be a failure?"

"Of course not. I don't idolize him so much that I wish to fail alongside him. I think west is the only place to go."

The song ended, and Will hated that he only had stolen moments with his wife. He hated even more that another bachelor was waiting at Molly's side, greedy eyes on Fenna.

Will surrendered her with numb hands, wishing more than ever that he could channel whatever blood he shared with Ben, could demand Fenna just be his wife already. But Fenna had had so much taken; he wouldn't take her agency too.

"She's a desirable woman." Molly's voice came at the same time as her hand weaved its way into the crook of his arm.

Will could only look down at his cousin. Anger kept his words at bay.

"Dance with me?"

Will nodded and led her so they were right next to Fenna and her partner. But, despite Will's efforts, the waltzing steps of the dance took them away from her.

"You want to win her back."

Will glanced down at Molly. "Of course."

"This is one dance. Let her have some space to breathe. She's had Bridgers crowding around her whole life." Molly laughed. "Don't look so broken; I don't think she minded. It's just"—Molly drew her brows together, considering—"I think she needs to find her worth without you lot."

Her worth. "And you think pressing her into the arms of every bachelor in Harrisonburg is the answer?"

Molly laughed again and Will had to mindfully keep his hands from clenching. "It's something. I believe in Charlotte she was part of your family. Perhaps not your fiancée any longer, but still part of you. She needs to see that there is a life for her without you."

"No." Will breathed, considering his words. Now wasn't the time to tell Molly. He wasn't telling anyone else, not until he told Fenna.

"She's afraid of losing your mother."

That swept the anger right out of him. "What do you mean?"

"I mean she's spent the last few years trying to find a place to belong. Even now, she's an interloper. She's going west, but not as the daughter she wants to be."

"She can—"

Molly cut him off. "She wants to be loved as herself. Not as your bride-to-be. Think of all the people who love you. It's not because you're so great." She squeezed his shoulder. "It's because you're family. Nobody loves her like that. If she missteps, she runs the risk of losing everyone."

Will's heart clenched. Molly was right. There was no way he could begin to understand what life as an orphan was like. With every blow life had dealt him, he'd had his family to turn to. Every disappointment, every misstep. Even going west... it wasn't so much an invitation as it was a demand. He'd never considered how the chains that made his family feel inescapable could also be an anchor in the storm, strong and unyielding when the crashing waves came.

Molly must have seen the understanding on his face

because she patted his arm. "I know it's difficult. But let her have just a glimpse of life outside your family."

Will sighed. What was worse was that now that they'd told his mother, Fenna was no longer bound to come to him tonight. Or any other nights.

CHAPTER 13

Back home, in Molly's room, Fenna lay tucked between the bedcovers and listened to Molly gush about the men who had expressed genuine interest. "I haven't had this much fun since my sister Anna was hunting for a husband."

Fenna couldn't help but laugh at Molly's phrasing. "Hunting? Did she shoot one from the sky?"

Molly lifted an eyebrow. "Hers wasn't nearly as high as Richard McAllister. His pa owns factories up north. If this war grows, they'll be set for generations. Not only would your children be rich, but their children's children and their children's children."

Fenna held up a hand. "Richard doesn't matter."

Molly scoffed. "That's because you've never had so much. You looked incredible tonight. I hate to agree with my mother, but it is an utter shame that you hide behind those drab browns and grays. You were made for pinks and shimmering blues."

Fenna chewed her lip. "I did have a man, back in Charlotte."

Molly paused climbing under the covers, the quilt hanging mid-air.

Fenna caught her lips between her teeth, instant regret filling her. *Will's team.* She begged her mind to remember that no matter how much she enjoyed Molly, no matter how close they were growing, Molly was still Will's. She would always be Will's.

Molly found herself, quickly nestled in close, and said, "Tell me everything."

"Well, he was rich. He bought the Bridgers' plantation from them."

"Oh, he did?" Molly's tone was teasing, and Fenna couldn't help but smile.

"He wanted me to stay, to marry him."

"You would have been mistress of the Bridgers' plantation?" Molly let out a low whistle. "Not bad, Miss Jennings."

"I never wanted that."

"I know. Family is all you want."

Fenna's gaze shot to Molly's face, searching for the sliver of teasing her words held.

Molly shrugged. "You aren't such a puzzle."

"Yes. I wanted family, but his mother…" Fenna shook her head.

Molly turned so she was facing the ceiling and fluffed her pillow. "It's always the mother. She can be the death blow to a marriage. I've seen it more than once. You want a man who is good to his mother, but if he's still clinging to those apron strings…" Molly slid her thumb across her throat and shook her head.

Fenna laughed, thinking of Edward. He had never seemed *too* attached. It was more that when she was around his mother, Fenna felt like a ring of scum to be scrubbed from a pot. After living in a house where the sons respected their mama's opinion so greatly, it was difficult to believe Edward didn't share her mind in this matter at least a little.

"Richard McAllister doesn't have a mother."

"Oh." Fenna thought of the dashing man who had claimed more than a few dances with her that evening.

"Don't feel sorry for him. He lost her so long ago. He's got a stepmother, and she's young and quite enjoyable. She might feel a bit more like a sister than a mother."

Fenna laughed. "I'm not marrying Richard McAllister."

Molly gave a dramatic sigh. "I wish you had less opinions."

"Me too."

After the conversation had slowed and Molly had dropped off to sleep, Fenna pulled back the covers before she realized she didn't have to go to Will's room tonight. Their deal was done. Each had fulfilled their portion and now the only place she had to be tonight was in bed, sleeping off the delicacies she'd indulged in that evening.

She glanced at the wall that stood between the two rooms. Was he waiting for her? Had he too forgotten their ruse was over? Should she knock just to make sure he wasn't waiting up? Or was that presumptuous? Perhaps he'd already fallen asleep. He hadn't danced as much as she, spending most of the night at his mother's side, but they'd all been yawning on the ride back to the Marx home.

She smiled. Did Molly consider Will was too close to his mother? Fenna didn't think he was. He'd left her for several years, after all, but for all the time since her accident she'd watched them correspond via letters. They were closer than one might have expected for living so far away from one another. She couldn't remember if that closeness was a newer thing, or if it had existed before she'd lost her memory.

She could ask, but what business was it of hers? If she

were in his room right now, it would be the type of thing that came naturally to their conversation. She might not remember much about this man, but she did know he was easy to talk to. If there weren't history between them, history that made Fenna aggravated if she thought on it for too long, she imagined their time in his room would have been that much easier.

As she tucked herself back into bed, she sighed, trying to imagine what their courtship had been like. Had it been casual, like this new friendship forming between them now? Or had it been passionate and consuming? She knew the timeline; he'd come home from school for the summer and in less than eight weeks they'd been engaged, would have been married if their parents had allowed it. She shook her head, her hair caressing the pillow.

The one thing she could be grateful for was the fact that they hadn't actually gotten married. It had been difficult enough to encourage everyone to get over an engagement. What would things have been like if there'd been a wedding? She supposed a vow made before God didn't account for amnesia. Perhaps God and everyone else would have expected her to hold to it. To live in a stranger's house—well, not a stranger, but not quite a lover.

She tried to think of the old Will, the one she remembered from her childhood, but as easy as it had been to conjure him up on the train ride here, now those memories were fogged with new ones. Visions of him on his bed, his hands in his lap, his eyes on her curled up in his desk chair with a blanket over her shoulders. He was right that those late nights had altered her memory. Will was no longer in the past, but part of the present, and an inevitable part of her future.

Their last week in town turned out to be busier than expected. Besides the hustle of acquiring Molly's provisions, the dance had invited guests to the Marxes' home. The Weathers family came on a day Will was at home. Fenna had seen one of the daughters dancing with Will, but once they were all crammed into the sitting room, Fenna could see there were a few more, all who blushed and laughed at the slightest attempt at humor from Will. Fenna told herself her annoyance with the ladies was merely due to the fact that such simpering could not possibly tempt Will and therefore these women were of no use to her plan to find Will a wife.

Fenna glanced over at Molly. Why must they be here when these ladies had obviously come to see Will? Molly discreetly opened her book. If only Fenna had been in here with a bit of embroidery so she could do the same.

Mrs. Weathers voice rose an octave. "Your brothers aren't coming here, then? I thought for sure…"

"They're heading right to Independence," Will said. "There is much to do before we leave, supplies that can only be acquired by those who know how to prepare for the Oregon trail specifically."

Fenna looked at each daughter with understanding. Their mother had brought them here especially to meet the Bridger boys. She glanced at Will, wondering if he wasn't as deterred by their behavior as she'd assumed. Perhaps he'd not been as devoted as Aunt Harriet had hinted. After all, Fenna had certainly had an affair Mam hadn't known about. It wasn't as though young folks told their elders everything.

If he had a bit of a relationship already, she could marry him off before they even left…but no. Three days was not enough time. The thought of leaving him here and breaking Mam's heart was too much for Fenna to bear.

When Will glanced at the clock, Fenna felt only relief at knowing he had no intention to marry any of these women.

KATE CONDIE

The way he was tapping his fingers against his knee made her wonder if his patience with their company was nearly spent.

When it was finally time for them to leave, Will escorted them out of the room.

Molly collapsed back in her chair. "That family is exhausting." She shook her head. "It's no wonder no man wants to marry any of them."

"They're pretty enough," Fenna offered.

Molly scoffed. "Would you want to sit through all that every night? It's a circus."

Fenna didn't sit. Instead, she stretched her back. Cooking over an open fire also meant keeping far enough away from the flames that her skirt didn't catch, which meant leaning far over to reach the center. Her back was cursing her for such a posture.

Harriet bustled into the room and clapped her hands. "Thank heavens they've gone. The McAllisters will be here in a quarter of an hour. I was afraid their parties would overlap. No doubt the Weathers would have driven him away before he had a chance to speak with Fenna."

"M-me?"

Harriet rushed over and tucked a loose hair into Fenna's bun. "Heavens, child. You smell of smoke." She ran her gaze down Fenna's front. "Go get on one of Molly's dresses. Your hair will keep the smell, but perhaps with a different dress..." She placed her hand on Fenna's back and pressed her toward the exit.

Fenna had barely made it to the stairs when Harriet's voice came again. "Go on, child. She cannot button herself."

When Molly appeared at the bottom of the stairs, Fenna smirked. Over the last week, she'd discovered a new pleasure, which was foiling Molly's plans to spend the entirety of her life with her face in a book. She didn't doubt Molly found real joy there, but with a family like this one, she often missed too much fun.

Molly helped her into a deep blue dress with ivory stripes. The dress's many cuts and seams put those stripes in just the right places, in such a way that though the dress was free of frills and had been deemed sturdy enough to take up space in the wagons, it was also quite feminine. Fenna had every intention of making a pattern out of the dress and trying to make a second one once life settled down a bit.

Once the dress was on, Molly turned her attention to Fenna's hair, undoing and redoing the knot to contain the strands that had loosened when she and Mam had been in the yard working.

"Why is he coming? Everyone knows we are leaving soon."

Molly shrugged. "Leave times don't matter to a man like Richard, who owns the world."

Fenna scoffed. "He does not."

"No, but his parents have done a poor job teaching him that reality."

"He thinks I'll stay and let him court me?"

Molly nodded.

"Miss my train west just on the chance he'll like me enough and want to marry me?" Fenna chuckled but when Molly didn't counter her, she stopped laughing. "Truly?"

Fenna blinked. What must it be like to be so sure of oneself? Edward had been sure as well. He'd not even considered that Fenna would join the Bridgers in going west. Perhaps it was a male thing, to be so confident. Another image appeared—the hurt on Edward's face when she'd told him she was leaving.

The image disappeared the moment Harriet burst into the room. "They're here. Now, mind your manners." She looked right at Molly, then turned to Fenna. "You look lovely, darling."

Fenna followed the Marx women down the stairs and into the sitting room. Molly returned to her spot and plucked her book from the table. Fenna was again without her needlework, but of course she couldn't have done it anyway. Reality breathed hard on her neck. Richard was coming here. For her.

Will entered the room just as the bell sounded. "McAllister?" His gaze flashed down the length of her gown and back to her eyes. "You changed?"

Fenna nodded, her throat dry. She'd loved the dress a moment ago, but Will's question made her wonder if it was too much. Was she making a spectacle of herself? She cleared her throat. They were leaving in three days. It didn't matter what Rich McAllister thought of her. But Molly's insight had made him feel huge, like a fellow that a woman didn't dare disappoint.

Before Fenna had even sat, Richard entered, and with Will standing just inside the doorway, the room felt far too small.

Will turned and shook Richard's hand. "Afternoon."

Richard's eyes quickly moved from Will to Fenna as he stepped farther into the room, putting distance between himself and Will and easing a bit of the tightness in her chest.

He took her hand and placed a kiss on the back. "You look lovely this afternoon."

Fenna dipped her head. "Thank you."

He took a seat and, finally, Fenna did too. The only spot left was next to Molly, so Will took that one with a glower on his face. Perhaps he thought Richard had come to see him and he disliked being cast into the background.

"How have you enjoyed your time in Harrisonburg?"

"Oh, I've enjoyed it very much. Molly is an excellent companion."

Richard's attention moved briefly to Molly, then fixed on Fenna again. "I had hoped to take you for a ride in the park, but the weather seems to have disagreed."

Smith stepped through the doorway with a tray of tea and cakes. She tracked his movements, using his entrance as a chance to slow her breathing.

"Allow me." She stood and poured tea for Molly first, then Richard. When she passed him his cup, she saw his gaze dip down the length of her body, appreciating her figure. To a man like this, her actions would appear the same as Molly's stroll across the dance had been: a chance to display herself for the world to see. She longed to be back in her gray dress, smelling of smoke, to see if Richard still had the desire to stare.

Finally, she brought a cup to Will. He took it clumsily, his hands draping over both of hers as he took the cup. Their eyes met briefly, and his brimmed with earnestness. She swallowed and looked away, but the heat of his gaze lingered.

Taking her seat again, she cupped her tea in her hands, but she didn't dare drink it, not with Richard studying her. He was nothing like Edward. She knew the Perkins family, had seen Edward countless times in her life, so he wasn't such an intimidating partner. Richard, on the other hand... She glanced at Will. He wore a disgruntled expression as he too ignored his tea.

"So," she said, desperate for any conversation, "you and Will must have gotten to know one another these last few years."

Richard made a show of turning to look at Will and chuckled. "Few know Will well. The man is a hermit, more so than Molly here."

Molly's only response was the ruffle of a turned page.

Richard's attention returned to Fenna. She wished she could render a covert kick to Molly's shin, anything to receive a sliver of help in conversation. Will, too. Why was he so irritated if he barely knew this man and had no interest in striking up conversation?

Fenna recalled Will's words from the dance. *You don't want to get too close to Richard McAllister.* She'd done the same for Will's brothers, warning them away from the unsuitable women back home. It seemed Will was intent upon bestowing the same courtesy upon Fenna. Not that she needed it. This man wasn't a real option for her. He was going to chat with them today and she would never see him again.

That thought brought courage, and Fenna smiled boldly at Richard. "Molly says your family owns factories a bit north?"

Richard nodded. "We're often traveling. In fact, I believe we will be at the train station on the same day, one headed north and the other headed west."

"Molly seems to think the rails will reach the west very soon. Do you agree?"

Richard considered, his handsome face tilting slightly. "I hate to disagree with a lady, but the war will stall all work on the railroad. It will reach the Pacific one day, but not before Molly has read through whatever book she's bringing west." He turned slightly. "Miss Marx, are you sure about going west? You'll have to reread a few of those."

Molly gave him a mock glare. "I am sure." She nodded meaningfully at Fenna. "So is Fenna."

Richard fixed his eyes on Fenna. "I admit I mourn the fact that I only met you last weekend. To know such a beautiful flower was among us all this time, and now she's about to leave."

Fenna blushed and found her embarrassment had

rendered her unable to speak. She'd heard flattery before, but it had never come from a stranger. Richard knew nothing of Fenna's past. He had no need to be overly courteous to her. Anytime she'd received a compliment, she'd understood the person giving it did so partially because they had known her for most of her life and wished to be kind to her. But hearing it now, from Richard's lips, made her wonder for the first time if it was truly so. Was she a beauty? Was she one to take the attention of a man like Richard, handsome and wealthy, who could have his pick of maidens in this county?

"When you leave, where are you going?"

"All the way to New York on business."

Perhaps he had his pick of women even farther than this county. She ached to look at Will again. Was that why he disliked this man? Had he spurned a girl Will was close to? She stopped her errant thoughts and focused more intently on Richard. "Do you travel often?"

"Yes. My father always did, and he's trying to pass the reins to me. It isn't easy at a time like this. Everything is changing, even from what my father knew."

As he continued on, speaking of how the impending war was affecting his family business, Fenna couldn't keep from cutting a look at Will. He was staring over the rim of his tea at the back of Richard's head. But, in a moment, his eyes flicked to Fenna.

She flinched, but she held his gaze for a long moment, until she couldn't stand it any longer. Anger fairly pulsed off Will. Was his anger truly all for Richard, or was Will angry with her as well?

When Richard finally left, Fenna turned back to Molly and Will. "You two were little help." She spun and marched to Molly's room to get out of the dress, but Harriet appeared at the bottom of the stairs. "How did it go? Does he want to see you again?"

Fenna turned and gripped the handrail, not yet done being angry with Will and Molly. "He wanted to take me for a ride in the park today. He said tomorrow the weather might be better."

"Oh, darling. That would be wonderful."

It certainly wouldn't be worse than handling the conversation alone as she'd just done in the sitting room. Fenna longed to reach Molly's room, but without Molly, Fenna wouldn't be able to rid herself of the dress. "Is Eliza still out?"

"Yes. Do you need anything?"

"No."

Harriet nodded, and Fenna took the dismissal. She continued up the stairs and sat on the edge of the bed. Molly's torso was longer than Fenna's, and the bodice cut into her hips, so she let herself fall backward, arms splayed.

She certainly wanted Will to express disinterest, but now that he had, she didn't like it. She didn't want him to be entirely careless of her. He'd obviously hated Richard, yet Will had done nothing to make Richard look bad or to take the conversation away from him and Fenna. If anything, Will's angry silence had only allowed Richard to have full control of the conversation, flattering Fenna one moment, then covertly mentioning his wealth in another. Traveling to New York. Harrisonburg was the farthest she'd ever been from home. People like her didn't take trains often, and when they did, they traveled in passenger cars, not the kind Richard would be in, with cabins and beds for comfort.

There was one world where Fenna belonged, and just now she felt she'd left that world far behind. That realization filled her with a mucky uneasiness. Too recently, she'd left her memories behind and the world she'd woken up to had been much changed. This time she would remember what she was leaving, and that knowledge burned away all the muck and gave her hope amidst the fear.

CHAPTER 14

Will wished his time at the clinic wasn't over. He wished Dr. McFarland wasn't so angry with him for leaving that Will could go, just for the day, and help. But the new intern was trained, and Will would leave for Independence in two days.

Two days of agony, as it seemed he'd finally had opportunity to be around his family just in time to watch Fenna be courted by Richard McAllister.

He sat in the study, empty for once since Mama had coaxed Molly to learn a bit of cooking outside. But he wasn't alone for long.

Mama appeared in the doorway with her hands on her hips. "Molly says Fenna is out with the McAllister boy."

Will gave a miserable nod.

Mama bustled in, smelling strongly of woodsmoke. "You cannot let her do this."

Will wanted to agree, but Molly's voice was stronger, telling him Fenna needed to discover her worth outside the Bridger family. A man like Richard McAllister was sure to imbue her with plenty of confidence. "We're leaving in two days. He won't propose before then."

"Is that all you're worried about? He's a handsome fellow." Mama stepped closer, her whisper growing harsh. "They are alone in a carriage."

The images Will had been doing his best to block out were back in full force. "I cannot tell her. Not yet."

Mama's eyes blazed. "Why not?"

The set to her jaw made Will's hackles rise. "Because she's not ready. The last thing I want is for her to hop a train back home."

"So you're waiting until we're on the trail and she cannot turn back?"

Will winced. "You think me so conniving? My intention is to make her fall in love with me again."

"Oh?" Mama's dander was up, her voice filled with all the heat of those fire-peppers she grew in the garden back home. "What will you do when she is finally in love with you? Tell her 'How convenient! We don't even have to see a preacher. You can just come live with me.' You don't think that's going to make her want to run away?"

Will hated the jest in her tone. Truly, he hadn't thought of how Fenna would feel to learn he'd been withholding this information all along. He couldn't expect her to feel *only* relief. "She may not be thrilled about it, but it beats feeling trapped now. She's had enough taken from her. I won't take anything else."

"By keeping this information from her, you are taking one more thing that should belong to her. The truth."

Mama spun on her heel and was out the door. Will hated that she was right. Hated everything about this situation. Fenna hadn't remembered anything from their time spent together. The things she lost were never coming back and his mama was right. Here was a memory Will *could* give her.

When she returned from her ride with Richard and entered the house, Will was waiting at the door.

Her face was flushed and her eyes bright as she lifted them to him. "Oh, Will. How are you?"

Will glanced up as Richard's carriage drove away. "How was your ride?"

"Oh, it was wonderful. Harrisonburg has the most beautiful park." She deposited her parasol in the corner and tugged on the fingertips of her gloves.

"Did Richard make you an offer? Does he want to see you again tomorrow?"

She looked up with wide eyes, the lace glove only halfway up her hand. She held his gaze for a moment before narrowing her own. "He did not make me an offer. Did you expect as much?"

"I don't know what he wants with you when you are leaving in a few days."

"Am I not an entertaining companion?"

Will's chest twisted at how much he'd missed her companionship. He could scarcely remember the days and weeks before the accident, but he sharply recalled their time in his room as of late. Multiple sweet evenings, and now they were done. "You are a fine companion. Of course he wants to spend time with you. Only I don't understand what he hopes to gain."

Fenna shifted and picked up her gloves once more, running them through her hands.

Will tried to catch her eye. "Did he tell you his intentions?"

Her throat bobbed. "He asked me to consider staying."

"Here?" Will couldn't help but laugh. "At the Marxs' while Molly leaves? You hardly know them."

Anger flashed in her eyes. "I didn't say I would. Of course, I have no place asking to stay here."

Molly's words were in his head again. *She has no place outside the Bridgers.* "Do you want to?"

Her expression softened. "No." She breathed, and Will waited for whatever was brewing in that clever mind of hers. "I just... it's nice to think I have options."

"Options? Could you not have stayed in Charlotte? Surely Josie Allen's family would have taken you in."

The corners of Fenna's mouth twitched. "I believe Josie will be engaged any day."

"Was there no one else?"

Fenna's chin hiked higher. "You wish I had stayed?"

"No!" He couldn't resist; he stepped forward and gripped her arms. "I cannot tell you how happy I was to hear you were coming."

She slipped gingerly out of his grasp. "Will, I am never going to be the girl you proposed to. I hope you know I do not hold you to that promise. And I hope you will not hold me to anything."

She turned and made her way up the stairs.

Will watched her retreat with misery in his gut. He'd pressed and she'd run away. So long as she didn't go too far. As long as his mama still meant everything to Fenna, he could wait until he meant as much too.

CHAPTER 15

Too soon, Fenna found herself standing on the train platform, waiting while Bridgers embraced Marxes, and both matrons wiped tears from their cheeks. Even Mr. Marx had a glisten in his eye as he released his hold of his youngest daughter.

He turned to Will, not for a hug. "You take care of Molly, you hear? Just get her safely to your pa and she'll be all right."

Will nodded and they gave one another a firm handshake. Harriet approached Fenna and touched her cheek. "You will do so well wherever you go. You're a resilient thing. You teach Molly a few things, all right?"

"Yes, ma'am."

They boarded the train and Mam looked at their tickets. "Molly, dear, your father upgraded our seats last minute. Let's see…" She walked along the hallway, checking compartment numbers as she went. Molly, Will, and Fenna walked along behind her, helpless ducklings while Mam held the tickets. "Here we are." She opened the door and gave a dramatic gasp. Too dramatic. "There are only two seats in this compartment."

Fenna leaned in to see that though there was ample space within the cabin, there were in fact only two seats.

Mam pressed a palm to her chest. "Will, I promised your aunt and uncle I wouldn't let Molly out of my sight. You and Fenna take these tickets and find your seats."

Will cut his mama a look but took the tickets anyhow, letting her press him back until they were out into the hallway completely. She slid the compartment door shut, nearly catching Will's coat.

"I guess we find our seats." He looked down at the tickets, then up at the compartment numbers, then started down the hall.

As Fenna followed him down the tight corridor, she had to focus on breathing deeply, otherwise she might just burst into tears. After the confrontation with Will when she'd returned from the ride with Richard, she knew he still had feelings for her. She'd suspected it, but after spending a few evenings in his room, she had allowed herself to believe he might only be interested in rekindling the friendship they'd once shared. Now, she suspected otherwise.

Will was merely grieving the loss of his fiancée. Just because she was now traveling with his family didn't mean he had any chance of getting her back. That girl was gone, buried as deep as her pa.

Will stopped and checked the ticket once more before opening the door to another large room. "Uncle Sven even upgraded *our* seats. I thought maybe Mama was just taking the good seat for herself."

Fenna took in the large space. Again with only two spots on a bench seat. She had an idea of what Mam was doing, and it had nothing to do with comfort.

Will entered first and set down his doctor's bag and another knapsack. Fenna set down her own traveling case. Molly had filled all the extra space with books, and it wasn't until this moment Fenna wished she'd asked for one she'd like. She figured she, Molly, and Mam would be chatting for most of the ride while Will sat in the corner of the cab, a lone man with a bunch of twittering women.

A whistle blew and Will sat on the bench seat with a strained smile for Fenna. She too took her place at his side and soon the engine groaned. They were off slowly at first.

The silence was nearly painful as Fenna forced herself not to fidget. "Are you excited to see your pa and brothers?"

Will's tight expression loosened into a boyish grin. "Yes." He glanced at her, but his eyes didn't linger, instead settling on the tickets still in his hands. "You?"

"Oh, yes. I've been away from them, of course, but never so far. It's odd, you know?"

Will nodded. She couldn't help but feel he was mourning something. Perhaps he had friends in Harrisonburg he was going to miss. It must be difficult to leave his aunt and uncle after living with them for so long.

Fenna was a poor companion, for she hardly knew this man. She didn't know how to comfort him. She didn't even remember how good of a relationship he had with his pa and brothers. Obviously, the hope of seeing them was not great enough to tamp down whatever was pressing on his heart.

After an eternity of stilted conversation and weighty silence, they arrived at their last stop for the day. Will checked everyone into an inn and Fenna found herself in a room with two beds. Mam in one and Molly, of course, sharing with Fenna.

"I cannot sleep," Molly whispered, laying her arm across her forehead. "I can't believe I'm actually going west. Are we really doing this?"

Fenna chuckled quietly so she didn't wake Mam.

Molly shifted under the covers facing Fenna. "Let's go out."

Fenna jerked to gape at Molly. "What?"

"Come on. It's my first night away from my parents. I can do anything."

Fenna glanced back at Mam. "We can't just leave. What if she wakes and we are gone?"

Molly climbed out from under the covers and lifted her clothes off the back of the chair. She tossed Fenna her clothes and nodded at her to get dressed. Fenna slid out from under the covers, uneasy, but she too was anxious about the idea of going to Independence. Sleep wouldn't come for hours, and a bit of distraction might be a good idea.

She slipped her clothes on and had barely buttoned the top of her shirt when Molly tossed her a shawl and opened the door. With one last look at Mam, Fenna followed Molly out.

The inn was quiet, most of its guests either out for the night or abed as she should be.

They came into the foyer to find a young man sitting with his feet up on the desk. He let them drop to the ground and leaned forward, adjusting his vest. "Good evening, ladies. How may I be of service?"

Molly stepped forward, "Yes, we would like to know where two ladies might go for entertainment on a night like tonight."

He took them in. Fenna's skin crawled at the way his gaze lingered on her chest.

"Mighty's Tavern is the place to start. Drinks and cards. He won't mind serving two women." He nodded toward the exit. "Across the street and four doors down. Hard to miss this time of night."

"Thank you." Molly settled a coin on the desk with a click and walked for the door.

As soon as they were through the doors and out of hearing from the boy, Fenna caught Molly's arm. "I don't know what sort of place will serve drinks to a lady, but we cannot possibly go."

Molly kept walking and merely grinned. "I agree it's not a reputable thing to do, but I feel this is the only time in my life I'll have the chance to do something so reckless without consequences."

"Who says there won't be consequences?" Fenna hated to hear Will's voice in the back of her mind saying Molly was reckless and foolhardy. Then he'd been talking of going west, and they were all a bit reckless to take such a journey. But going out alone was different. Fenna's fear twisted her gut with each step they took across the empty street.

"Well, there is never a guarantee of *zero* consequences. But without risk, what is life?"

Fenna disagreed. She was perfectly content to live a simple life. She didn't need bawdy houses to feel alive.

Molly pushed through the doors, and at this point Fenna knew she was no longer here to enjoy herself, but rather to protect Molly from her own recklessness.

The bar fell silent, and Fenna's gaze ran along the men spread throughout. There was a set of stairs along one wall and at the top stood a woman, dressed finely, but her stern look told Fenna she wasn't a friend.

Molly cleared her throat and Fenna was glad to hear a bit of a tremor when she spoke. "The young man at White's Lodge told us we might come here for a bit of entertainment."

Nobody spoke, so Molly strode forward to the bartender. He narrowed one eye at Molly, then did the same to Fenna. "Rusty sent yer?"

"Yes," Molly lied.

"D'you want a drink?"

Molly shook her head and scanned the room. "Is it only cards?"

"And liquor." The man's voice was hard, like he'd seen too many things in this bar of his.

Fenna found her voice. "There was a woman upstairs. Is that where the ladies play cards?"

A coarse laugh came from behind her, and she turned. A thick man had risen, his cards lying face down on the table. He stepped closer, pushing chairs aside, their legs screeching against the rough wooden floor. The noise made the hair on Fenna's arms stand up. "I'm more'n happy to escort you upstairs, Miss."

His breath reeked, and he swayed the moment he stopped walking. He glanced at the bartender. "Mighty, let me take her upstairs. I'll be real gentle."

Fenna stepped closer to Molly, her heart jumping like corn in a frying pan. "You are no gentleman." Fenna squeezed Molly's arm. "Let's go."

The man laughed and his breath turned Fenna's stomach. She closed her eyes against the smell, and in the darkness, she saw a flash of that night. It was the same as ever, dark, as though the memory was cloaked in black fabric so she couldn't see any of it clearly.

A hand gripped her arm, and Fenna was relieved that Molly had finally seen sense. She lay her hand over Molly's hand, but hair tickled her palm. Glancing down, she saw it was the man, not Molly, who had taken hold. She glanced up to see his leering face too near her own. She tried to take a step back, but he held firm.

"Release her!" Molly's tone was more aghast than commanding, and she whirled around him and pulled at his arm in a feeble attempt to free Fenna.

He only yanked Fenna closer, until she collided with his chest. The whole of him smelled much the same as his breath, as though the alcohol was leaking out of every crease of skin. He took her other arm and held her against his front.

"Yer friend wants to see the upstairs and I'm going to show her."

He shoved Molly and she stumbled backward, catching herself on a table.

"Mick," the barkeep warned, eying the man who held Fenna, but he didn't move out from behind his glistening bar to help the two women.

"If Rusty sent them here, these girls were asking for a good time." He leaned closer and spoke near Fenna's ear. "I hate them to leave disappointed."

Fenna arched her back so the only part of him that touched her were his hands on her upper arms. She dared not close her eyes again, afraid if she did the images would return. But the fear that surged through her was familiar. Like too much of what she'd forgotten, all she had were impressions, and the ones coursing through her now were the same as they'd been that night. She squirmed in his grip, trying to keep her mind present, and looked around at all the men in the room. All eyes were on them, but none seemed to care. One even lifted his glass and took a drink, as though this were a show to entertain him while he finished his beverage.

Molly recovered and came charging back, waving a finger in the man's face. "You listen here. You let us go or I'll have the law on you so quick you'll wish you hadn't let your drink get flat."

The man laughed at Molly's bluff. They didn't know the law, and one thing she'd noticed as she scanned the men was that the one holding her seemed to be the largest of them all.

The door opened and Fenna looked up with desperation on her face. Would anyone in this town help them?

Will stepped through, his face worried even before he took in the scene. "What's going on here?" Will took long strides toward Fenna.

The foul man released Fenna's arm long enough to push Will backward.

"She was lookin' for me," Mick answered, his round stomach brushing against Fenna's back.

"No, I wasn't." Fenna jerked her arms, not even caring at how his grip pinched the tender skin on the inside of her arm.

Molly reached Will and tried to take his arm, but he shook her off, his gaze intent on the man who held Fenna. "Let her go." He ground out the words with such hatred, Fenna expected to be released immediately. But this man had probably never been intimidated in his life.

"I'm so sorry, Will." Molly's voice was small, and Will ignored it like it was a fly on a window.

He extended a hand to Fenna. She couldn't take it, not the way the man was holding her. Will's eyes weren't on her anyhow. It was like he was asking the man for permission.

Mick's grip tightened.

Fenna's heart dropped.

A voice came from above, and Fenna saw the woman still standing there, watching the scene with the same blank expression she'd had when Molly and Fenna had walked in. "I'll not have you bring her up here, Mick. This ain't that kind of place."

Mick's hold loosened briefly, causing a pinprick sensation in Fenna's fingers. Then he tightened them again. "'S fine. My house ain't far."

Mick stepped to the side and Fenna's boots dragged along the wooden floor.

Will followed. "I won't ask you again."

The upstairs lady spoke again. "Don't think your wife will take too kindly to that plan."

Fenna continued looking up at the woman, praying she

would keep talking and with every word, Mick would lose a bit of his swagger.

But instead of loosening his hold, a sickening smack came from behind her. Mick jerked and Fenna's world spun as he pulled her backward. Not stepping, but falling. He crashed to the ground, chairs skittering away, and Fenna landed on top of him. His grip finally loosened and Fenna rolled away.

She scrambled farther, her hands still numb from the way Mick had held her arms. Her movements were clumsy, and she hit her head on a table leg, seeing black spots for a moment before she could safely crawl out from the wreckage of Mick's fall. She turned to see men hauling Will off Mick.

The man wiped at his bloody nose and glanced from his hand to Will. "I'll kill you." Mick ran at Will, who was helpless with men still holding each of his arms. Those men quickly released Will as Mick toppled on top of him, hitting his face and body.

Fenna and Molly both screamed and threw themselves on Mick's back. He easily swiped them away and continued his assault on Will. Those same men came forward and hauled Mick off Will, a service they'd denied Fenna.

Will used a table to bring himself to standing. Blood criss-crossed his features and Fenna's stomach lurched as she rushed forward, surveying the damage. Her hands hovered, unsure where she could touch without inflicting more pain.

Mick spat on the ground near Fenna's feet. "Get out of my town."

Fenna turned with a glare, but it was Molly who spoke. "Gladly."

Will gripped Fenna's wrist and hauled her out of the bar.

Molly was at his heels, talking, her words tumbling over one another as she tried to apologize to both Fenna and Will.

Fenna's hands no longer felt like they were being stabbed by tiny needles. Instead, her chest was shaking, like she was out in a snowstorm. The shaking spread to her shoulders and by the time they reached the warm interior of the inn, her hands had started too. She lifted the hand that Will wasn't holding and held it in front of her eyes. "I'm shaking."

Will took her hand and pressed it to his mouth. "What were you thinking?" The heat of his words breathed into her skin. Will turned to Molly. "Get back to your room before Mama notices you've left. Lock the door."

"But Fenna…"

Will growled. "Go."

Molly met Fenna's gaze and Fenna nodded, releasing Molly from whatever it was in her that vacillated between her friend and her family. Will still held both Fenna's hands, and among all the things she didn't know, she knew Will was no threat to her, no matter how angry he might be.

CHAPTER 16

Fenna watched Molly's back as her friend made her way down the hall, leaving Fenna alone with Will.

Will faced Fenna, his voice no kinder. "You're in shock. I need you to take a deep breath." He pulled air through his nose and blew it out his mouth. "Do this with me."

She tried, but her breath was as shaky as the rest of her, and each small intake of air quickly rushed back out again.

"Again," he commanded, and she found the strength in his tone strangely soothing. He was a doctor, and she could trust him to cure whatever was wrong.

She'd only gotten one more breath in when he wrapped an arm around her shoulder and led her down the hall. They passed her room and she tried to stop, but he kept on. "You're not sleeping in there tonight."

She dug her heels into the thin carpet, but Will continued.

She tried to roll out of his grip, but though it was far gentler than the grip Mick had held her with, it seemed she was just as unable to break free.

He stopped at his room and released her, digging in his

pocket for his key. Once the door was unlocked, he pushed it open and gestured for her to go first.

She eyed him, not because she didn't trust him, but because she couldn't figure out why she did. He'd rescued them, but just because he didn't want some greasy man to have his way with Fenna didn't mean Will didn't have his own ideas. If tonight had taught her anything, it was just how vulnerable she, a woman, was to a man's strength.

"I need you to look at my hand."

Fenna glanced at his other hand and saw his first and second fingers were bent unnaturally. "Oh, Will."

He only gestured again, and she entered without hesitation. She saw his medical bag on the floor near the door and scooped it up. The lantern was already lit on his bedside table, and she set the bag down on the quilt, then turned up the wick for more light.

Will followed and sat next to his case. He tried the buckle, but the leather strap kept falling out of his fingers.

Fenna sat on the other side. "Let me." She undid the buckle and opened the sides.

"There are ivy leaves to reduce the swelling."

Fenna glanced up. "Will, you need a real doctor. I think your fingers are broken."

Will nodded. "They are. But I already made an enemy out of the clerk. Had to hold him up by his collar to get him to tell me where you two had gone. I'm not going to find a doctor tonight, not with those men out there. They know where we are staying." He cut off his speech and breathed through his nose, the same way he'd just been instructing her. "I don't know what you were thinking."

Fenna swallowed, ashamed. It had been Molly's idea, and Molly had already explained as much, but it was Fenna who had known better. Fenna who had ignored her gut and followed Molly into that tavern. Fenna who, though she might not remember it, had been in a similar situation before.

"I'm sorry." She wanted to cradle his hand, to make it quit looking so red and angry.

"The leaves," Will repeated, fatigue etching his words. Fenna dug in the bag until she found the bottle.

She unscrewed the cork and looked up at Will. "What do I do now?"

Will met her gaze. "You know."

She did, but she looked around the room and didn't see a bowl. "I need something to mix the poultice."

Will nodded toward the bag. "I have one."

Fenna looked through it and, sure enough, he had a tin bowl. "I'll have to go to the front desk for hot water."

Will shook his head. "Cold will have to do."

"It won't steep the leaves and they'll be less effective."

Will was quiet and when she looked up, his anger had softened into a gentle smile.

"What?"

"I just... wasn't sure if I'd ever see this again."

"See what?"

"You, being a nurse."

Fenna blinked, "A nurse? You said I helped you. It's not the same."

"You were learning." He sighed. "We had dreams, you know?"

Fenna poured a bit of the broken leaves into the bowl and stood to get the pitcher. She didn't *know*. And it had been a while since anyone had told her something new. She'd forgotten how unnerving it was to learn something about herself. Especially something like this, that she'd never considered before.

"Mama said you've been nursing my brothers all these

years. You might not have realized, but that potential was always in you. Before and after."

Fenna couldn't look at him. Instead, she focused on mixing the poultice until the leaves were a fine pulp.

She sat down on his other side and looked at his hand. Her insides puckered at the sight of his misshapen knuckles. "Will, this is too bad. It's already swelling, and if it gets too big, you won't be able to fix it tomorrow."

"I know."

She snapped her eyes to his.

He nodded toward his hand.

"You want *me* to fix it?" Her voice was reaching a pitch that was closer to a squawk.

"I was going to wait until you offered."

"I didn't offer."

"I didn't ask."

Fenna opened her mouth to argue, but he was right. She closed it and let out a long breath through her nose.

Will laughed, the sound tense as though it was squeezing through a tight throat. "I'd be mighty obliged if you'd set these bones before I pass out from the pain."

Fenna chewed her lip. She'd never set a bone, at least not to her memory, and as much as she might be disposed to nurse others, any knowledge she'd learned before her accident was gone. "I— I don't know how. I can't."

Will took the poultice from her hands. "Those are two very different sentiments." He set the poultice next to his case and waved the fingers on his good hand. "Give me your hand."

She did, and he laid it on his thigh. She swallowed at the contact, trying to settle her nerves. He was just a man in pain. He wasn't an ex-fiancé who may or may not still be hoping for a life with her.

He grasped the top knuckle on her first finger. "You're

going to grasp here and give it a hard tug." He pulled a bit on her finger. "Pull straight and don't stop until you hear a pop."

Her mind cringed at the instructions, but surprisingly, her body gave no reaction, not the way it had when she'd first looked at his mangled hand. She could do this, and with Will's help, she *would* do it.

He released her finger and laid his good hand over hers, giving it a gentle squeeze. Then he laid his broken hand next to hers.

She swallowed. Her fingers hovered over his first finger. "This one first?"

Will nodded. "I'm not sure if you'll be able to fix the second one."

She glanced at the other one. It had swollen more, and she wasn't sure how Will could even tell what was wrong beneath all that bloated flesh.

One at a time. She breathed the same way Will had shown her in the lobby. In and out slowly. She glanced at him. "I'm not shaking anymore."

"No, you're not."

If she didn't know any better, she'd have thought she heard a shred of pride edge his words.

She took his first knuckle and felt around, trying to get a firm grip. She knew she'd need to pull harder than if it were her own finger. Will would feel as though his finger was breaking a second time.

She looked at him. "I'm so sorry."

Will's gaze flicked up from his finger to meet her apologetic gaze. He looked away, then right back again, as though he saw something unexpected in her face.

"I'm sorry for so much," she continued. "For going to that bar, for getting myself into a situation where you had to break your hand to get me out. I'm sorry for forgetting you, for going into those woods, for getting my pa killed." Her voice cracked, and she let her swell of emotions give her the strength to pull his finger. She both heard and felt a snap, and he gave a howl of pain and cradled his hand as he breathed in the short gasping breaths she'd been doing before.

She opened her mouth to tell him to breathe slowly, but her chest was also heaving, though not in fear. It was electrifying. She'd felt this before—it was the rush of an almost memory, a feeling of familiarity, if not complete remembrance. He was right. This feeling that accompanied healing, it wasn't new.

After her accident, she'd often recall something, the name of a flower for example, only she didn't actually know it. It was like the name would fill her mouth, but she couldn't speak it no matter how long she contemplated its name. She drew an odd sort of comfort from that, knowing that she'd known it once and part of her even remembered knowing it. That was how she felt now, and it was exhilarating.

She lifted her gaze to Will, but his face was still a scowl of pain.

Fenna couldn't help but smile. "I thought maybe if I distracted you..." Her look fell to her hands as she remembered the words she'd said. She'd meant to fool him, like when she played with the Bridgers' dog back home, a hand up high when she threw the stick down low. But distractions weren't always a ruse. Her words had rambled, moving from apologizing for tonight to apologizing for so much more.

When she looked up, his gaze was on her. Then he lifted his hand and let the light fall behind it. It was swollen but straight. By comparison, the second finger looked worse than before.

"Do you want me to try the other?" she asked.

Will was still drawing and releasing intentional breaths. "Not just now." He gently touched either side of the break and nodded. Then he laid back on the bed with his hands against his stomach. His eyes were closed when he said, "You didn't get your pa killed."

Fenna stood and scooped the poultice from where it sat on the bed. She lifted his doctor's bag and set it on the floor, then crawled onto the bed, scooting to kneel at his side. With gentle fingers, she applied the poultice to the finger that had been set.

When she was through, Will said, "There is a roll of bandages in my bag. We need something for a splint."

She found the bandages, but all she could find for a splint were instruments he would no doubt need to use before his hand was healed. She stood and walked around his room. "There's nothing in here. I could go break some branches from the tree out back."

"No." Will lifted his head from the bed, his eyes aflame.

With all that had transpired within the walls of this room, she'd forgotten how very recently they'd made enemies in this town.

She put her hands up, palms out. "Okay." Unwilling to suffer the heat of his gaze, she let her attention drop to his finger, calculating the length she'd need. She scratched her head as an idea came to her. With practiced movements, she pulled the u-shaped bobbins from her hair, letting her long tresses tumble down as she held the three bobbins up for Will to see. "Will these work?"

Will remained silent, his stare a mixture of pain and longing. With the light behind her, she allowed herself to watch him study her in wonder. She wasn't even embarrassed for him to see her with her hair down. Was this what it was like to be adored? Had he looked at her like this before?

She crawled back on the bed and used his stomach as a surface to wrap the finger. She wound the bandage around his finger a few times, covering the poultice and being careful not to jostle his other broken finger, and after a few passes, she laid the bobbin along the top of his finger. Then she wound the bandage around several more times, securing the makeshift splint in place.

"Do you have any plaster in your bag?"

"It's in my trunk at the station."

She sighed. They'd have to deal with that tomorrow. She eyed the other finger, far worse than the one she'd just fixed. "Ready for the next one?"

Will's throat bobbed, and he didn't answer.

"Do you want to instruct me, or shall I just go ahead?"

Will let out a slow breath and closed his eyes. "You'll have to guide the set. One hand on the break and the other hand pulling the first knuckle like before."

Fenna swallowed, glad he wasn't watching her. Surely, he would see her nervousness written plainly on her face, and he had enough pain to consume his mind.

"You'll squeeze the break to guide it into place as you pull."

Fenna could hardly tell where to grasp; only by figuring the widest part of the swelling did she guess where she should place her fingers. She took his knuckle again, and when she touched the swelling Will sucked in a sharp breath.

She snatched her hands back, guilt rolling over her at having caused him pain. She wasn't ready to inflict it again, but still she asked, "Ready?"

"No."

Fenna looked at him, but his eyes were closed, as though he was trying to escape.

"I have two more bobbins, which is good since I think this one might need a bit more structure. Do you have any laudanum?"

Will shook his head. "I don't want it. I won't be able to

wake in time for the train tomorrow. Just do it." He set his teeth, pressing his lips into a line.

With a gulp she took his fingers again, ignoring the way his breathing stuttered as she felt around the swollen flesh, trying to find the break. She closed her eyes as well, letting her instinct guide her. Then she felt it, like a knot in thread, slightly raised from the rest. She gripped the first knuckle and pulled.

Will groaned again and cradled his hand, but she wasn't done. She reached for it again, finding the spot more easily this time and tried again, harder. This time she felt the bone slide into place. Will moaned again, leaning his face into her lap as he curled around his hand. His frame swayed as waves of pain made their way through him.

The heat from every breath seeped through her dress and stockings, warming her thighs as he exhaled. Fenna brushed the hair from his face, and it was several moments before he opened his eyes to meet her gaze.

She smiled. "It's official. You're the toughest of the Bridger men."

He laughed, but it was laced with a whimper, and he stayed put with his head in her lap. She had the strange desire to run her fingers through his hair, just to feel its texture. To trace the wave that went from his hairline, up and around his ear, and down the base of his neck.

His breathing slowed, and before he fell asleep Fenna whispered, "I need to wrap it."

He knew this, but Fenna knew how pain could steal even the most basic knowledge. Was he even in much pain anymore? She didn't doubt he could have fallen asleep had she given him a few more minutes. Pain could also do that, wear a man down to exhaustion. Surely that's why he seemed so comfortable in her lap. Pain. Exhaustion. Nothing more. By allowing him to lie there, she wasn't giving in to any expectation. She wasn't leading him on. She was merely giving him the basest comforts for an injury she'd contributed to.

He lifted his head, allowing her to slide out from under him and collect the poultice and more bandages. Kneeling next to the bed this time, she wrapped the finger, and he took the pain in stoic silence. She'd seen Ben handle similar pain with the same hard self-control. Perhaps all the Bridger brothers were made of tougher stuff than the rest of the world.

When she was through wrapping it, she pulled back the covers. "Here. Climb in."

He opened glassy eyes. "No. You're sleeping there."

Fenna scoffed. "I am not."

Will closed his eyes again. "I'll feel better knowing you're safe."

"I'll be safe with your mama and Molly."

Will hauled himself up and walked to the wicker chair in the corner. It was woven with sloped sides. As Will settled into it, he slid down so his head was resting on the back and his bad hand rested safely in his lap.

"Will, you need to rest, and I cannot possibly sleep in here. What will folks think?"

"You didn't seem to care when you entered that bar."

Fenna glared, but his eyes were closed.

"Besides," he continued. "Who's to say you aren't my wife? Mama and Molly aren't going to doubt your reputation." He gestured with his good hand. "Tuck in. It's late and we have a long day of traveling tomorrow."

Fenna stood in the center of the room, contemplating leaving anyhow. He wasn't likely to drag her back to his room like those men Molly spoke of. Neanderthals. But his remark about the bar had reopened that wound of guilt.

Sure, she'd not been the one to break his fingers, but she had known better. She could at least do this one thing.

"You take the bed. I'm small. I'll fit in that chair better."

Will only snorted and gave a dreamy smile.

When he didn't move, Fenna huffed. Though she'd not had her fingers set, exhaustion was weighing heavy on her too, and she didn't care to argue. She walked to the bedside and slipped off her shoes. Then, with a glance at Will to be sure his eyes were still closed, she quickly removed her outer clothes. She was to wear them again tomorrow, and it wouldn't do to arrive at the train station looking like she'd slept in them. Once they were off, she draped them across the foot of the bed. She climbed in and pulled the covers up to her chin.

She watched Will for another moment before reaching up and turning down the wick, blanketing them in darkness.

With her sight gone, her ears perked up, listening to his breathing. The medical bag was still on the floor, and she could smell the sharp scent of herbs and tonics.

So she'd wanted to be a nurse. Was it before or after she'd agreed to marry Will? Had that been her dream, or his? If it was his, why did her heart still thud in her chest with the exhilaration of setting his fingers? Of fixing something broken? She'd tried so much to fix her own cracks and had failed each time.

She let the idea of nursing tumble along the open field in her mind. Since deciding to go west, she hadn't thought much about what her future would hold. She'd be with Mam; that was about all she had considered. She'd find a man out there. Everyone kept saying how there were thirty men to every woman. When the time came that she was ready for a family of her own and the husband that would come along with it, she would have plenty of options.

For the first time in her memory, she didn't long for a

family, but for the idea of nursing and what life would be like if she knew the things Will knew. If she carried a bag with her and administered remedies to those in need. The best teacher for such an endeavor was in this very room, and he was about to spend every day for the next six months with her.

CHAPTER 17

Will woke before the sun, his neck aching nearly as much as his hand. But both of those pains were nothing compared to the way his heart lurched when he spotted Fenna, asleep in his bed. Last night flooded back to him. As angry as he'd been about Fenna and Molly's recklessness, the chance to rescue Fenna from that situation had healed a part of him. The part that was still angry with himself for shortcomings that night. For not having a gun on him, for not telling their families about the wedding, for not holding tighter to Fenna as he'd fought to keep her in the saddle.

His gaze ran the length of her blanketed form and stopped at the foot of the bed where her dress lay draped. She was in her undergarments beneath the quilts. His throat grew tight and he turned away, searching for a clean shirt. When one didn't magically appear before him, he abandoned the idea, all the while doing his best to ignore the urge to lie down and hold her, to kiss her brow, to kiss her mouth.

He snatched his hat off the hook and tugged the door open. The moment he stepped into the hall, he took a deep breath, closing it softly behind him. He pulled his hat low over his face in case the same gentleman was still at work at the entrance, then set out to search for a bakery, knowing they would be up before the sun as well.

He left the bakery with a pastry in hand and directions for a physician's home. As much as Will hated to wake the man this early, he needed to know if a surgery was necessary before their train departed. Try as he might, he couldn't do the examination himself, especially not without crying out and waking the entire inn.

The good doctor nodded and came out on the porch to administer the examination without waking his own family.

"This first one is just fine, but on the middle one, it's hard to say if some of the bone didn't break off. You may never bend it again."

Will grimaced. He needed the full function of his hand. Not only to be a doctor, but to homestead the land he would be getting once he got to Oregon.

"If you'd like, I'll make an incision, poke around a bit."

Will's stomach turned at the image of being prospected like a gold mine. But he could tell by the doctor's examination that the man was humble and knowledgeable, two of the most important characteristics Will sought in a physician. What was more, there was no way for Will to know whether he'd encounter another doctor capable of performing the procedure. If he didn't do it now, he might lose function.

"I have a train I must take today. And women who need a guardian." A truth clearer than ever after last night.

"The trains are as safe as they can be, but if you get held up, you won't be much help with this hand."

Will sucked his tooth. The doctor was right; he wouldn't be of any use if bandits stopped the train. What was important was that he was *on* the train, something he wouldn't be able to do if he consumed the laudanum necessary for such a procedure. "Let me see if I can speak with the stationmaster. Maybe you can perform the surgery on the train and administer the laudanum while I'm already in my car."

The doctor's face lit up. "I must say, I didn't expect so much adventure this early in the day."

Will gave a soft chuckle. "I'll return when I know more. The train will have to be in the station for... how long do you need?"

The doctor tapped his chin. "An hour if there's anything to be removed."

Will tried to consider his own appendage with the careful disassociation he used with his patients, but it was difficult. The prospect of losing a function, even one so small as a single finger bend, was thick in his mind, making it difficult to see past his worries.

He let the crisp morning air do its best to clear his fears as he walked to the train station. He also couldn't help but glance at the inn as he passed, imagining Fenna in his bed. Though he hadn't ever actually slept in the bed, it still stirred something primal in him to think of her back there. He let himself imagine what every morning might have been like had he only taken a rifle with him when they'd gotten married. What if he'd been able to do more than just run away from those goons? He might have saved her pa's life, might have preserved her memories.

She blamed herself. She claimed to have said those things to distract him, but he heard the truth. As angry as he'd been, he could no longer voice his irritation with her and Molly having been out last night. Not if Fenna was already hard enough on herself. Now Molly—that was someone he wanted to chew on just a bit.

His dear cousin might be naïve, but she was smarter than that. And to endanger Fenna... He got hot and angry just thinking about that man's hands on his wife, of the crass insinuations he'd called out. The future that could have been Fenna's had Will not arrived. Will was glad those men had pulled him off the man, because Will might have broken more than just two of his fingers in his rage.

When he reached the station, he was glad to find it lit up. The stationmaster listened to Will's predicament and checked the schedule. The train would be in the station soon, leaving the doctor three hours to perform whatever surgery he deemed necessary and getting off before the train departed.

With a thank you to the stationmaster, Will went back to the doctor's home and slid a note under the door. Then he returned to the inn with visions of waking Fenna and seeing her blinking, bleary-eyed up at him.

Instead, he found her in Ma's room, getting more than a small scolding. When he entered, Ma took one look at his hand and gasped. Then she glared at Fenna, whose shoulders collapsed in on themselves just a bit.

"Ma, can I talk to you for just a moment?" he asked.

Her nostrils flared, but she followed him into the hallway. Once the door was closed, Will leaned close and whispered, "I don't want you speaking to her that way."

Ma opened her mouth to speak, but Will cut her off.

"She's carrying enough on her conscience. She feels bad, and she helped me with my hand last night. She still has it, Mama, the training we did that year. She doesn't remember it, but her hands, her ability is still there. Just let this be a step in the right direction for us. Let me work with her."

Mama nodded toward his fingers. "How is your hand?"

Will drew a deep breath. "That's what I'm here to talk with you ladies about."

Fenna was shown to her train cabin by an irritated attendant. He opened the door and Fenna tried smiling her thanks, but the man had his gaze fixed to a point on the doorframe. She stepped through and any embarrassment over the attendant's rude behavior vanished.

Will lay asleep, his bandaged hand draped across his stomach. The bandage was huge, much larger than the one she'd done last night, making his hand look like more of a lobster claw than a human appendage.

The door clicked behind her and she was alone. She twisted her fingers, wondering why Mam had insisted she ride in this cabin with Will. It wasn't like Mam to be so pushy, nor to allow the care of one of her children solely to another, even Fenna.

She lifted her suitcase from the spot next to the door and set it further in, nestling it next to Will's luggage. His was worn, but of fine quality, while hers had been cheaply made from the start and now boasted more patches than original fabric. She turned away, an odd bitterness swelling inside her. Who was she to reject this man if he wanted her to be his? Could she really find any other man in Oregon who was better than him? She was different, to be sure, but wouldn't it be his problem if she was no longer the woman he loved? Why should she be the one to hold him at bay? He had as much a risk in all of this as she did.

But the moment she thought the words, she knew them to be false. If he decided he didn't love her after all, couldn't love her again, then his life would remain the same, while Fenna would be in the awkward position of staying or going. As fanciful as it may seem, she wanted to be loved, truly loved, and the idea of a loveless marriage was too much to bear.

She turned to take her seat and realized there were no

other seats. Both hers and Will's seats had been transformed into a single cot for Will to lie on.

It was lucky that Mr. Marx had bought them all these better tickets, or what would they have done with an unconscious Will? They would have had to stay in this cursed town until he was able to travel again.

What they'd done really had been foolish, and Fenna determined she would speak up the next time someone tried forcing her into a reckless adventure.

She stepped nearer and slid herself onto the cot by Will's feet. There was only wall behind her, no padding. She narrowed her eyes, suspicious that Mam knew all about this seating arrangement and had still placed Fenna in Will's compartment.

Once the train got going, Fenna settled in with a bit of embroidery. She had to admit that once she adjusted her position and added a pillow for her lower back, then draped her legs over Will's shins, the position wasn't too uncomfortable. So long as she pretended this was just a lumpy cot and not a man lying as still as the dead.

When she needed to, she stood and paced the small space, then sat down again. By the time Mam came to collect her for lunch, Fenna had found she quite enjoyed the relative solitude. With Will asleep, there was no pressure to speak to him, no fears of leading him to believe there was a future. Just quiet contemplation and soothing needlework.

As she closed the door on Will's unconscious body, she felt a pang in her chest. She caught up with Mam. "Should we leave him in there, alone? What if he falls off the bed?"

Mam glanced over her shoulder thoughtfully.

Fenna saw the dining car just ahead. Surely, Will would be fine for a few moments while she collected her lunch. "I'll take my meal back and sit with him."

Mam nodded. "He said you did a fine job last night."

Fenna didn't think her actions warranted a victory. "I did a fine enough job getting his finger broken."

They entered the car to find Molly seated at a table. A gentleman stood nearby, one hand splayed on the table as he grinned at Molly. Mam cleared her throat and glared, effectively warding him off.

"Who was that?" Mam asked, sitting down and placing her napkin over her lap.

"He's also headed to Independence for business on the railway. I told you it would be finished soon." Molly spread a napkin over her lap and turned to Fenna. "How is Will?"

"Unconscious. Do you think I should take him a plate of food in case he wakes up?"

Molly glanced toward the kitchen. "I already ordered our plates. If he's hungry, you can come down at any time and get a bit of food. Can you believe they allowed a surgery on the train?" Molly shuddered. "I don't know how you set his fingers last night." She cleared her throat. "I am glad to hear he was well taken care of." She shot a glance to Mam, whose face was pinched. Ever since Will's visit that morning, she'd stopped haranguing them about their foolish behavior, but her disapproval was apparent in her stiff posture and her tight mouth.

A server arrived with plates of food, and Fenna winced as she asked if she could take hers to her room. The employee gave her a stiff nod and gestured for her to go, the plate held aloft in his flat palm. "I'll take it to your room."

"Oh." Fenna said, gulping at the idea of this man seeing her return to a cabin that was actually a room with an unconscious man. She gave Mam a pained look.

Mam reached a hand out and touched the server's elbow. "My son is in there, recovering from a surgery. Please be quiet."

The man nodded and Fenna turned to lead him to her

cabin. She opened the door quietly, playing into Mam's ruse. The server eyed Will, but handed Fenna her plate without hesitation. "Enjoy," he said with a stiff bow.

"I'm sure I will." Fenna smiled as he turned and slid the door closed. Fenna glanced down at the unseasoned scrambled potatoes and wished she'd taken the salt and pepper shakers along with her.

She set her plate down at Will's feet and slid her suitcase closer to act as a seat while the cot was her tabletop. It worked quite well so long as Will didn't decide now was the time for a thrashing awakening. He cooperated, and when she was through, she set her empty plate by the door, then settled once again with her legs draped over his. She had just taken her needle and thread in hand when he mumbled. She set the fabric down and leaned closer. Nothing.

"Will," she whispered, though there was nobody to disturb save the man she was trying to disturb.

He remained silent.

After a few more times of this, Will finally opened his eyes. Fenna clambered off the bed and knelt on the floor near his head. "Will, you're in a train. A doctor performed a surgery on your hand."

He opened his eyes and she waited as he found focus.

"Fenna." He breathed. A chill ran down her spine at the way he said her name. Like a breath. A lifeline. Salvation.

"Yes, it's me. We're on our way to Independence to meet up with your pa and brothers."

"My wife."

"No, not your wife. Your pa and brothers." She repeated herself a bit louder and he grimaced.

She remembered what the doctor had said. He would forget where he was and where they were going, and he'd have a headache.

"Sorry," she whispered.

He reached for her, but his eyes fell on his clawed hand. He stopped and lifted it up, surveying it.

"You had surgery on your hand. I have a bit more laudanum if you need it."

He laid it back down again and looked at her with such adoration that color rose in her cheeks. "You're my wife."

Fenna blinked, fear rising up her throat and threatening to choke her. Did Will have amnesia? The doctor hadn't said anything about imaginations or forgetting the past. Will hadn't even a head wound. No, it couldn't be.

"No, I am not your wife. I was your fiancée, but, well, I'm not anymore."

"You're my wife." His voice was softer, and his eyes began to droop. Soon, he was asleep once more. Fenna let out a huff and shook off his words.

In a different world, she would probably have been his wife. And, in that world, her pa was still alive. And Mam was her mother by law and Molly her cousin. If only that had been the life she'd lived.

That old ache to remember simmered, begging to grow. There had been a time when she'd longed to remember, but those days were gone. At least they had been until she'd come west. Being with Will made her wonder what those days with him had been like, what their romance had been, who she'd been. Maybe it wouldn't be so bad to find out and become that woman again.

CHAPTER 18

Finally, they stepped off the train onto the platform in Independence. It was the usual bustle of bodies, each clamoring to reach their loved ones, or even just to reach a café for a meal before the next leg of their journey.

Will scanned the crowd until he found Ben standing next to Pa and waving an arm, his head above most of the passengers jamming the platform. He caught Fenna's hand in his good one and called to Ma and Molly, then led the way through the throng of travelers.

As soon as they approached, Ben glanced at Fenna's and Will's entwined hands. Fenna must have noticed it too for she released it, tucking her hand into the folds of her skirt.

Will's hand was cold as he stepped closer to Pa and gave him a hug. Next, he pulled Ben in for a hug and a clap on the back. "I've missed you, brother."

Ben gestured to Will's bandaged hand. "What happened there?"

But Will didn't have to reply before Fenna cut her way in for a long, tight hug.

Will watched, wondering if all Ma's efforts had been in vain and Ben had fallen in love with Fenna.

Finally, they broke apart and Ben gave a similar hug to Molly, but there was one very important difference: Molly was family. Fenna was not.

When Molly stepped back, she had tears in her eyes.

Ben only smirked. "Ma said you were coming. I thought she was playing some kind of joke."

"No joke. Will here convinced me."

"I did not. I only suggested it. The only pressure I gave was in regards to making a decision and getting it approved." He turned to Ben. "We still need to purchase a few personal items before she's ready. How's it been?"

Ben sighed. "It's been tough. Glad to have a bit of extra help if we're going to make it out on time."

Ma and Pa were having their own conversation, and Will yearned to ask for more information about why things were so tough. The point of going west was to find a better life. But better didn't mean effortless, and it was never an easier life they were searching for.

The group made their way off the platform and through the train station. Soon they were on muddy streets, not at all like the ones in Harrisonburg. The scent of horse manure and other waste was instantly overwhelming. Will wanted to take Fenna's hand and help her pick through the muck so she didn't soil her skirts, but when he glanced at her, she was already arm in arm with Molly.

"I see you two found a bit of peace with one another?" came Ben's voice, low and close to his ear.

"A bit." Not as much as he'd hoped.

Ben huffed. "I'm just glad she didn't stay behind with Edward Perkins."

Will's head nearly snapped off his neck as he swiveled to look at Ben. "Perkins?" Will knew the Perkinses had purchased his family's home and property, but he didn't understand what that had to do with Fenna.

"I guess they had a bit of a romance going before she left. He asked her to stay, to become mistress of the house where she served. I told him Fenna didn't serve us anymore than his own mama did." Ben grinned. "He didn't like that."

"He proposed marriage to Fenna?" Will insides curdled, then twisted. Ma hadn't mentioned a beau. She'd promised to be vigilant in protecting Fenna. He stared at the back of Ma's head, trying his best not to blame her for the situation but doing a poor job of it. What if Fenna had agreed to another secret wedding and unknowingly become a bigamist? His stomach roiled.

Ben continued. "I don't believe there was a ring, but he thought they had an agreement."

An agreement. Will's head spun as he realized what such an agreement would have included. Stolen kisses were at the forefront of his mind. Will's imagination turned from Fenna loving some faceless stranger to Edward Perkins. His uneasiness turned to rage. It was just like that man to think he and a girl had an understanding before he'd even given her a ring. His head was so big it was a wonder he could fit through the doorway of their grand house.

As neighbors, the women in their families had always gotten along, but the men all stayed clear of one another. "How did Pa take the transfer of his land to a Perkins?"

"To be honest, I think Pa lost his pride a while back." Ben's eyes stayed on the road as he spoke. "The confederates are getting nasty, dressing up in bedsheets and doing as they please. They say the west is wild, but I think it's better if everything is wild; that way you expect the danger. Not like the way things are going back home. The law hardly bothers to investigate an attack anymore. Pa figures the Perkinses are some of the ones dressing up."

There were towns in Virginia that sympathized with the confederacy, but their aunt and uncle's city was firmly union. One didn't have anything to fear by being on either side. Though families often stuck to the friends that agreed with their beliefs on the matter, there wasn't violence.

Will clapped his brother on the shoulder. "Things will be better out west. You'll see."

Ben only blinked, and Will knew his brother had more on his mind than he had said. "Did you try to convince Jane Connor to join you? Fenna says Mama is more anxious than ever to see you boys married."

Ben cocked a brow. "Only us? Haven't you got a girl of your own by now? I'm sure you had at least one in that town who would take you on."

Keeping his marriage a secret from Ben had always been the most difficult, especially when they were together like this and Ben was being so candid. "As the oldest, I believe it is your duty to deliver on that desire before she can hassle the rest of us."

"Pa wasn't the only one toeing the confederate line. Jane wanted a soldier."

"She wanted you to fight?" Will grimaced. A girl sending her man to the fight rather than trying to keep him home safe? He imagined it had hurt a great deal.

Ben shrugged. "I think she wanted a show of faith, for her parents."

Will shook his head. It was always the parents. His brothers were handsome enough to turn the head of every girl in Mecklenberg county. It was the parents who were never convinced. The Bridgers were not rich enough; they were too different in their refusal to own slaves.

Will hoped that, even if their great-grandfather hadn't been sold in America as an Irish slave, they still would have refused the practice.

"Do you think you'll survive without her?"

Ben nudged him and laughed.

Their group reached an inn and went inside. The rest of his brothers weren't there. Things must be difficult indeed if it was supper time and all were not yet gathered.

"Are we having trouble procuring everything we need?"

Ben lowered his voice. "They have it all, but the prices are nearly double what they were back home." He shook his head. "I know folks got to run a business, but they're gouging prices as the last stop before the trail."

"I'll jump in tomorrow and help with whatever you need."

Ben nudged him. "You did your part just this week. When Pa purchased a spot on the wagon train, he learned they didn't have a trail doctor. Said his doctor son was coming along and we're going for free. For all our wagons, not just yours."

Will tried to be thrilled, but he only felt sick. "I can't do it alone. I've never practiced on my own. I'm not ready."

"What have you been doing all these years? Sucking your thumb?"

They reached a hall of rooms and entered the women's room. Setting down the items that belonged to them, Ben led Will to another room down the hall.

Will turned back. "We should be on either side of the women." He almost said *with our doors open just in case.* But he was trying to forgive Fenna and Molly.

But Ben didn't miss his tone. "Trouble on the road?"

Will shook his head. "Two beautiful women in search of entertainment in a strange town."

Ben's brows rose and he waited for more. Will relayed the events of the night, not to punish the women, but because he wasn't sure they were done pulling such antics. For all he knew, Molly was so deprived of real adventure she was going to search for it at every chance.

His hand was aching from the walk, and he was ready to lie down and keep it elevated. There would be no time for more laudanum. Not if his family needed help getting out on time. "When are we setting off?"

"There's a camp outside town for those who can't afford to rent rooms. As soon as we've all we need, Pa wants to head over there and start learning a bit. We need to see what else we need and to be sure our bedding will be warm enough. We can't pack extra unless we truly need it."

Will glanced at Molly and Fenna talking outside their room. "Even the women will be camping with us?" It was inappropriate for them to sleep among other men. It only suited on the trail because there was no other option. He didn't think it appropriate that they start any earlier than necessary.

Ben gave Will a long look. "You've been in the city a long while. And I don't know that I agree with your encouraging Molly to come along. She's been a pampered little girl her whole life. If she had a sensible hair on her head, she'd be married by now."

Will bristled. His brothers didn't know Molly like he did. Growing up, they'd had little chance to get to know their cousins, and even during the brief visits, the brothers hadn't meshed well with the family of rich sisters.

"She has her own ideas, that's for sure. But she's tougher than she looks."

Ben grumbled. "She better be."

Try as he might, Will couldn't keep his mind on any other problems. His thoughts were a divining rod, drawn only to Fenna and her relationship with Edward. The idea that Fenna could have had a relationship in secret shouldn't have surprised him. After all, they'd stolen away to get married in secret. She obviously wasn't opposed to a certain amount of subterfuge.

If it had to be someone, he tried to focus on just being glad it wasn't one of his brothers.

She had come west. He exhaled.

If she'd married Edward, or even loved him, she'd have stayed. The near miss unnerved him, just like a bullet whistling past a soldier on the battlefield. There was no time to worry. He had to recover, to pick up his ammunition and keep up his efforts.

CHAPTER 19

Though Independence was an unfamiliar town, having all the Bridgers present made it feel like home. The doubts Fenna had experienced in Virginia were swept away like a fall leaf caught in the river's current.

Strangely, not even Molly knew the Bridger brothers the way Fenna did. It caused her a sense of pride, and while she knew pride was one of the worst sins, she also knew this was a rare opportunity and she wasn't about to let this chance to feel like family slip away.

They'd spent a few days at the inn, but today they were hitching up a wagon and heading to a campsite outside town. Fenna hadn't yet met the wagon master, but Molly had been reading excerpts of the book she'd bought, and she was almost giddy to meet a man so experienced as to be able to lead others across the plains.

They hit a rather long delay, something about yokes and wagon widths. Fenna didn't pay it much mind, as there was plenty of washing to do while they waited.

When it was finally time to set off, Will came over, leading Fenna's horse, Red. He had become hers upon the passing of her father, but she had often lent the beast to the Bridgers for use and for exercise. She drew near, letting Red lip her palm, then rubbing his cheeks and behind his ears.

"You want to ride him?" Will asked.

Fenna glanced around. "Nobody else is riding."

"It's been a while since you've seen him."

Fenna's throat grew tight. How did Will know her love for this animal? Was it plain on her face? He couldn't have known from before. She hadn't grown to love Red until her pa had died. Being near this horse had healed parts of her.

She nodded and walked around to the side. Red was a tall animal, and she usually used a fence to reach the stirrup, but Will was there, his good hand in the shape of a cup, ready to give her a boost.

She placed her boot in his hand and Will lifted her without even a grunt of effort.

She arranged her skirts, taking extra time so she didn't have to meet Will's gaze. She was grateful for his thoughtfulness, but she couldn't identify the feeling that stuck in her throat like a dry pancake.

Crunching ahead told her the wagon wheels were turning. She gave Will a small smile and kicked Red forward.

The laundry wasn't quite finished and the heavy buckets of damp clothing rode in the back of the wagons. They were four wagons in total. Mr. Bridger drove one, then Ben with young Chet as his assistant, then the twins—Nate and Alex—and finally Sam. Will and Sam would share the job of driving the fourth wagon, as Will might often be off tending to a patient.

It was this wagon they followed all the way through town and across dry dirt that would soon be covered in tall grass. The camp was easy to spot, not only because of the wagons, but also the smell of campfire and even food. Dinner was fast approaching, and while they had plenty of laundry to hang, there was also grub that needed cooking.

Mam swiftly divvied up the chores, setting Molly on laundry duty with Sam as her assistant to get a line hung. Fenna and Will were tasked with finding firewood.

With something like thirty tents spread out in this temporary camp, it didn't take long to realize all the wood nearby had been gathered long ago. Will saddled a horse for himself, Fenna climbed back on Red, and the two set off toward the tree line.

Though this was civilized territory, Fenna still had the disturbing sense that she was heading into a wilderness with only Will as her companion. The last time she'd done this, she'd regretted it sorely.

As they gathered wood in the darkening forest, Fenna was both unnerved and soothed by the quiet stillness. After spending several days in the noisy inn with its parchment-thin walls, she was grateful for some solitude.

"Do you think it will be like this on the trail?" She heaped some sticks onto her pile and turned back in search of more.

"Do you mean will it be this hard to find wood? You can bet so. Might be harder. I'm not sure how many trees are on the plains."

"I mean the quiet."

Will stood and looked up. She watched as his chest expanded and she did the same, breathing in the fresh, crisp air.

"We have one hundred and fifty in our company. I suppose once everyone is asleep it will be quiet, but the babies don't sleep just because the sun is down."

"No, they don't." She watched him, the way his movements tensed when he spoke of the company.

"Are you worried about caring for that many people?"

He stopped and looked right at Fenna. "I'd be worried if I

were only caring for our family." He shook his head. "Every doctor goes out on his own eventually."

He was right, but Fenna could hardly focus on that fact. All she could hear was "our family," and she wasn't sure exactly how he'd meant it, but it stirred something in her to hear him include her as part of the Bridger family. Not because it was some lie to tell the girls who wanted Will's heart, nor to cover her sleeping in the same house as a single man, but because they had claimed her as theirs. They had done so before her accident and again afterward. Just because Will hadn't been there to watch the rhythm they'd found, didn't mean he didn't see it now and appreciate it for what it was. Family.

"From what Molly says, you could have gone off on your own long before now." She piled sticks into one arm. "Why does it seem like you put your life in a jar of preserves?"

She felt rather than saw Will freeze. The shuffling sound of his footsteps ceased, and she didn't dare turn to face him. She just continued picking up sticks until her arm was too full. She carried them to Red only to find Will there, tying a pile on to Red's back.

He took her pile and added it on top of his. "I was busy. I had work to do, and it seems *you* were doing the opposite. Ben told me you might have married Perkins."

Fenna's heart lodged in her throat. "H-how did he know?"

"Perkins told him, said he wanted to make a mistress out of a servant."

Her gut twisted. "I never wanted that."

Will snorted as though he thought her a liar.

She bristled. "If I did, do you think I would be out here scrubbing your brothers' laundry and darning their socks?"

"I don't know. Why didn't you say yes?"

Fenna's heart was beating a steady rhythm, warming up her chilled arms and hands. She supposed with Will by her side, making unfair accusations that made her blood boil, she could walk the Oregon Trail in the dead of winter without a care for frostbite. "I don't have to justify my choice to you."

"You sure don't. But my ma always said folks only hide that which they are ashamed of."

Fenna gasped at the direct rudeness, stepping around Red so she was standing directly in front of Will. "I was trying to protect her."

"From Perkins?" Will scoffed. His voice had that hard edge that made Fenna want to make his jaw go slack.

"You leaving meant all the pressure was left to me, you know. All your mama's dreams of a wedding between you and I?" She pointed at herself with her thumb. "Mine to manage. She didn't ever say it outright, but though I might have forgotten a lot, I haven't forgotten her expression when she's displeased. I've endured about all the disappointment I can stand."

Will turned and roughly tied the leather straps around the bundle of sticks. "Is that why you came? So you wouldn't disappoint Mama?"

A sinking in her gut told her the truth. Will didn't want her here. He might think of her as part of the Bridgers, but perhaps he no longer thought of himself as one. He sure dressed differently and even his language was more refined. Physical appearance alone spoke to his heritage.

Fenna marched closer, intending to climb into the saddle, but she still couldn't climb in without assistance. Unwilling to soften toward Will in any capacity, she lifted her gaze. "Pardon me." Her voice was tight, and Will knew her too well to not notice.

Will stepped backward, making space for her to move between him and the horse and take Red's halter in hand. "I came because I thought it was the best choice, but maybe I was wrong."

She led Red a few steps away to a boulder and used it as a stool to get into the saddle. As soon as she had her seat, she kicked Red forward, not caring one whit how much he saw of her ankles as she rode away.

As she came upon the camp again, she couldn't help but sympathize with Will just a little. She saw clusters of families all completing their various tasks as they readied for the end of the day. She saw harmony and endurance.

Will saw burdens. And Fenna was just one more.

Red took her right to the Bridger wagons, as though the horse knew where safety was. Fenna looped his reins around a wagon rib and went to find Mam. Will didn't need any help creating a fire, and she wasn't about to let him abuse her with any more words. How was it even relevant that she had refused Edward Perkin's proposal? Did Will expect fidelity from a woman who didn't even love him? Was he jealous?

She stumbled a step, then stopped, zoning out as she stared at the canopy of Mam's wagon. That was it. Will was jealous. She scoffed and continued walking. What on earth did he have to be jealous of? Perhaps if she'd agreed to marry Perkins, that would be cause for jealousy. Or even if Edward was here now pursuing her, but she was here and *that* made Will jealous? It didn't make a whit of sense.

Not two days into camp, Will had his first emergency. A young boy had been playing by the horses and fallen down, only to have his lower leg crushed under the hoof of one of the beasts.

A worried aunt had been sent to fetch Will, and when he gathered his medicine bag, he met Fenna's eyes over the campfire. "Will you help?"

Fenna nodded and set down her mending. She stayed

tight to his elbow as they followed the aunt through camp. This was the first time they'd been cordial since the fight in the woods. Would medicine be what bound them together, just like it had been before?

When they arrived, Fenna went right to the boy's mama and murmured softly to her while Will assessed the break. It was bad, but thankfully the bone wasn't exposed. Fenna moved to the boy's head and stroked his damp hair away from his face. "There now. Your mama says you've been a brave boy. Just a bit longer and Dr. Bridger here will have you fixed up in no time."

Will glanced at Fenna, displeased with the way she downplayed the procedure. This boy was in for far more pain than he'd already experienced.

She met his expression with a grim nod. She turned to his mama and said, "Go. Take your other children for a walk. There's a bit of grub back at our camp. Have some and when you're through, come on back."

The mother hesitated but eventually obeyed, her four little ones in tow.

Will glanced around the remaining adults. "Who is the father?"

A man raised a hand and stepped forward.

"I'm going to administer some medicine, then I'll need you to hold that arm."

Another man shuffled forward, concern written on his face. Will assigned him the other arm.

Will poured a bit of laudanum into a spoon and poured it between the boy's lips. He grimaced at the taste, but before long his little eyes grew heavy. Once his eyes closed, Will faced Fenna and took a calming breath. Though she was mad at him, she'd been the only person to ask how he felt about being responsible for the health and safety of one hundred and fifty souls. Just now, he needed someone to acknowledge how scared he was and if he wanted these folks to trust him. One look was all he was allowed.

She gave him a firm nod and he drew in a breath, straightening his shoulders. He turned to the two men who each held one of the boy's arms.

"Got him?" Will asked.

Fenna had the boy's head, and she nodded too.

Will felt the break, and when he was ready, he pulled. It cracked a bit, but when he felt it again, it wasn't quite set. He tried a few more times and finally had to ask the father to sit on the boy's upper legs while Will and the uncle pulled. Finally, it was in place, though Will feared his first attempts might have caused more harm. There was nothing to do now but wait and see how it looked in the morning. There would be bruising, but if the wound was red or hot, there wouldn't be much they could do.

Will wrapped the break. They would put it in a plaster cast once the swelling reduced.

The father walked to his wagon and pulled out a long barrel rifle. "Thank you." The man said with such sincerity, Will felt his chest swell. He offered the rifle, but Will waved it away.

"Just remember my family and help us when we need it."

"I will." The man set the butt of the rifle on the ground and watched as Will gathered his supplies.

Fenna gave the father a few last-minute instructions. "Don't jostle him. He's going to wake up in pain; just help him breathe through it." She glanced back at Will. "We'll be by in the morning?"

Will nodded.

Fenna faced the man again. "If you need Will before then, you know where to find him."

As they made their way back, Will had an overwhelming urge to take her hand. Ever since hearing the news of

Edward, he'd wanted to touch her, to stake his claim, but just now his need for her was different. He wanted her comfort, he wanted to tell her she'd done well. Mostly he just wanted her near. The last few days of silence had somehow been harder than the last couple of years in Virginia without her. Losing something twice was bound to be worse than just the once.

"You did well." Her gentle voice cut into his dark thoughts.

He gave her a sharp look. She'd stolen the words from his mouth. "*You* did well. We used to work that way always."

She nodded. A bitterness shot through him. Duller than the jealousy regarding Perkins, but heavy and painful. He'd won her affection once, yet doing so again seemed impossible. Had she changed, or was he a lesser version of himself since training under McFarland?

"I'm sorry." The words were out before he could consider whether to say them.

She glanced up at him, her expression one of confusion.

He swallowed the emotion clogging his throat. "Sorry I didn't stay."

Her brows lifted in comprehension and she turned forward again, watching the ground in front of her as she walked.

"I should have fought for you. I should have been the one to tell you what we were, tried to gain some of it back."

"I couldn't look at you."

"But you can now. Why wasn't I there that very day?"

Fenna gave a nervous laugh. "You were there, in the church."

Will couldn't join her laughter. He may have been there, but it had only been a visit, and he'd left before anything had been revealed.

"Will, you had to stay away. If you hadn't, you would have

put me in the asylum. Did you know your ma never told anyone about that? Just told them all I needed time to heal. She was afraid of them knowing, and I never quite figured out why she cared. Except that maybe she still wanted us to get married and didn't want to make everyone think you were marrying a mad woman."

"Ma doesn't care what they think."

Fenna cocked an eyebrow. "She also didn't tell them we were alone in the woods."

Will blushed. He could figure out what Fenna had assumed, and the way her neck colored confirmed his suspicions. "We never. I never."

"So you've said, but still, she was worried about my reputation."

They reached the campsite, and Ma approached them with a bowl of soup for Will. "How was it?"

Will shrugged. "Fine."

He passed the bowl to Fenna, who beamed at Ma. "Will did wonderfully."

He tried to ignore the look of pride that brightened Fenna's face when she said it, but it was impossible to stop the swell that grew in his chest. Once they started on the trail, the pressure of caring for all these folks would be immense, but if he had Fenna at his side, believing in him, the burden would be a sight easier to bear.

CHAPTER 20

Will rose early to check on the boy whose leg he had set. The family was already about, as was much of the camp. Today was the first day on the trail and this family would be starting with a passenger in the wagon. How many more bones would Will set before they reached Oregon?

When he returned to his family's section of camp, jobs for the day had been assigned. Will would start driving his and Sam's wagon. With Fenna's permission, Sam rode Red along with a few other men to play cowboys as they herded the cattle for the entire train. As they went along the trail, they would be required to go further away for good grass. As it was, the animals all had full bellies and were able to stay close.

Molly and Fenna walked along the side, companions still. They stayed between his and his parents' wagon, and Will got to watch the back of Fenna's bonneted head and her familiar gait as he drove his team.

By midday, jobs were shifted, and Will was granted the chance to walk alongside Fenna and Molly.

"How are your feet?" he asked them.

Fenna glanced down. "They stopped hurting a few hours ago. I'm not entirely sure what to think."

Molly's voice was weary. "It means tomorrow is going to be worse. My trail book says we will do anywhere between eight and twenty miles a day." She glanced up at Will. "Has the wagon master told you how far we're going today?"

Will shook his head. "Ben would know." He had found a friend in a man who was experienced on the trail. He wasn't the wagon master, but he knew at least as much as the man.

Molly sighed. "I would guess twenty. The trail is flat, and we've all got the most energy. I supposed those eight-mile days are saved for the hilly areas or river crossings."

Will smiled. He hoped she'd had a similar conversation with Ben. It would go a long way to curing his judgment of her. She might be dressed in fine clothes and breaking in new shoes on the trail west, but she was no dummy about what they were undertaking. She might even be able to beat that guide in a timed test.

Will turned to Fenna. "You can ride in the wagon, you know?"

"I know."

Molly cut in once more. "She cannot climb in while we're moving. That's a cause of death. Folks trip when they climb back out and"—she clapped her hands together—"they get run over. Broken bones or worse."

Will blinked. "Molly, you might learn a bit of bedside manner if you're going to be spouting your discoveries."

Molly glanced around. "I see no one about. Fenna is tough enough to hear it." Molly linked her arm through Fenna's. "I'm just protecting my own."

A small smile spread across Fenna's face, and Will was glad to know she wasn't put off by Molly's brash personality.

Ma was ahead, walking with Chet and Nate. He guessed

that's where Fenna would be if it weren't for Molly. He smiled. Fenna and Molly had become quite a pair. With Molly joining them, Fenna would be less often left out, as though they'd formed a little band of their own.

Soon they reached a creek crossing and Molly climbed up into the bench seat next to Ben while she crossed. It wasn't a dangerous crossing and riding in the wagons was more to save their shoes than anything. Will helped Fenna into the back of his and Sam's wagon, then climbed in himself.

"I have a bit of balm I can put on your feet tonight," he offered.

Fenna looked up at him through her lashes. "You're bound to have others whose feet need tending."

"Every group should have balm of their own. I tend to my own first, and you're lucky enough to share a wagon with the trail doctor." He winked, elated at the smile it drew from Fenna's dry lips. He had to grip the edge of the wagon to stop himself from wrapping an arm around her.

The wagon bounced across the creek and Will watched as the wagon behind them did the same. The slowness of the crossing left enough space between wagons that he and Fenna could hop off again without fear of being run over by the next wagon.

Will jumped down and reached up to Fenna. She took a deep breath and leapt off. He didn't so much catch her as he held his hands out in case she needed them. As they both moved out of the way, he thought of the way he'd been treating her since he discovered she could look upon him. Keeping her near, just in case she needed him, but not overstepping or doing anything she could do herself. What if she never needed him? What if she continued to find her own way? Forever?

Molly stayed up in the bench seat with Ben, and he could hear muffled conversation. At least he could hear Molly's voice, but it looked more like a one-sided conversation. He laughed and Fenna looked up.

Will pointed to Ben, whose mouth was set in a grim line. "Ben is having the time of his life."

Fenna let out a soft chuckle. Just then a gust of wind picked up, blowing her bonnet nearly off her head. Will clamped a hand on his own hat and cinched the strap tighter. Fenna tried to pull hers forward again, but wisps of her hair fell down with it, tickling her eyes.

Will scanned the area and spotted a copse of junipers standing just off the trail. He took her elbow and guided her over. When they were close enough that the wind was mostly blocked, he tugged the strings of her bonnet loose. Fenna lifted it off and tried to smooth her hair.

"I must look a mess." Fenna tucked the cloth bonnet between her knees and used both hands to work with her hair.

A few pieces were stuck to the sweat that dampened the skin along her hairline. Will ran his fingers along those pieces, loosening them so she could tuck them in with the rest. He could remember touching her like this, but for his life, he couldn't recall the last time he'd done so. He wanted to duck in and press his lips to hers. See if she remembered that, or better yet, kiss her in a way she would never forget.

She took the bonnet from her knees and placed it on once more. Will adjusted it so it was straight and she tied it tight under her chin.

"Ready?" he asked.

Fenna merely nodded and they set off, both of them still using one hand to hold their hats on as they easily caught up to the wagons. The walking wasn't so bad. The wagons moved slowly, and so long as they didn't stop, there was little need to rush. They were following the Platte River, and Will had seen a few holes he wished to fish.

TO WIN HIS WIFE

He hadn't fished his entire time in Harrisonburg, and he found being outside made him miss his childhood. He and Ben used to finish with their chores and set off with cane poles.

As they got further into the trail, he was sure they'd be aching for fresh meat. It might be worth falling behind the wagons a bit to fish during the day.

Fenna asked, "What things are you expecting to encounter, doc?"

Will smiled. "Well, sickness for one. Snake bites. As Molly said, broken bones. Honestly, I figure to encounter just about everything. There's a woman very pregnant. I expect all this walking is going to put her into labor."

"Why did they come? There are a few more weeks to get on the trail."

Will shrugged. "Didn't think it my business to ask."

"Maybe it *is* your business, seeing as how you'll be the one leaving your wagon to deliver her baby."

"Could be there's a midwife among us." Will wondered if Fenna remembered her own time working alongside the midwife in the county next to Mecklenberg. It had only been a few times, but Will had seen Fenna's eyes shine with possibility. She could have been more than an assistant. If she still wanted it, he hoped she'd find that once more.

Fenna's voice was light, with none of the hopes and fears Will was considering. "It's funny, this company of ours. Molly claims we'll be quite close by the end of it. Like a family."

Will nodded, his heart sobering at the idea of what would bring them closer. Desperation and sorrow. He tried for a lighter topic. "What do you see your life being when we get to Oregon?"

A smile played at her mouth. "Much the same as it was in

Charlotte. Me at your mama's side, and now Molly there too." She gave a little laugh.

"For all Molly doesn't want to find a husband, I wonder if working with Ma will change her mind."

Fenna laughed. "Your mama is wonderful."

Will smiled. "True, but Molly ain't used to that kind of work."

Fenna turned and looked at Will. "You just said *ain't*."

Will winked. "Don't tell my mama."

Fenna turned back to the trail. "Is it odd being back with your own again? Will you miss the sophistication of Harrisonburg?"

Will shook his head, but she wasn't looking. "I'm ready to start my life, to have a place of my own." He swallowed the part about a wife and children, but Fenna must have heard the omission.

"And a family of your own?"

"Perhaps in time." He watched her, certain one of these times she was going to surprise him by saying she knew about the marriage.

"Molly thinks you all should have stayed in Harrisonburg for a year and found yourselves wives before coming all this way. She thinks you'll be picking brides from this wagon train, or else posting an ad for one."

Will laughed. "I won't be posting an ad for a wife."

Fenna gave a dramatic shiver. "I can't imagine the type of woman that would reply to such an ad."

"I suppose a desperate one."

Fenna nodded.

"Be careful. There is a group of mail-order brides in this company."

Fenna gawked at Will, who chuckled. "Are you scandalized, Miss Jennings?" The name had been meant as a tease, but the moment he spoke it, a dagger twisted in his gut. It was wrong. She was Mrs. Bridger and she didn't even know it.

"You cannot think me such a prude as to be scandalized. I only imagine such women must not have known real love in their lives. Otherwise, they could never find the courage to agree to a loveless marriage."

Is that why she'd rejected Edward's offer? She didn't love him? Try as he might, he could not rid his mind of the situation. She wasn't desperate, yet she'd agreed to come west. Perhaps she had already learned a bit of who she was outside the Bridgers, as Molly had suggested. Perhaps she would be ready for the truth sooner than he'd anticipated.

He knew better than to say anything about Edward after the way she'd reacted the last time he'd brought it up. The memory did make him smile. She hadn't been such a spitfire before her accident. He'd loved her then, but something about this new version spoke to him in a different way. He hadn't thought it possible, but he was growing to love the Fenna at his side more than he'd loved the one he'd married.

CHAPTER 21

Their first day on the trail was drawing to a close. Fenna found herself once again at Will's side, their steps peppered with the occasional conversation but also with long stretches of silence.

There had been much talk of the group of brides ordered and delivered like they were a parcel to be taken on the Pony Express. She doubted any of the Bridger brothers would need mail-order wives. She'd seen the other men in the train and none of them could hold a candle to a Bridger. Strong, handsome, and they had a doctor in the family, something any woman would be glad to have. In addition, they had four wagons, which was more than any other family in the train. True, they also had the largest party. Some also had six children, like Mam did, but those were younger families with smaller bellies to fill.

As Fenna surveyed each group, she saw many young couples with bright eyes facing the west. The Bridgers had lost much by living with folks who didn't respect them. Their sons should be married by now. Most of them, anyhow. By going west, they were salvaging a future as well as a large portion of pride. They were worth so much more than the folks in North Carolina had allowed them to believe.

When they stopped for the night, Fenna wanted to be the one to brush down Red, but there was too much to do—cook dinner, arrange tents, feed and water the animals. Plus, it looked as though a Bridger would be asked to start on guard duty so Red was brushed by Chet, fed and watered, then saddled once more before Nate took him out.

She was glad they'd brought Red along, and of course every creature was required to do its part, but she longed to hop on his back and take a gallop across the wide prairie, to feel herself moving in a way that wasn't on her sore feet.

As she watched Nate ride away on Red, Sam's dog, Boomer, came over and nosed her hand, vying for a rub behind the ears. Fenna obliged, scrubbing at his head then running her hand along his butter-soft ears. "How are your feet doing, bud?"

Boomer's tail thwacked the ground once and Fenna nodded. "Mine too." She turned back to camp and joined in the work.

The men got the tents set up while Molly, Mam, and Fenna prepared dinner. When they all finally sat to eat, Fenna couldn't take it any longer. She took off her shoes and groaned at the sight of fat blisters glistening in the firelight. Will came over and set his doctor's bag down.

When she looked up, he gave her a winning smile. "I told you I would help."

Fenna didn't dare look around the fire. She was embarrassed to have even taken off her shoes and showed her ankles, but this was too much. "Will, no."

He pulled a tin can from his bag and twisted off the lid. The smell of camphor and herbs reached her nose. She whimpered with the promised relief and nodded.

Leaning back in the chair, she let Will take her feet into

his lap and, with the same gentle fingers she'd watched mend so many folks, he mended her aching soles. His strokes were light over her blisters and heavy on her arch and her eyes fluttered with just how good it felt.

She forced them open once more and searched her mind for conversation, anything to keep her from falling asleep in this chair with her feet in Will's hands. "Did you always want to be a doctor?"

Will gave her a rueful smile, then turned back to her feet. "I wish I could say so. There are many men I met in school, ones who felt like helping others was their calling in life." He gave a small shake of his head.

"And you?"

Will paused his ministrations to look up at her and shrugged. "I just find the human body interesting." He went back to rubbing the salve into her feet.

"More than interesting. You've spent how many years learning your trade?"

Will's face fell, but it was so slight Fenna could have convinced herself she hadn't seen it at all. But she didn't want to convince herself of anything. She didn't want to ignore him any longer. Something about this man pulled at her, drew her in.

"Nearly six."

"I enjoy embroidering, but I haven't dedicated my life to it, nor have I moved away from home to pursue it."

Will paused again and, despite how good his hands on her felt, she appreciated his attention. This moment was too big for him to be distracted with anything, even doctoring.

"You think I shouldn't have left?"

Fenna chuckled at his obtuseness. "Oh, Will. I'm saying you have been every bit as called to this vocation as any of your peers." She flung a hand out, gesturing to the many wagons making camp all around them. "These people have been blessed by your knowledge, and many more will be blessed in the months to come."

She lifted her feet from his lap and set her toes on top of her dirty socks where they lay folded on the ground.

Will's mouth quirked thoughtfully. "I only hope I am enough."

"You are. And you care greatly for your patients. I've seen it." She wanted to reach out to him, to catch his hand in hers and press it tight until he felt it as strongly as she did. She thought of his brothers, always teasing one another, never serious. Maybe that was the language he understood. She leaned down and pulled her stockings over her feet. "At the very least, you're better than nothing, which is what they would have without you here."

Will narrowed his eyes, and Fenna released a laugh that cut the tension as thoroughly as these wagons were cutting their way through this prairie.

He lifted her other stocking from the ground and let it pass through his fingers, determining which way it went. Mortification rolled through her. She knew how badly they smelled after spending a hot day inside her boots.

She reached out and stole it from his hands. "Will–" But she was too embarrassed to say the real reason she took it from him. "Thank you."

He just smiled, his gaze holding hers for a beat too long. For just a moment, she let herself think what it would be like for this man, strong and tender, to be hers. If she hadn't lost her memory and she was here now as his wife.

She couldn't blame Mam for having hopes. Fenna had them too. Only it was just as she'd told Molly—how could she risk it? What if there was something about her, something she'd gained over the last two years, that would repulse Will? That would make him wish to run away or, worse, to send her away.

Molly took the chair next to Fenna with a huff. Will passed her the tin of salve, and she gladly leaned back and pulled off her boots and stockings, lifting one foot onto her knee while she applied the salve to her own blisters.

Fenna risked a glance around the camp. She had been so desperate for relief from her aching feet, she hadn't thought how public her encounter with Will was. She was already getting used to life on the trail, where there were no secrets. Not with the many hours spent walking and the precious few ones spent asleep with only canvas for privacy.

Mam came over with a bowl of dinner in her hands for Will. He took it gladly. Fenna wished she'd served herself a bowl before coming over here to sit down.

With an exhausted breath, Fenna put her feet back into her boots and learned her first lesson: don't remove boots until bedtime.

CHAPTER 22

Four days into the trail and the bugle sounded as it did every morning. It took no time for Fenna to rip away from her dream, and the moment she opened her eyes, whatever she'd been dreaming was forgotten.

She nudged Molly, who groaned but rose, and the two women started their morning by rolling up their bedding in the dark. On the trail, the day started before the rooster was even awake.

Together, Molly and Fenna packed and took down the entirety of their tent, setting the trunks and bedding at the foot of the wagon and tying the canvas tent to the side. Already, there was a rhythm to their days, and it was easy to see how this rhythm would turn monotonous very soon.

Wake, pack, breakfast, tend stock, walk. Walk. Walk. Sleep.

But today was different. In the afternoon, when the sun was relentlessly beating down on them, Fenna heard talk of a river crossing. They'd followed the Platte and, every once in a while, they could see it as they walked, but today they would be crossing it.

Once the lead wagons reached the river's edge, the train stopped. The guide pulled his wagon off to the side and climbed on the back to shout instructions on how to cross.

Folks could cross on foot, using the rope that was located downstream. Anyone with a horse could ride across, but he didn't recommend giving rides, because if the horse lost its footing, two would be harder to save than one.

No matter what, folks were not to go upriver of the wagons. Fenna and Molly stood in the crowd that had gathered along the bank to watch as the first wagons splashed across. A rope had been strung between two stout trees, and eventually one soul was brave enough to use it to walk across. After that, a line formed, and Molly and Fenna queued up. Those in front of them gasped as they entered the water, then slipped and stumbled their way across. Fenna's heart was in her throat by the time she neared the front of the line and crouched down to unlace her shoes.

Molly joined her. "Too bad it's so muddy. I could use a bath."

Fenna laughed. Molly was right. Crossing downstream from the wagons, though safer, meant the water was so churned up they would all come out worse than when they entered.

Fenna tied her shoelaces together and draped her shoes and stockings around her neck. The line moved and she shuffled forward, her bare toes reaching the muddy riverbank and sinking down. She closed her eyes, curled her toes into the soil, and let the cold soothe her endless blisters.

As the family ahead of her stepped into the water, the mother started shouting at her four children to stay close. The oldest was maybe ten years old, and the mother was with child. By the size of her belly, Fenna guessed this was the woman Will anticipated was going to give birth very soon.

She lifted the youngest child to her hip and took the rope with the other hand.

Fenna rushed forward, the cold of the river shocking her feet as she stepped in. "Please, let me put him on my back. You need both of your hands."

The woman looked back at Fenna, her mouth turned down. "Will you help me get him on my back?"

Fenna smiled at the boy as she hefted him under his arms and onto his mother's back. The boy clung to his mother's neck, and Fenna tugged gently at his arms. "Not too tight." She moved his arms lower so they were on the woman's shoulders. "Hold tight here. Your mama needs her neck."

"Thank you," the woman said, though her voice held a quaver.

Another boy came over, clinging to his mother's skirts. This one couldn't be more than two years older.

Fenna squatted down so her eyes were his level. "Your mama needs her legs to cross. Would you like a ride on my back?"

He shook his head and buried his face in his mother's skirt.

"Ronald, you let this good woman put you on her back or your father will tan your hide."

The boy's fear instantly shifted from Fenna to the threat in his mother's voice.

Fenna jerked her head, gesturing for the boy to climb on. He did, his skinny arms clinging to Fenna much the same way his brother had done to their mama.

Fenna moved his arm from around her throat and stood, shifting his weight on her until he felt secure.

Behind her came Molly's voice. "You better hop on up here too, little one."

Fenna turned to find a third boy climbing onto Molly's

back. He wasn't nearly as shy and smiled wide, showing his two missing front teeth.

The mother started into the water, followed by her eldest child. Next was Fenna. The first step into the water wasn't bad, but once it passed her hips, Fenna couldn't stifle the gasp as the water tickled its way under her corset and chilled her core.

Molly didn't bother suppressing her vocal displeasure. Her cries were peppered with irritated comments to the boy of "stop choking me" and "no, hold tighter."

Fenna's own passenger didn't alter his hold, not even when the river reached its deepest point and his legs brushed the chilly water. Soon enough, the rocky riverbed started up again and they made their way out of the water.

"Thank you," the mother said, holding tight to her youngest's hand while she reached for the boy Fenna had carried. The daughter fetched the boy who had crossed with Molly. Wet, the family looked much thinner than before, and Fenna longed to offer for them to come to their wagons and have a meal. How could they endure what was to come if they were already so thin?

"You're welcome." Fenna smiled at the woman, trying not to let her fear show. That mother needed all the strength she could get, and Fenna wasn't about to steal any of it. As the family moved toward the wagons that had started to circle for camp, Fenna hoped they had enough for a hearty meal tonight.

Molly came to Fenna's side and tried wringing out her skirts. "It might be better if next time we just go down the river a ways and cross without clothes."

Fenna laughed. "Shh. You'll scandalize the lot of them."

Molly glanced around and at least one girl was staring at them. "If we get far enough away from the sand the wagons are kicking up, I don't see how it's any different than a bath, so long as the men don't see."

"They're so afraid of Indians, they aren't going to let us walk down and cross out of sight."

Molly gave up wringing out her skirts and lifted them up, gathering them in her arms and showing too much ankle. Fenna couldn't help but follow her friend's lead. She gathered her own, and on bare feet they made their way to the half-circle of wagons.

The Bridger wagons had been near the front and were among the first to cross. They found Mam and Mr. Bridger. They'd already erected one tent for changing. Molly and Fenna collected some dry clothes and took their turn inside. Fenna found that, despite the muddy water, she appreciated the short bath she'd gotten. In just a few days, no crack or crevice had been spared from the dust that the wagons kicked into the air. Her ears were filled; her nose and even her teeth felt gritty.

As she pulled on the dry clothes, she was grateful at least her lower half had gotten a bath of sorts. But there was no time to rejoice. There was wood to gather and a fire to build. Others were doing the same, and by the time the sun had set, little orange fires spotted their camp.

A cry rang out and talk of Indians must have gotten into Fenna's head, for she first looked outside their corral of wagons. More screaming started, and Fenna stumbled toward the ruckus to find a woman ablaze, her family using blankets to smother the fire. Fenna rushed over as the flames were finally snuffed. The woman was shaking and crying softly. Her stockings had been burned, and beneath were angry black and red splotches of charred flesh.

She turned to see Molly standing nearby, her shoulders folded in and her head turned like she couldn't take looking at the woman's wounds.

"Go get Will. Hurry."

Molly spun and disappeared in the crowd of onlookers.

Fenna glanced around at the bystanders. "If you aren't family, go back to your own camp." She turned back to the woman, who held a shaking hand out, as though she wanted to cup her damaged legs. "Don't touch them."

She'd seen burns as bad as these, she was sure of it, but just now she couldn't remember. As much as she'd wanted to remember her lost memories all this time, now was the first time she'd longed for them on behalf of someone else.

She glanced up and found as many folks as before. Fenna stood, looking at the lot of them. "If you're not this woman's kin, scram." One man looked particularly worried. "Do you belong to her?" He nodded. "Get her a blanket. I need to get her stockings off."

What remained of them anyway. She glanced around and didn't see Molly or Will. *Oh, hurry.* She turned back to the woman and started unlacing her boots.

Her voice shook. "I'll be able to walk, won't I?"

The burns were superficial. Fenna doubted it would impede her physical abilities, but she would have scarring. "I'm hopeful. When the doc gets here, he'll fix you right up."

The man returned with a blanket. Fenna was glad to see her harsh words had cleared out all but a few bystanders.

"Clean, hot water and cloths," Fenna said to the man, who hurriedly turned and jogged to the back of a wagon. "That your husband?"

The woman's face was pained, but she spared a glance for him and nodded. "Yes. Married just a few weeks ago."

"Lucky you. And you're going to start your family out west?" Fenna hoped to keep the woman talking as she peeled the stockings down and off her feet.

The woman laughed. "Lord knows he's trying hard enough to start one."

Fenna glanced up, and when the woman's meaning sank in, Fenna's face warmed.

The woman's eyes widened and she cupped her stomach. "You don't think…"

Fenna glanced at her belly and back up to her eyes. "You expecting a little one?"

The woman shrugged. "I suspected, but I wasn't certain. Not yet."

"So long as you take it easy, little ones are resilient." Were they? Fenna had no idea where those words had come from. Was she spouting nonsense to ease this woman's worries? Or was it a truth locked somewhere deep?

"What do we have?" Will skidded to a stop, dust from his hurried steps rising up and settling over the woman's legs.

Fenna shot him a sharp look. He glanced around sheepishly. The dust was such a daily companion, it was easy to forget about it.

"Burn. They put her out quickly; I believe it's only surface."

Fenna had managed to remove the woman's boots and the remainders of her stockings. The skin underneath was barely touched. Likely the thick wool socks had saved her from a more serious burn. If only she'd been wearing the taller boots that the horsemen wore, she might have been spared any burns at all.

Will scooted the lantern closer and leaned in to inspect the skin. "See how there is white forming around the edges? Her body is trying to clean and heal." He looked at the woman. "Do you mind taking a bit of medicine to dull the pain while I clean the wounds?"

"I don't mind anything you tell me."

Her tone was bawdy, and Fenna glanced up to see the woman a bit starry-eyed as she looked at Will's profile.

Will didn't react, only turned to Fenna. "A dram of laudanum will do."

The woman's husband returned, and Fenna hoped she would curb her attention to Will now.

The husband set a pot of water at Will's elbow. "Fresh water, doc."

Fenna dug in Will's bag and found a small bottle. *Doc.* It was odd to hear him called that. It gave him some authority, but she supposed he *did* have authority. Most folks in this camp would need him one way or another. She worked the cork out of the bottle of laudanum and poured the contents into the woman's mouth.

Just as she swallowed it down, the woman sucked in a breath and lifted her head to see Will wiping at the burns. The cloth came away dirty with blood and dust, so Fenna rushed to his other side to dip the cloth and offer him a clean one. They worked that way, him dirtying and her cleaning, until Will stopped. "Let's smother them in calendula and wrap it to keep it from festering."

He reached into the bag and pulled out a tin. Fenna watched as he applied the balm with those long, gentle fingers. She looked away, trying to clear the memory of him tending her own sore feet. Instead, she assisted him in wrapping each leg. By the time he'd finished, Fenna realized she was standing there, not even needed. She turned and made her way back to camp.

Will was right. She was a good nurse. They worked well together. But her desire to learn from him directly contradicted her hope of distancing herself from him. She should find another woman to be his assistant. A single woman he could fall in love with.

She came back to find dinner had been cleaned and Molly was in their tent, just her head poking out to steal a bit of lantern light to read.

Fenna roughly climbed past Molly and said, "I need to talk."

Molly moved to sitting, ducking her head inside. "What is it?"

Fenna glanced around. The canvas sides of their tent were hardly a barrier for sound. Worse, they couldn't see who was out there and if anyone was close.

Fenna leaned forward, putting her lips to Molly's ear. "I need to find Will a wife. Soon. *She* should be his assistant."

Fenna sat back and surveyed Molly's thoughtful expression. "Fenna, he didn't ask you to run to that woman's aide."

Fenna blinked. Why *had* she run to her? Because she could help. Surely countless others could do the same. "If he had an assistant, they would be responding to those events."

Molly merely raised her brows.

Fenna hated her friend's expression. She vowed right then to stop responding to cries for help. If she didn't, surely someone else would go to their aid. Fenna could be the one to fetch William; that was her place as a member of the doc's family. Not at his side, admiring the deft way his fingers worked and wishing they were on her instead.

"Fenna?" Will's voice came from just outside the tent.

Fenna's eyes looked pleadingly at Molly, as if her friend could save her.

She gathered her will to avoid this man and stuck her head out of the tent flap. "Yes?"

He gave her a gentle smile. "You did well."

"Thank you." Fenna moved to pull her head back in, but Will spoke again.

"You had it all in hand before I got there."

Fenna nodded.

"There will be times when I'm not available. I'll be out with the cattle or with another patient."

"Yes. Molly here has agreed to be your assistant on the trail."

Inside the tent, Molly's hand clamped around Fenna's ankle, and she was glad her face was hidden from Molly.

Will's voice came again, halting and incredulous. "Molly? No, Fenna, I need you to assist. I thought—"

"I can't. It's not in me to help with that."

Will was silent for a moment, but his silhouette remained. "Fenna, you have it in you."

"I'm not the old me. I cannot be everything I used to be."

"I didn't say—"

Fenna adjusted the flap so no light came through. It was the closest thing she had to closing a door.

Will could have kept talking, a lecture like her father used to give her, but there was only silence. Then, eventually, the shuffling of feet as he retreated.

"Cold," Molly said, but her brows showed admiration. She leaned back on her pillow, her arms behind her head.

Fenna shook her head. Her stomach ached with regret.

Molly adjusted the blankets around her legs. "I won't be his assistant. I almost fainted when you pulled that woman's skirt up."

"You don't have to look at the patient's wounds. You just need to do what Will asks. It takes no skill at all."

"And yet he came here and suffered your indifference just to tell you how good of a job you did."

Fenna lay back and dropped her voice low. "He's looking for excuses."

Molly matched her volume. "Excuses?"

"To talk to me."

"Fenna, he doesn't need excuses. You two talk every day. He walks with you. I heard him bribing Sam to drive extra yesterday."

"That's because the dust is thicker by the wagons."

Molly stared for a moment. "You don't even believe that. Will isn't one to shirk his duties, not even with Sam."

A fiddle started and Molly lifted her head, turning toward the sound. "I read there would be dances."

Fenna looked at the side of the tent, listening to another fiddle join and the long pulls of sound as they adjusted their strings. "It's an early stop."

They lay in the dim light of their tent while the fiddles played softly and the voices grew louder. Eventually, the music started in earnest.

Molly sat up and shook Fenna. "We cannot miss our first prairie dance. The book says this is what keeps our spirits up."

Fenna groaned. She wouldn't be able to avoid Will if she went.

"How else do you think you'll discover which woman to match with Will?" Fenna sat up, and Molly laughed at her sudden eagerness. "You're too easy." Molly smirked as she ducked her way out of the tent.

Fenna followed and as she exited the tent, she saw a group of folks in the center of their makeshift corral talking and laughing. A few were in the middle, dancing the way they did back home, with stomping feet and bouncing steps. This was a gay affair, and Fenna felt her heart lift, just as Molly's book had predicted.

CHAPTER 23

*B*en pulled Will toward the sound of the fiddles, ignoring his protests about being too tired. Fenna was tucked in for the night. She clearly didn't want to speak to him.

They got more than a few flirtatious glances, and Ben slung his arm around Will's shoulders. "Having the doc as my brother is the best luck. Everyone knows you."

Will brushed him off but gave an unwilling chuckle. They found Sam, already with three girls around him, though by their matching hair and dresses, they looked to be sisters. He glanced up and waved Will and Ben over. Ben nudged Will and picked up his pace. Will hung back and searched the crowd.

Perhaps the fiddles had drawn Fenna out, just as they had Ben.

Sure enough, as he scanned the folks he saw first Molly, then Fenna. Her face was tight like she, too, had come unwillingly. Only she didn't have the same reasons for not wanting to attend.

Chet approached her and offered his arm. Her face softened as she took it and let him lead her onto the dance floor. They danced together with such ease it made Will's heart ache. He almost wished he hadn't fallen in love with her before, that he and she could start fresh. That he could be as familiar with her as his brothers were. That he could use that friendship to make her fall in love with him. For the first time.

He'd thought they were building something, but then she'd refused him, closing her tent flap as if it were a wooden door to shut in his face. She didn't want to help him, didn't want to be near him. He was always the one who sought her out. She had yet to come to him.

Ma came and stood at Will's side. "She loves you. She just doesn't remember."

Will laughed at her uncanny way of reading his thoughts. "Ma, I think someone has to remember it for it to be so."

"Of course not. There are plenty of people in love who don't even know it yet." She gestured to a young couple dancing. "Them."

Will gave her a doubtful look. "Do you know them?"

"No, but can you see how he looks at her?"

"What about her? Love can remain one-sided forever." It was sure looking like that was to be the case between him and Fenna.

"Not if he tries hard enough."

They were no longer talking of the two strangers.

The song ended and Chet led Fenna right to them. Will offered Fenna his arm, and she took it with the briefest of hesitation. Her throat bobbed, and Will sent up a silent prayer for a slower tune, one where he could hold her close the entire time.

He led her to the center and they shifted around as other dancers joined the crowd. Soon the musicians started again, but they must not have heard Will's silent plea, for their song was as raucous as the one prior. But somehow it was better than the one he'd wished for. The quick movements meant Fenna had to hold tight, and when she spun back toward him, he got to feel the press of her shoulder in his chest, his one arm looped around her middle.

As they moved, Fenna relaxed by degrees, first her hand in his, then her neck swaying to the tune, and finally, her face, a wide smile gracing her lovely features. And best of all, her laugh, which was the perfect medicine. A balm to his broken heart.

If she was happy, he could wait. He could let her fall in love with him by degrees the same way she embraced this dance.

Fenna softened in Will's arms and did her best to pretend he was just another Bridger brother. Someone who had once pulled her braids and helped her onto a horse. Whose dirty shirts she'd scrubbed and whose socks she'd mended. Except she couldn't remember any of those things, and whenever she looked at him, she realized that memories were where comfort came from. It wasn't the person; it was the time spent with that person.

Will spun her back toward him and into his arms for a dip. He leaned close with the momentum of the move, and she let herself stare into his dark eyes. The light was low enough that she couldn't see color, but she knew what she would find. Brown with flecks of green.

He pulled her up again and they continued dancing, but Fenna was lost in thought. If she couldn't see his eyes in this light, when had she discovered their color? Even so, how could she be sure she hadn't just made it up? Imagined it?

When the dance was over, Will started for the same spot

where Chet and their mama stood, but Fenna slid her hand down his arm and caught his hand in hers, tugging it to change their direction and pulling him toward the musicians.

They had several lanterns around them like lights on a stage. She stopped and took hold of Will's shoulders, angling him so he faced the light. "Let me see your eyes."

She placed her hands on both sides of his head and raised onto her tiptoes. Dark brown and there, at the center, flecks of green. They were so faint she wasn't sure how she would have noticed. Perhaps in the daylight they were more obvious. She released him, like he was a blanket with a snake inside.

Will gave her a quizzical grin. "Do they pass the test, doc?"

Fenna rested her hand on his chest. "They have green in them."

"Do they?"

Fenna nodded. "Has nobody told you that before?"

He shook his head.

Fenna cocked her head at him. She knew the Bridger boys. Some girl must have looked deep into his eyes. "Have you courted any girls besides me?"

"No."

"Not even before?" Surely there was someone, and whoever it was would have been close enough to notice his eyes.

Will twisted his head in thought. "I may have given a bit of attention to Beth Mallery."

Fenna dropped her jaw in mock surprise. "No wonder she never liked me."

Will laughed, and Fenna had the strangest desire to make him do it again.

"Did she never look into your eyes and tell you they weren't only brown?"

Will placed his hand on top of hers and she could feel the thump of his heart. "Never."

Fenna swallowed, appreciating that the light was behind her and he wouldn't be able to see her flush. Now wasn't the time to swoon over her hand on his chest. "Will, I knew they had green. How did I know that?"

Will slipped an arm around her waist. "Do you remember something?"

Fenna drew her hand away and stepped back so his hand slipped off her waist. "No." She searched the crowd and found Molly, already looking her way. Fenna widened her eyes, attempting to communicate the need for rescue.

Molly nodded and marched right over and caught Fenna's arm. "Come with me. I have someone for you to meet."

Fenna feigned a sorry look toward Will and skipped away with Molly. When they'd gone far enough, Fenna leaned into Molly's ear. "Thank you."

"I doubt my cousin will say the same. You need to steer clear of him. Even I'm not sure where you are with him."

Fenna shook her head. "It's all confusing. Did you find someone? The sooner we can find him a girl, the sooner it can get un-confusing."

Molly shot Fenna a skeptical look, one brow lower than the other. "That's not a word."

"You understood what I meant. I think that's the very definition of a word."

"Communication and language are two different things." Molly pulled Fenna into a group of young women. "Take your pick," she whispered in Fenna's ear.

Fenna surveyed the women, judging them solely on their appearance. Normally Fenna would be opposed to such superficial judgements, but just now she was desperate. There was one woman with long yellow hair and dimples. Fenna approached her. "Hello, I'm Fenna Jennings."

"Delia Camp." The woman bobbed her head.

Another girl touched Fenna's elbow. "You're with that family of brothers, aren't you?"

Molly came closer. "Yes. And they're all single."

Fenna felt the group cinch tighter around her and Molly. She almost laughed at the power that surged within her, like she was some witch capable of bestowing gifts upon whomever she deemed worthy.

Fenna pressed closer to Delia. "One of them is a doctor. How are you at handling sick people?"

"Oh… I don't really… I tend to my family just fine when they're ill. It must be difficult for him doing that every day."

Molly must have understood Fenna's intention, for she came to Delia's other side and slowly, they drew her apart from the group of women. Fenna searched the crowd for Will and found him already looking their way.

She swallowed and gave him the smallest smile. It worked. Immediately, he was moving toward her.

Fenna's heart beat faster than fingers playing a fiddle. She weaved her way between Delia and Molly and whispered in Delia's ear. "Do you see the man coming toward us?"

"Yes," Delia said, ducking her head close.

"That's Will. He's a bit shy and so busy because of all the work he has to do as trail doctor. But he needs a wife most of all. Someone who can…" Fenna floundered, wondering why it was he wanted a wife before. He'd proposed to Fenna, so he must have wanted one. Only now, as she tried to spin a tale, her imagination had stalled.

Molly jumped in. "Any one of them is a prize, but Will is my favorite."

Fenna smiled at Molly. She knew it was true. Will and Molly had a special bond.

Will had reached them and all conversation ceased. He looked right at Fenna, expectation bright in his eyes.

Fenna pressed her hand into Delia's back, pushing the girl forward. "Oh, Will. I'm glad you're here. Delia needs a partner."

Delia glanced at Fenna, her cheeks aflame at Fenna's lack of tact. Fenna shrugged and waved the girl closer.

Will gave Fenna a stern look, then his face softened as he turned to Delia. "It would be my pleasure." He held an arm out to Delia, but his smile was as stiff as an Indian's arrow.

He shot Fenna another hard look as the pair made their way onto the dance floor.

Fenna swallowed, watching how Delia fit perfectly with Will. Even their size was complimentary. He could rest his chin on her head if he had a mind to do so.

The girl followed Will's lead with grace, and Fenna ignored the snakes in her belly. This was exactly what she wanted. Delia would help Will. She would claim his attention. The two of them together would claim Mam's attention. And Fenna would be left alone to be whoever she was.

Too soon the song ended. Will glued his eyes to Fenna as he led Delia back to them.

Fenna swallowed the anticipation. Surely, he wouldn't say anything to her, not in front of Delia. And yet he came at her with such determination…

"Dance with me?" He stared right at Fenna.

There was something about the command in his voice that stirred her insides, but when she looked down to accept his hand, it was Molly he was reaching for.

Molly placed a tentative hand in his open palm, her gaze bouncing between him and Fenna.

Finally, Will broke his stare and swept Molly onto the floor with a whoop.

His mouth wasn't a line anymore. It was bright and smiling, like the sun dawning a new day. Fenna watched the cousins move through the other dancers with a deep dissatisfaction climbing her ribs like the strands of a morning glory.

"He is such a handsome fellow." Delia's voice came from Fenna's side.

She forced her gaze away from Will and turned to Delia. "Yes." And he was. Fenna had never tried to deny that fact. But his brothers were too, and she wasn't in love with any of them.

She blinked at that errant thought. Nor was she in love with Will. It would be madness for a woman in love to attempt to match that man with another woman. Fenna wasn't mad, just desperate.

She linked her arm through Delia's. "He needs an assistant with his doctoring. Someone who can find what he needs, clean water, towels, search in his bag for the remedy he seeks."

Delia winced. "I don't know anything about that. I mostly just give my brothers water when they're thirsty."

Fenna waved away Delia's concerns. "Will can teach you. He's quite remarkable." She clamped her lips together and glanced at Delia. Had she laid her admiration on too thick? She didn't need Delia thinking Fenna longed to be at Will's side.

"Delia, will your family be going to Oregon, or splitting off for the California trail?"

"Oregon."

"Good." Fenna settled her arm tighter around Delia's. The last thing Fenna wanted was to be responsible for separating Mam from her son a second time.

The next morning, before the wagons started moving, Fenna was tending to the chickens in the coop attached to Mam and Mr. Bridger's wagon. They weren't laying but two eggs a week, but she hoped as they grew accustomed to the trail, they would start laying in earnest. Just the thought of an egg fried in butter made her mouth water.

The overcast sky hung low and close, making the wide prairie feel like a cramped kitchen. Will approached her with a tentative step. Did he regret the way he'd left things last night? Or had he discovered her and Molly's plan to match him with Delia? It couldn't be that. She'd seen the fire that lit him when he'd been provoked, and his posture held none of it now.

"Can you come see the woman from last night?"

Fenna's hands stilled on the coop. Was he speaking of Delia? Had more transpired between them than Fenna had witnessed? "Is she all right?"

Will shrugged. "Her husband has asked us to come."

Husband? Realization snapped, and she recalled the burned woman. That was who they were going to see. Fenna glanced at the wagons ahead. Some had already pulled out and were bumping their way west. "We're about to start."

"Fenna, she knows you. You will be a comfort to her. I understand you no longer wish to help, but you should finish out this last one."

Fenna eyed him for just a moment, wondering if he was playing on her dedication to a patient. Did he know her heart longed to explore that missing puzzle piece? Even as she pondered it, she shook away her own concerns. This woman needed her and surely one more visit with Will wasn't going to change anything. She could keep her distance in other ways, starting by keeping her eyes away from Will's hands as he worked with the patient. She latched the coop and nodded, stepping around the wagon to Will's side.

The husband hovered just beyond their camp, and they followed him to his wagon. The rigs on either side were hitched and ready to pull out. This delay meant they would likely be at the end of the train today.

Will gestured toward their oxen. "You should get your team harnessed. We'll take care of your wife."

The man nodded and his step seemed lighter as he made to tackle a different responsibility.

The burned woman was set up in the back of the wagon, tall walls of supplies stacked on either side of her and tied down with rope so they wouldn't fall and crush her once the jostling started.

"Your husband says you aren't well this morning."

Fenna reached out and lifted the quilt off the woman's legs. A few spots of blood showed through the cloth bandages, but not so much that they warranted a change.

"They hurt." She grimaced.

"They'll hurt for a few days more."

Fenna touched Will's shoulder. "Maybe a bit of alcohol?" She knew laudanum was a supply Will was terrified of running out of. Alcohol was a remedy this woman could administer herself.

Will nodded. "Can you speak to her husband?"

Fenna nodded, but before she climbed out of the wagon the woman spoke, her voice raspy with lack of sleep. "What about that stuff she gave me yesterday? I slept like a babe last night."

"Laudanum. I cannot give it away freely. I don't know how my supplies will last the journey."

The woman's face darkened. "But what if you don't use it all, and here I am in pain on this bumpy ride?"

Fenna drew back in surprise, no longer inclined to leave Will's side and speak with the husband. That could wait. Will might need a friend on his side of this wagon.

For all she remembered, she must have forgotten the times when the patient turned from grateful to hateful. Pain could do that to a person. Same as ignorance. And yet Fenna found herself angry at this woman.

Will lifted his doctor's bag from the floor of the wagon. "You might change your bandages when we stop this evening." He glanced around the wagon. "You're right that the bumpy ride will be difficult. I recommend walking as much as you can today."

"Walk?" The woman's voice still held that hateful tone. "But my legs."

"The wounds are surface. They'll be scabbed over in the next day or so. They're not so bad that you and your husband should risk falling behind."

Fenna stiffened. They'd all heard stories of what happened to a wagon that got left behind. The trail guide had been sure to warn them not to risk separating from the company. Will was right. Death was the only reason to fall behind, and even that could wait until nooning or nightfall.

Will climbed from the wagon and offered a hand to Fenna.

She gave a final glance at the woman before reaching out and taking Will's shoulders as he took her waist. She was at once reminded of the way they'd danced last night before she'd upset him with her shenanigans with Delia.

How the fear of attracting him had bled away and she was able to enjoy herself dancing with a friend. Their eyes met and Will gave her a stiff nod that told her he hadn't forgiven her yet for forcing Delia into his arms, and he didn't even know the whole of it.

Wind blew around them and tiny raindrops fell sharply against her skin. Will approached the husband who was wrestling an ox into its harness. "I cannot do more. Give her alcohol, as much as she wants. You can resupply when we reach the next trading post."

The husband nodded. "Thank you."

Will nodded and the husband turned back to his task. At least *he* hadn't turned sour on them. Will reached out an arm and ushered Fenna along the path. All the wagons had started, and it would take them a bit before they caught up to theirs. She hoped the Bridgers had found a place near the front where the dust wasn't so bad.

But as they made their way forward, the wind and rain picked up more and more. Fenna's skirts blew hard against her legs, acting like a ship's sail and slowing her down.

They came strong enough that she accepted Will's offered arm and even gripped it tightly as she ducked her head against the wind.

A cry came from ahead and Fenna raised her head to see what it was about. The sky had darkened, as though the sun hadn't risen just half an hour ago.

Another cry came and she heard the word.

Twister.

CHAPTER 24

Will stopped. Fenna had such a tight hold of him that she stopped too. Her heart was pounding, her body unable to do more than cling to him. The strong wind lifted more than dust in the air, and tiny rocks pricked at her face. She searched the skies, but she saw no proof of what others had claimed. There was no twister. Not yet.

Will tightened his hold, pressing her arm against his ribs. "We have to get to the wagon." He started running and Fenna clung to him, letting him half-drag her across the wide prairie.

Shouts and screams swirled through the air, and when a piece of clothing caught Fenna in the face, Will stopped and helped her untangle herself. He scanned the ground and led her to a slight dip in the landscape. He sat down, pulling her down too. Once on the clumpy prairie grass Fenna knew—they weren't low enough. She wanted a root cellar or a river wash, but there was nothing, not in this wide prairie. Not even their heads were below ground level.

Fenna scanned the wagons, each of them looking exactly

alike, and she couldn't find the chicken coops that would identify Mam's.

"Your parents," Fenna shouted over the wind.

Will shook his head, his eyes raking the wagons in the same desperate way.

They had set off before the Bridger wagons started, and now there was no way to tell where the rest of his family was in the line.

Will caught her head and pressed her ear to his mouth. "A funnel cloud."

She looked behind the wagons to see a u-shaped dip in the gray clouds. The dip stretched toward the earth until the end of it was out of sight behind the line of wagons. Folks were rushing to remove their canvas bonnets, but as dirt flew into Fenna's eyes, she closed them tight, blocking out whatever the others were doing.

Will kept hold of her and tucked her close to his body, shifting so they were lying flat on their grassy bowl. They waited as screams from others in their group mixed with the howling wind. Cries came from all around them.

"Will," she whimpered, but she knew he couldn't hear her, not even with how close they were. She merely clung to his coat and pressed herself as tightly to him as possible.

She imagined his eyes, those flecks of green in the yellow lantern light. Pictured his face between her hands in that moment of wonder. She hadn't had a chance to get a good look in the daylight, and now she might never know.

Except she did know. She knew it like she knew the feel of his body against hers. None of this was new to him. He remembered her eyes, he remembered embraces, kisses, and promises. And some of those she remembered too. The way she felt now, it was different than if she were pinned to the ground with one of his brothers. Her heart felt something for Will, even if her mind was a bit slower to recognize it.

The wind came stronger now and Fenna ducked closer to him, her nose brushing against the skin at the base of his neck. Even his smell was familiar. Whether it was because of the time spent at Molly's or not, he was no longer the stranger he'd once been. But he also wasn't her fiancé. The wind pummeled them, buffeting her clothes and zipping into every tiny opening in her dress, her neck, her sleeves, even her seams.

And then, in a breath, it was gone. Fenna kept holding on to Will, waiting for it to start again. But even through her closed eyelids, she could tell the daylight was growing, like it had merely been a cloud shifting between them and the sun and now it was moving away once more. Will lifted his arm from where it was draped across her middle and lifted his head, his eyes raking her frame. "Are you hurt?"

Fenna shook her head. She looked at her fingers curled so tightly around his coat lapels. "Will." Her hands were frozen in fear. Or maybe it was desperation that bound her to him. She didn't want to lose him. Didn't want to go through with the plan to find him a wife, nor did she feel confident enough to tell him she wanted to try, to see what they could salvage from whatever she'd lost the night she lost her memory.

He placed his hand on hers, and the heat from his grip did something to her own, his touch speaking to her in a way that proved her body remembered him even if her mind didn't. Bit by bit her fingers relaxed, but now that she could, she didn't want to let go. He pressed his forehead to hers and closed his eyes, letting out a sigh that warmed her chin.

His eyes may have been closed, but Fenna didn't want to close hers. She wanted to look at Will, so close, so warm, and so alive. She lifted her stiff fingers to touch the stubble on his cheek. He opened his eyes, searching hers. That ever-present question lurking behind those green flecks, only noticeable when she was close enough to feel his breath.

Over the past two years, she'd wondered about why they had been alone in the woods that night. It wasn't difficult to guess and just now, so close to him, she understood. Lust was powerful, and it could make a person forget what was right. Or maybe it was that it made everything feel right all at once.

Slowly she lifted her chin, bringing their mouths close enough that his shallow breaths warmed her lips. Her body was still pressed so close to his she could feel his chest rise and fall. And yet, he didn't move to kiss her. He'd been doing that for so long, waiting for her to come to him. Just now she didn't understand why she hadn't. Yes, it was a risk, but the reward was the greatest one, the potential everything.

A shout came, and Fenna's mind was yanked from Will's mouth. She lifted her head to survey the wreckage that lay before them. Wagons lay on their sides, their canvas ripped and contents pouring out like tipped sacks of grain.

As her attention swept the destroyed prairie, she noted that some wagons stood hale and hearty, as though the winds had passed them by without even a puff in their direction.

She had no idea the fate that had touched the Bridger wagons. Fenna spun to Will, and he met her gaze with ferocity.

"Where are they?" she asked.

He stumbled to his feet and reached for Fenna, gripping her hand and hauling her onto wobbly legs. Her mind was spinning as fast as those winds, incapable of logic. She held his hand and wasn't sure if she was more afraid of being left alone, or of him reaching them without her there.

They ran together, awkwardly, since she refused to surrender her hold and he didn't seem inclined to shake her off.

They reached Sam first, the same wagon Will would have been driving had they not been called for the woman's burns. It stood on four wheels, untouched.

"Sam!" Will called as they jogged past. There was no reply, and Fenna's stomach dropped, but Will didn't stop. Next was the twins' wagon. Theirs too was untouched, but they didn't answer their calls. Finally, they found Ben's wagon and though it was still upright, the canvas had been torn and supplies littered the ground.

"Ben!" they both called, running around the wagon in search of him.

The absence of every brother so far made Fenna sick. She bit her fist as she scanned the prairie. There were dark clumps scattered everywhere and no way to tell what was a person and what was an overturned crate.

"Ben!" Will called, his voice cracking.

A man waved from the other side of the wagons.

"Will, there." Fenna pointed and Will released her hand, leaving her behind as he ran to his brother.

Fenna's heart was in her throat as she chased him, dying to reach them and dreading whatever she would find.

When she caught up to him once more, Will was on his knees, his arms curled around his pa, rocking him. Mr. Bridger's hand lay palm up on the prairie dirt, lifeless.

Fenna fell to her knees. *Gone.* How could she take losing any more people? Ben knelt by her and gathered her in his arms.

Fenna clutched his shirt and sobbed into his shoulder.

Soon, someone else came, and Fenna felt more arms wrap around her.

When she looked up, Ben had gone, and it was Molly who had replaced him, a hollow look on her face.

Fenna wiped her face with her hand and sniffed. "Anyone else?"

"Auntie Eliza is hurt."

Fenna turned, but her movements were slow, drained. "Where?"

Molly's bottom lip was quivering, her eyes filled with tears.

Fenna pulled her friend in for a hug.

Molly spoke into Fenna's neck, her words muffled but audible. "I barely knew him. Only in the briefest of childhood memories."

Fenna held Molly tighter, knowing more than ever that it didn't take a memory to love somebody. Sometimes a body felt it.

Will lay his father down on the ground and rose to sit on his haunches. Fenna untangled herself from Molly and went to him. She placed a hand on his shoulder. Such a weak gesture, but she knew better than most that nothing took away the pain of losing a father.

Will jerked his face up, startled at her approach. His face was so broken. He turned, his knees bracing themselves on the ground as he hooked his arms around her waist, burying his face in her skirts. His shoulders didn't shake. If he was crying, it was the silent clinging kind, and her skirts were drying the tears as soon as they formed.

Her heart longed to return the embrace, to hold him like he was holding her. She shifted and loosened his hold enough for her to lower herself and take his face in her hands the way she'd done last night. Instead of searching his eyes, she let him see the apology written in hers.

Tears fell from both their eyes as they stared at one another.

Then a call came from her left. Sam was waving them over. Will rose and Fenna held his hand, able to keep up with his now sluggish steps. That desperate rushing fire from before had been snuffed at his pa's demise. Mam was lying on the ground, her head in Sam's lap. A dribble of blood leaked out the side of her mouth. Still, she smiled up at Will and Fenna.

Ben lifted from where he knelt by her head and sniffed, wiping tears away and making room for Will to take his place at their mama's side. Fenna knelt at Will's side and Mam placed a hand over their entwined fingers. "You two be together, as a proper husband and wife."

She coughed into a handkerchief and pulled it away, bloodied.

Will caught her hand and took the cloth, uncrumpling it to reveal more blood. "Mama," he breathed, reaching both hands to prod her ribs. Mam winced and sucked in a sharp breath. "You've broken a rib."

She took a shuddering, labored breath. A bit more blood escaped her lips. Fenna wiped it away with a bit of her skirt, but Mam only had eyes for her son. Her face was so sad, like she'd given up and knew she wasn't going to live to look at his face again. After all those years of Will being gone, now it was Mam's turn to go away.

"My bag." Will glanced around.

Fenna did too, before realizing he would have left it all the way back in their bowl, that is if it hadn't gotten swept away by the winds. "I'll get it."

She stumbled to her feet, surprised at her own litheness when her heart was a heavy lump in her chest. Mam dying and Fenna without even a scratch on her. She ran on weak knees down past the crying families, all grieving their own losses. Past the wreckage that was greater than anything she'd ever known.

She found their bowl and skidded to a halt, twisting until she finally located a dark lump down the way. She ran down, a sagebrush root catching her boot and causing her to trip and fall to the ground. Her knees screamed in a way she hadn't allowed her mouth to do. She pulled her hands off the earth and turned them over to reveal bloody scratches down the heels of both hands. She stared at the blood. Angry. Why Mam? Why did the last person she loved have to go away?

Fenna clasped her bloodied hands together, savoring the ache of pressing her wounds together, and prayed. "Please let her stay. Please, God, I need her." But even as she prayed, she recalled the way Mam had been breathing, the whistling, strained sound she'd made with each intake of air.

There was no time to cry. Will needed his bag, and Mam needed him. She made her way to the bag and gripped it by the handle. It was still closed, though everything inside had been displaced and was now rolling and rattling around the bottom.

She rushed back, shifting the heavy bag from one hand to the other as she ignored the cries for help. *We help our own first.* Will had said that to Fenna when her feet were aching.

He'd said it, and she wasn't even theirs. Did it ever matter that she wasn't truly theirs? They were hers.

Finally, she reached Will and found Mam and Mr. Bridger laid out next to one another. Both eyes closed, their sons standing in a line, shoulder to shoulder, faces stoic with grief.

Fenna dropped the bag, and the clank drew Will's eyes only. She mouthed, *Will,* and he held her gaze for another breath, then switched his gaze back down to his ma and pa.

Molly wrapped an arm around Fenna's waist, leaning her head against Fenna's.

Fenna stood strong, fighting her tears. If Mam's sons weren't crying, it wasn't Fenna's place to do so.

Ben broke away and walked past their bodies all the way to his wagon. He slid a spade from the side and brought it back, cutting into the earth with sad ferocity. Alex joined him and Will broke away and did the same, taking the spade from his wagon. The other brothers worked on righting Mam and Frank's wagon, but they couldn't do it alone. Ben,

Will, and Alex stopped and helped. As Will started back for his spade, Fenna caught him on his chest.

She didn't say anything, just looked into his eyes. She knew what it was to lose a parent and no words could ease the ache.

He sighed and placed his forehead to hers, that same way he'd done before, and she knew without him saying it that this was something they used to do. For the first time, she didn't feel lost in forgetting the past.

CHAPTER 25

His forehead was pressed to Fenna's, their breaths mingled, and yet he drew no comfort in Fenna's proximity. Like this body had been drained of the ability to emote.

The hiss of Ben's spade cutting through the dry ground pulled Will from his trance and he stepped away from Fenna, letting her hand fall away from his chest. The skin beneath his shirt was cold where she'd touched him, the loss of her tangible even if his mind couldn't grieve it.

Will joined Ben and relished the pain that shot through his broken finger with every turn of dirt.

When it was time to lay their bodies into the ground, Fenna came to his side. She didn't touch him, just stood there strong, as though she hadn't lost someone too.

Just now he didn't care about concealing the truth. He slid an arm around her waist and she leaned into him as Nate and Alex lowered Pa first, then Ben and Sam lowered Ma into the same, large grave. On the other side of Fenna, Molly had her arms around Chet's waist and his face was wet with tears.

"Doc," a voice came from behind. Will and Fenna both

turned. "Sorry to disturb. My daughter…" The man turned, and for the first time Will surveyed the scene, truly taking in the destruction of the twister. Of course, there were folks who needed him. He let out a heavy breath and released his hold on Fenna, but contrary to her words last night, she took his hand, wove their fingers together, and said, "I'll go too."

Fenna watched Will work with patients. Bandaging the bloody, comforting the grieving, and explaining what was to come.

Many of the families were cursing this prairie. Cursing the decision to take this savage journey. By the time she and Will had worked their way back to the Bridger camp, Fenna figured more than half of the wagons were decided against going to Oregon.

When they returned to camp, Fenna was shocked at how it looked exactly the same as it had last night. Unchanged. Tents were set up and a fire built. Instead of Mam over the fire, Chet was doing his best, but the smell of burned cakes stung her nose.

Fenna wrapped an arm around his shoulders. "You did good. I'll teach you some in the morning."

"You were needed out there." Will's voice was raspy, but there was an underlying harshness that was unfamiliar to Fenna. "Chet can cook just fine. Molly too. They cannot work with patients the way you can."

Fenna nodded, somehow understanding his words weren't a compliment. Maybe he was remembering her desire to find him a new assistant. That conversation felt like it happened a thousand days ago.

Will left her by the fire and disappeared behind a wagon.

"Was it bad?" Chet's voice was small, and it felt as wrong as backwards boots.

Fenna thought of the dead. Young and old. The storm having no care for which souls it took. "Plenty of folks lost loved ones, just like we did." And plenty would lose more in the days to come. There were certain patients whose bandages Will didn't take as much care with, and his face was grim when they left. Those were the ones Fenna knew he couldn't help. All he could do was give them hope, a bit of happiness before their world became dark.

The wagon master had died, and without him there was no hope for continuing on. They hobbled back to Independence. Though the family was silent with grief, they had picked up a few new friends, including one woman, Ellen, who had lost her husband and knew as little as Fenna did about driving oxen.

Sam and Ben took turns driving Ellen's wagon while the twins and Will drove the remaining three. Mam and Mr. Bridger's wagon had cracked an axle. Rather than fix the crack, they distributed everything between their remaining wagons and even squeezed a few things into Ellen's wagon. The plan was to bring a new axle back with them when—if—they came back through.

Will was needed more than ever, and though he wanted Fenna to come along, he seemed colder than she'd ever known him to be before. Like he was a tin cup without any coffee.

In addition to sharing the space in her wagon, Ellen knew how to cook almost as well as Mam had. Oftentimes, Fenna and Will would return from working with a patient to find Molly and Ellen over a fire, Ellen instructing poor Molly. Fenna couldn't help but grin at the idea of Molly learning something from a person instead of a book. It might be the first time in her life.

The three women were scrubbing dishes together one night when Molly spoke. "I'm sorry you lost your husband. It must be a mighty challenge for you. What will you do when we get to Independence? Is your family there?"

Fenna was beginning to wonder the same thing. What were the Bridger brothers planning to do? Surely Molly would go back home. Fenna had an urge to do the same. But her home had never been hers and was even less so now.

Ellen replied, not lifting her eyes from the pot she was scrubbing. "I don't rightly know. My family is back east. My first husband brought me to Independence, but he died shortly after."

"Oh, Ellen." Molly set her dish down and went to her but stopped short. She glanced at Fenna, who shrugged. Then Molly wrapped her arm around Ellen's shoulders. Ellen endured the embrace and finally Molly let go. "You're too young to have been widowed twice."

Ellen just sighed. "I'm doing just fine. I appreciate your men driving my wagon for me."

"It's nothing." Molly waved away her gratitude, but Fenna knew it wasn't nothing. Driving a wagon was difficult work, and without Pa to drive theirs, the brothers had no chance to trade off and rest.

"You should learn to drive it," Fenna suggested, lifting her gaze to see how Ellen took this suggestion. Was she the type to take and take and feel no guilt? Ellen's sharp glance was worried enough that it soothed Fenna's fears. "Not that they mind helping, but you might want to know how someday."

Ellen nodded and went back to her scrubbing. Fenna watched her for a moment longer, wondering what she was thinking. Widowed twice. She couldn't imagine. She knew the grief of losing loved ones, but a spouse must be different. A companion, one she shared her life with, and her bed. It was bound to be different.

Fenna looked in the direction of their camp. Will had hardly spoken a word to her since the day of the twister. She tried not to be hurt, to understand this was how he was grieving. After all, she hadn't allowed him to comfort her while she grieved her own pa's death. Though the situations were different, Fenna knew if he could endure that, she could endure a few days of being ignored.

Eventually, they made it back to Independence. Most wagons continued driving right into town, but many folks corralled the wagons, just as they'd done before, and camped at the very spot they'd been living before the journey began.

Somehow, the idea that they'd not only wasted time, but lost their family as well, brought Fenna so low she wanted to lie down in the dusty grass and water it with her tears. She helped Molly set up their tent and climbed into her bed, praying for sleep even though it was mid-day.

As she lay in her bed, she let the tears run down her face. She missed Mam. Missed her easy way, how she had comforted Fenna just by existing. Why had Fenna come on this journey? Losing Mam in Charlotte would have been devastating, but here it was somehow worse. Fenna wasn't even allowed to grieve because everywhere she turned there was work to do. Even now, she cried into her pillow to muffle the sound against the walls of canvas.

She'd agreed to come because she figured this was what Pa would have wanted, but as she lay in her tent, she wondered if she'd been wrong. Perhaps Pa would have wanted her to live, not die along the Oregon trail.

Voices drifted in from outside the tent. She strained to listen. Ben was taking Ellen and her wagon home. Fenna considered climbing out and saying goodbye, but she knew her face must be puffy with tears she wasn't entitled to shed. Instead, she let her mind consider borrowing some funds from Ben and doing the same. Going home.

She must have fallen asleep, because the next thing she knew, Molly was shaking her awake. "Fenna, you better come quick."

Fenna rushed, bleary-eyed, out of her bed and into the late afternoon sunlight. Then, as though she was still dreaming, Edward came to her, pulling her into his arms. His breath was hot on her scalp as he spoke. "I heard about the twister catching a wagon train. I had to come to see if it was you."

He shifted his hold from around her waist to just her shoulders, staring into her face.

"Edward," was all she could say. He was so out of place, this far from North Carolina. She hadn't thought to see him again in her life. A sharp pang of homesickness overtook her, and her chin quivered. She was so tired of pretending everything was fine. This journey was becoming the worst mistake of her life. The Lord hadn't preserved Mam, but maybe he'd provided Fenna with means to return to Charlotte.

Fenna's gaze was drawn to a figure entering the clearing. Will.

His face turned from the practiced blankness he'd clung to these last few days to shock to outrage. He took several quick steps toward Fenna, brushing Edward's hands from where they pressed on Fenna's shoulders. "What is this?"

Edward frowned. "Will." He clapped him on the shoulder. "I heard about your folks. I'm sorry."

Will knocked Edward's hand away. "What are you doing here?"

"I came to be sure Fenna was well." He turned to Fenna. "And see if you would reconsider my proposal."

Molly, still standing at Fenna's side, gave a loud gasp. Fenna blinked at Edward. She wanted so badly to go home, to undo the awful she'd just endured. But no matter where she went, Mam would still be buried in that prairie.

Yet the same reasons still remained. She didn't love Edward, didn't want to be mistress of his house. He might help her get home, but she was no longer a woman to consider a marriage merely for convenience's sake. She'd felt something in that prairie, with the storm raging around them, and again when she'd touched foreheads with Will. She had known love before, even if she couldn't quite remember it. Will was watching her with such intensity, she had to look away again.

What she needed was options of her own, without either of these men. She opened her mouth to speak, but Will cut in.

"She cannot go with you. She's my wife."

Edward took a hurried step backward, like Will had just confessed to having smallpox.

Fenna let out a small laugh at Will's desperate attempt. Though she didn't mind the ruse, it wasn't fair for Edward to think her rejection was a lie. He had come all this way and he deserved the truth.

"I am not." She smiled, trying to convey her gratitude to Will, but he didn't smile back.

"You are."

Fenna's brows drew together and she shook her head.

Will drew a deep breath and looked around. Molly was standing there, but so were the Bridger brothers, all but Ben.

"Fenna is my wife. We married two years ago, the day of the accident."

Fenna's feet went cold and the sensation crawled up her body, freezing everything in its wake.

His voice softened, like he was only speaking to her now. "Only Mama knew."

Fenna's knees felt like puddles. She glanced around and

found one of their canvas camp chairs close. She stumbled over and Molly met her there, a hand on Fenna's elbow. But Fenna couldn't take her eyes from the two men glaring at one another.

This revelation hadn't been for Fenna's sake; it had been for Edward's, to chase him away. And yet the way Fenna's heart was thumping wasn't because Will's words were a lie. It was because she somehow knew them to be true.

"Married?" she whispered to herself. Her mind wouldn't believe it, but once again her body hummed at the word, as though it was trying to show her the truth of it.

Edward's voice was hard. "Grant her a divorce."

"Never." Will stepped closer, he and Edward nearly nose-to-nose.

Edward swung his hand in Fenna's direction. "You cannot protect her." He cast his gaze around their hasty camp. "Look at her, look at this. She'd be better off coming home with me than being buried by trash like you."

Will and Edward collided, but a fight in the dirt was quiet and nothing like the one in the bar, where bones hit the hollow floor and chairs and tables skittered and toppled over. Each blow was muffled by flesh, each step a shift in the too-familiar dust.

Fenna rose and slipped behind the tents and wagons, taking slow steps away from camp and into the town.

CHAPTER 26

Fenna stumbled through the streets of Independence. The twister had hit here too, taking parts of buildings and, in some cases, the entire thing. The smell was the same as before: manure and woodsmoke. Folks still bustled about, though the sun was dipping below the horizon. This was the jumping off point for the Oregon trail. Surely there was work here. Perhaps she could stay and build a life of her own.

Like family.

She'd spoken that phrase so often. But there was nothing *like family*. There was family and there was non-family. There was no in-between.

Will's revelation only proved her insecurities. Mam hadn't taken Fenna in out of love; it had been obligation.

Fenna stopped at her destination. A dressmaker. Rather than step inside, she tucked around the corner and drew a few lungs full of air. Mam may not have loved her for herself, but she'd done a fine job at helping Fenna heal from the loss of her father, and from her memories. She'd cared for Fenna, and that would just have to be enough.

Fenna fanned her eyes, drying the tears that were doing their best to ruin this opportunity for her.

Before she lost her nerve, she rushed inside the dressmaker's shop. A bell above the door tinkled and a smiling woman stood behind the counter, looking at Fenna expectantly.

"How may I help you, dear?"

Fenna glanced around the place. Not much detail. These dresses were meant for the trail. They would not need embellishment. No matter. Fenna was still a dab hand with a needle and could sew better than most women.

"I wondered if you might be needing some help around your shop," she said.

The woman's face softened. "You from the wagon train that just returned? I heard many were lost. I'm sorry for your loss."

Fenna swallowed, unsure whether she was worthy of accepting this woman's pity. Fenna had merely lost a close friend, not a mother, no matter that it felt like a tumbleweed had made its home in her throat and she could not draw a full breath without her eyes watering.

The woman must have taken Fenna's silence as grief.

"I wish I could help, but you're not the first person in here today asking for work. There will likely be more tomorrow."

Of course. Fenna nodded and, with a quiet thank you, she slipped from the shop.

Most women knew how to sew. It was an obvious job and one that should be given to someone truly in need. Someone who had lost their family in that tornado. Someone who had nobody to turn to. An orphan.

And why shouldn't Fenna have it? Just because she was orphaned long ago? It didn't mean she was any less needy.

Except she wasn't needy. It was only her pride that stood in her way. And her desire not to be a burden to the Bridgers.

But the expression on Will's face when he'd clashed with Edward…jealousy, she was certain. He'd gotten to know her over the last few weeks. He knew her already, but he had a taste of who she'd become over the last two years. And he'd still argued to prevent her from going with Edward. That had to mean something. It had to mean he at least wanted to try making things work with her. Not just a courtship. A marriage. He was her husband.

The sun was lower now and though she passed other options for work—a café, a schoolhouse, a bawdy house—she knew every one of those options would take her away from the Bridgers.

Fenna didn't dare risk anything more by staying out past nightfall. She might feel desperate, but she wasn't reckless. With a wince, she remembered setting Will's fingers.

Along with that memory came the knowledge that he still trusted her. He saw the old parts of her, and he was willing to see if she still possessed them. And yet, with Will, she'd never felt the way she had with Mam and so many others back home, like she was falling short of expectation. Every memory made with Will felt like a fresh start. She'd warned him early on, when they'd spent evenings in his room, not to talk of the past, and he'd never needed another word on the subject. It was as though he was glad to let the old Fenna remain in North Carolina.

She turned her feet toward the camp, no longer willing to ignore the pull she felt to the sanctuary of the Bridger wagons. They weren't *like* family. They *were* her family by law. Unless Will meant to grant her a divorce, she no longer had anything to fear.

She might not remember their wedding, but she'd attended enough ceremonies to remember some of the vows made. *Until death* being one of them. Death may be swirling around them like that twister, but she and Will were miraculously still alive.

As the camp came into view, Fenna didn't bother trying to stop the smile that spread as she drew nearer to the wagons. To Will.

Everything she'd lost, even the bits she hadn't remembered, seemed to be within her reach once again. The way folks had mourned the loss of her and Will's love, it was hers again. The weak position she thought she held within the Bridger family, stronger than ever. And Pa... He was still gone, but she was to spend the remainder of her days with someone who knew Pa, who loved him too. He was not completely lost, not while they remembered him.

CHAPTER 27

*F*inally, Edward was on the ground, wiping at his bloody nose. Will stood above him, chest heaving. "Are you done?"

Edward spit and crawled to his feet. Will's fingers throbbed. The splint on one of them had busted.

"Your wife?" Edward wiped at his mouth.

For a brief moment, Will pitied this man. He knew what it was like to love Fenna and not have that love returned. He too would have come all this way to ensure she was safe and beg her to reconsider.

"I have the certificate."

Edward gave an angry shake of his head and brushed at his clothing, too fine for this far west. Edward spit at the ground and turned away, stomping back toward town.

Will watched him go, then turned to Fenna. But her chair was empty—only Molly stood to the side. He scanned the camp; plenty of onlookers had come to watch the fight, but Fenna wasn't among them. His gaze settled on Molly. "Where is she?"

Molly glanced around as if she only just noticed Fenna's disappearance. "I don't know."

With a growl of frustration, Will shouldered past Molly and the others and went to Fenna's tent. She wasn't there either. Soon the whole family was searching for her and when they decided she was nowhere in the camp, Will made for the town.

As he searched the stores, the sun dipped lower in the sky. All he could think of was their first overnight on the train ride over, when she and Molly had gone off and Will had ended up with broken fingers. Wasn't she smart enough not to go off on her own?

Guilt swelled in his gut. He should have told her earlier. He should have told her privately when all his attention had been focused on her. She'd run off because her world had altered, and he'd been too busy using his fists to convince Edward. It was impossible to tell how she'd taken the news, but she surely hadn't been overcome with joy.

The clouds gathered, making darkness fall sooner than expected, and rain fell in a slow drizzle. It was pitch dark by the time Will returned to camp, sodden and muddy. He tried to suppress visions of Fenna in a tavern with a greasy man's hands on her. Surely she was smart enough not to try that escapade again. But wherever she was, it wasn't right. She belonged by his side, within his family. She's always belonged there; she'd just forgotten. And he'd failed to convince her of that truth.

Most of the lanterns were dimmed, not just in his family's area, but the entire camp. Everyone had taken shelter from the storm.

Will longed to tear his way into Ben's tent and demand they all rise and help him find Fenna. But when he reached his family's area, he saw it was tidy, as though this was a normal night. His anger abated as clarity settled in. They wouldn't be resting, not if Fenna were still missing. She must have returned during his absence. He glanced at her and Molly's tent, imagined her there, sleeping the way she'd done that night in his hotel room.

He started toward the tent, but when he tipped his head, a run of water dripped in front of his face. He couldn't go in there sopping wet as he was, not when he knew it would wind up being someone else's responsibility to clean everything he ruined.

Instead of going right to her, he trudged to his tent in search of dry clothes. He untied the flap, hardly of the mindset to be grateful to whoever had set his canvas up for him. But when he pulled back the door, he found a form asleep inside. He ducked out, glanced around, counting all the tents and checking the poles on this one. It was his tent. He ducked back inside and tried to look at the figure inside, but the blanket was tucked tight and the night was too dark to see anything but vague shapes. He could hear breathing, too. It was shallow, not the deep noises Ben made. Chet, maybe.

Will removed his boots and hat and slipped inside, knowing he was still making a mess that would need to be cleaned come morning. He stripped his clothes off, missing the warmth, even though he knew their wetness only leached heat from him. Even his underwear was wet, so he took those off too. Naked, he rummaged in his trunk and found his spare pair and stepped in, pulling it up and slipping his arms through before working the buttons.

He didn't bother with anything else before nudging Chet. "Hey, what are you doing in here?"

"Will?"

But it wasn't his little brother's voice that lifted up to him. "Fenna?"

She rolled over and moonlight glinted off her lighter hair.

Will twisted on his haunches, keenly aware that he wasn't properly dressed. "Is there a lantern in here?"

Fenna crawled out from under the covers, tucking her feet under her and looking around the space. "It's here, but the fire is out. I waited for you."

Will nearly laughed. "I was looking for *you*. Where did you go? And why did nobody come fetch me?" As his eyes adjusted to the shadowy interior, he could see Fenna's white shift in the dark, her skin a dusky gray in comparison. Heaven only knew what she could see of him. "Get back under the covers. You'll freeze."

"Will, nobody knew. Are we truly married?"

Will sat back, hugging his knees. He took up too much room in this tiny tent. "Yes."

"Why didn't you tell me?"

That was the question. All his reasons seemed foolish now. "I wanted you to love me."

"Oh, Will." She reached up and ran the tips of her fingers along his jaw.

He couldn't stop himself, and he didn't want to. He caught her hand and leaned into her touch. Turning his face, he kissed the inside of her palm. Her hand was warm against his still-chilled cheeks. "Edward was right. I have no business keeping you here."

Fenna pulled her hand away. "You mean you want to try for a divorce?"

"No." Will scooted closer, hating the distance she'd put between them and wishing he had her hand again. "I mean..." What did he mean? If Edward was right, Will was endangering Fenna with this trek west. Should he find someplace else for them to live? Somewhere back east, safe and settled? "Do you still want to go west?"

Fenna was quiet, fiddling with the corner of the quilt. Will watched, longing both for her touch and the warmth those quilts promised. But he wasn't about to climb in next to her in his underwear. Just because she now knew they were husband and wife didn't mean she was ready for anything so intimate.

Still, he couldn't suppress a shiver. His hair was still damp and his skin chilled.

Fenna scooted over and lifted the quilt. An invitation.

Will looked at her eyes, hardly visible in the dark. "Are you sure?"

Fenna nodded and Will didn't waste any more time. He slid under the covers, doing his best not to let his icy skin touch hers, but the space was narrow and Fenna didn't make any attempt to scoot away from him. She settled in, too, adjusting the quilts so each of them were covered to their necks.

Fenna rolled onto her side, placing her palm on his chest. "Ben needs you. He brought Ellen back with him."

Will turned. "Ellen?"

"Yes. She's in my tent with Molly."

Will took in the information with quiet breathing. "Is that why you're in here?"

"I'm in here because I was waiting for you."

Will dared not hope that she'd expected this very outcome, each of them dressed down, lying next to one another.

"Why were you waiting?"

"I was worried, for one. How are your fingers?"

Will hadn't been able to feel them since shortly after the freezing rain started.

He lifted his broken fingered hand out of the quilt and held it up. "I don't know."

Fenna touched the heel of his hand. "Did you break them again?"

"No." Will let his hand fall to the pillow between them

and her hand stayed with his. Her other hand came up and rested on his wrist. He'd done his best over the last few days to allow her space to grieve his mama when all he'd really wanted to do was tell her the truth and hold her in his arms.

After burying both his parents, he wasn't sure he could handle the other reaction she might have had, the outcome that led to her not embracing him, but turning away from his whole family. He wouldn't run that risk, wouldn't take everything away from her at once. So he'd stayed away. Again.

"Do you think me a coward for not telling you?"

Fenna was silent for a beat and Will's heart grew tighter with every moment that passed. "I wish you had."

"Truly?" Will's chest refused to expand to hold the regret that filled every crevice. He'd been such a fool.

"Everything makes sense now. The devotion, the way you took no interest in Delia."

"Interest? I hardly met her."

Fenna laughed, her hot breath warming his injured hand. "I might have told her you were interested and needed a bit of a push."

Will's breath left in a whoosh.

"I feel terrible, especially now. Sending a woman to tempt my husband." Her hand on him clenched tighter. "Will, what if I had married Edward before I left?"

Will shook his head. "Mama was supposed to keep an eye on you. I guess she did a poor job."

Fenna gave a small laugh. "She didn't do a poor job. I knew she was watching me. I was careful to not let her find out."

"I should have known you were capable of it."

"Tell me about our wedding. Why did nobody know?"

"Our parents wouldn't let us. We decided to do it anyway. I found a preacher down in Tearson and his wife agreed to be the witness."

"Neither of them knew us. How did he know that I hadn't been forced against my will?"

"You were more than willing." Will's face warmed at the thought. "Anyone who looked at us could see we were in love."

"And I lost it all."

"We both lost it."

Fenna breathed in and out for a few moments. Will was lost in memories, the wood paneling of the church where they were married, the flowers in Fenna's hair.

"Did my pa know?"

"Nobody did. Not even Ben. We were on our way home when your pa found us." Will remembered the way her pa had yelled, but he didn't want to taint Fenna's memories of her father. "Then the tramps came."

"And they shot him?"

"Fenna, are you sure you want to hear this?"

She nodded and shifted closer, her knees brushing against his.

Will swallowed, hating the fact that he had to tell her everything. It was one thing to withhold information before, when he thought her fragile. But now he knew better, and it was time to give her the entire truth. "Fenna, they said things, they planned to hurt you in a way worse than death."

"Your mama did mention that." She bowed her head and placed her forehead against their entwined hands.

Will slipped one hand to cup her head, his fingers twining in her hair and lifting her face to press his forehead to hers. Her breath mingled with his in a heat that twisted down to his core. "Your pa told me to get you out of there. I had no choice. It was you or him."

Fenna shook her head. "I would have never left him. I know I don't remember, but I would never…"

"You didn't."

She drew back, meeting his eyes.

"I had to hold you on the horse as we rode away from him. You were screaming to go back." Will's voice broke. His heart breaking all over again at what he'd had to do that night. Go against Fenna's wishes, allow her father his demise. But that still wasn't all of it. "You fought so hard you fell off the horse. Cracked your head on a buried stone. I believe *that* was when you lost your memory."

Fenna lay in her shift, the cold from Will's foray out in the rain still chilling the space under the quilt. But that was nothing compared to the frigid realization that she'd been the one to erase her memory.

"I did it? I stole my memory?"

Will's hand came up and brushed her cheek. "You wanted to save your pa."

"And I didn't." Her tone was hateful.

She wanted to curl into herself, to be left alone. She'd spent the evening wondering what Will wanted from her. Wondering why he'd kept their marriage a secret. Only for him to return and break her heart in an entirely unexpected way.

"Not for lack of trying. Fenna, you are the bravest person I know."

Fenna scoffed. "Except I wasn't even brave enough to look at you." A flash of realization illuminated her mind. "Is that why you didn't tell me? Is that why you left?"

"At first, yes. Every bit of research I did told me that forcing the memories on you would have made them disappear forever. If I had stayed, the trauma might have prevented you from remembering those last few years with your pa."

"But I still didn't get them back."

"No."

"Do you think I ever will?"

"It's difficult to say. There's so much we don't know about the brain. But the more time passes, the less likely they are to return."

Will shifted and his leg brushed against hers.

The contact and attention she'd been craving from him these last few days was being given now in large doses. "I'll never remember you falling in love with me."

"Fenna, I fall more in love with you every day. Everything you remember? That is the same as before. It wasn't some turn of a coin. It was a hundred moments, and it was nothing compared to the rest of our lives."

She wished she could see him, that she hadn't snuffed the lantern and gone to sleep. But his quilts were infused with the smell of him, and she hadn't been able to stop herself from burrowing deep into his domain.

The rest of her life. With this man, with his hands on her jaw, his legs next to hers in the bed, his chill ebbing away, being replaced by the steady beat of his heart.

"Am I the reason you agreed to go west?"

Will hummed. "I would have gone wherever you were."

"If I'd stayed in Charlotte?"

Will adjusted the quilt on her shoulder. "I would have come to you there."

"And told me?"

Will sighed. "I would have had to." He huffed a laugh. "I cannot believe my mama didn't know you were accepting Edward's advances. How often did she send you to their house?"

Fenna chuckled. "Plenty of times."

Will drew a deep breath and let it out slowly. "I know I cannot care, but I must know if you love him."

"Love?" Fenna almost choked on the word. "I do not love him."

"You didn't refuse his proposal to take you back to Charlotte."

"I didn't say yes."

"You hesitated."

Fenna felt a tiny flame of anger flick to life. "I didn't know what lay ahead of me. No matter what I chose, I was dependent on somebody. I wasn't sure if you and your brothers wanted me now that you had no parents and already Molly as an added burden to the journey. I thought I could make it home on my own, but I had no money. Then Edward arrived."

Will scooted closer, wrapping an arm around her and pulling her snug against him. "Fenna, I love you. I have always loved you, and if you'll have me, I'll protect you all your life. My family will be your family and you will be a Bridger by law and by love."

Fenna snuggled into the space between his neck and his shoulder. "You're very bold, Doc Bridger."

"I wish I'd been bolder sooner."

"No." She ran her fingertips along the sinewy muscles that ran up his neck. "I'm glad I had the chance to know you again, to choose you for myself."

Will pressed away so he could look at her eyes. "I thought you were sending Delia after me?"

"That was before. When I was worried you wouldn't love me."

"Why would you think such a thing?"

"I'm different now. I'm not the girl you fell in love with."

"You are right. These last few weeks I have fallen in love with an entirely different woman."

She closed her eyes, conjuring that pull she'd been feeling toward him, the one she'd foolishly tried her best to ignore, letting it guide her mouth to his. She brushed her lips against his, savoring the warmth that she knew would be there. Not because all kisses are warm, but because Will was. He was tender and gentle, but a lion when she needed him to be. And yet he'd been patient, licking her wounds as she wrestled with herself these past weeks.

Will let out a shuddering breath, one of longing and uncertainty.

Fenna curled her hands in the fabric of his long underwear, pulling him closer to her. She leaned farther into the kiss, hoping he understood he didn't need to fear any longer. He didn't need to rein in his affection for her. She'd given up her idiotic hunt for a replacement wife. She would have to be the lion now, keeping other women away from her man. Her husband.

And for the first time, Fenna knew who she was today was enough, was right, and she didn't have to pretend any longer, didn't have to study the expressions of those around to see if she was meeting their expectations.

She was getting a fresh start with Will, and a chance to be loved for the Fenna she was now—today. And the surety that she would still be loved for whoever she would become tomorrow.

EPILOGUE

Molly insisted on a celebration, since not only did Fenna not remember their wedding, but neither of them had gotten the chance to celebrate. She rallied the same musicians that had played at the dance on the trail, the ones who's lanterns Fenna had used to spot the green in Will's eyes. Then Molly pulled Fenna toward their tent.

Fenna glanced back at Will, who was accepting congratulations from one of the families who would be joining them on their next attempt to reach Oregon.

"I should be at his side," Fenna said.

"You will be." Molly tugged her inside.

There, on the floor, stood one of Molly's trunks, and laying across the top was that same blush-colored dress she'd worn to the dance in Virginia.

Fenna huffed and turned to Molly. "This wasn't on your packing list."

Molly just grinned. "I knew you didn't have its equal in your trunk, and a woman needs at least one fine dress."

Fenna fingered the quality fabric, remembering the

luxury of Molly's life back home. Dances with carriages and plenty of food. And her mother and Mam there, smiling. Mam was gone. Fenna's throat grew thick and tears stung her eyes. She sniffed and Molly turned, grasping both Fenna's elbows.

"You don't have to wear it."

Fenna shook her head, hating for Molly to think her ungrateful. "It's lovely. You're too good to bring it."

Molly gave a dry laugh. "I had to remove seven books just to make room. Seven." She shook her head in mock disappointment. Or maybe it was true disappointment.

Fenna smiled. She didn't have Mam, but she had Molly, and as much as she regretted not spending more time with Mam before she was gone, she appreciated the relationship she was building with Will's cousin.

"Come on. Let's get you dressed."

As Fenna removed her dress, she couldn't help but feel shy wearing such a showy dress when everyone else would be in their trail duds. But she supposed a wedding celebration was an acceptable time to be overdressed.

She stepped into the gown, and Molly helped her adjust it around her shoulders and tied up the back. Molly circled to Fenna's front and pinched her chin, her lips twisted. "I wish we could do more with your hair."

Will's laugh floated in from outside the tent. "I don't want my hair done." She just wanted to be at Will's side again, holding his arm, feeling the heat of his breath when he pressed a kiss into her hair, watching him look at her without holding anything back.

She passed through the tent flap and scanned the space for Will's familiar form. She spotted him a few yards away from where she'd left him. Though he stood in conversation, his gaze locked on her and didn't break as she made her way across the prairie in a dress too fine to be worn in the dust.

When she reached him, he snaked an arm around her waist and tucked her close to his side. He introduced her around, and Fenna accepted congratulations from the folks they encountered, but all she longed to do was retire to the sanctuary of Will's tent, to the blankets that held his scent, to remove this dress and just be Fenna and Will.

She almost whispered as much to him, but the musicians started and Will pulled her into the space in front of the band and held her in promenade position. She couldn't help but smile as he looked at her with mock seriousness. Then he moved them and he was easy to follow, his every step foreshadowed by a slight tilt of his hand on her hip.

They danced a few songs and Fenna looked around. She'd expected his brothers to have cut in by now, but only Chet stood near a cask with a cup in his hand. Fenna narrowed her eyes at him, but he was too consumed with his beverage to pay her any mind.

Then Sam stepped between two wagons and into the light, a slight frown on his face. Next was Ben and Ellen. Fenna's feet stopped moving and Will did too, following her gaze.

Ben made his way toward them and dipped his head close to Will's, his voice a low whisper. "I couldn't leave her there with him."

Will grimaced.

Fenna frowned. Who was Ben speaking of? "With who?"

Will's gaze shifted to her. "Ellen's brother-in-law." He turned back to Ben. "Won't he come for her?"

"He thinks we've married."

Fenna's jaw dropped, but Ben wasn't done. He leaned closer. "Everyone has to believe it, even in camp."

Will shook his head. "The company is too tight. There are no secrets." But his eyes flicked to Fenna, and she understood that he'd been able to keep the biggest secret of all.

"Just for a few weeks, until we're far enough west that he can't come for her."

Will sighed and shook his head. "I don't like it."

But Ben was not asking permission.

Fenna's hold on Will's arm tightened. "Surely he's not a danger to her." This seemed quite the ruse for a woman who was so recently widowed. She should be able to take shelter in her family at a time like this, not be protected *from* them. While Ellen hadn't seemed overly distraught at losing her husband, she'd never mentioned danger when she spoke of returning to his family.

Ben turned his harried gaze on Fenna. "Trust me. She couldn't stay there."

Fenna's mind concocted several different meanings to Ben's words. In the end, she trusted his judgment and nodded. "Okay."

Ben drew a deep breath, his shoulders lifting and falling. He looked over her shoulder where Ellen was speaking to Molly. For a moment she thought she saw longing in his eyes. "Could you not have married her in truth?"

Ben turned sharply. "No, and I don't want you or anyone to meddle."

Will pulled Fenna closer. "Ben, we aren't a danger to you or to her." His tone was a warning, and Fenna almost laughed. She didn't need protection from Will's brothers. She'd dealt with them on her own for years now. Nevertheless, it felt good to have a Bridger on her side. Not just in this moment, but forever.

She shifted, standing in front of him and interlacing her fingers behind his neck. "How long do we have to stay at this party?" His hands on her waist tightened and she knew he understood her meaning.

A scoff sounded behind her and she heard Ben's retreat.

Will leaned closer, his voice low in her ear. "That's one way to end a conversation."

"He was stalling."

They swayed to the music, a soft melody that made Fenna want to lay her head on Will's chest and listen to the beat of his heart.

The twins, Alex and Nate, joined the circle, their eyes lit with whatever they'd done to contribute to Ellen's rescue. Neither brother wasted time finding a girl to dance with and escorting her into the open space meant for dancing. Ben escorted Ellen onto the floor; Sam did the same for Molly.

Fenna looked up at Will. "I think Molly will find a husband out here. She's more of a romantic than you might think."

Will chuckled. "You didn't watch her expertise in rejecting offers of marriage."

"Surely she wasn't so bad."

Will just shook his head.

Fenna glanced back at the family, all of them dancing nearby save the youngest. "We'll have to keep an eye on Chet."

"A bit of hop juice won't hurt him."

Fenna nodded, but with Mam gone, she knew they would all have to take their turn watching over him. He was old enough to have his own mind, but young enough to be a dummy about it.

Will caught her chin and stole her gaze away from Chet. "If you're worried, I'll speak with him about it."

"You Bridgers are always making trouble." She smirked. It was true—they'd given their mother a large dose of grief, but she'd never been disappointed in her sons.

Will snaked his arms around her waist. "Can't say you didn't know what you were getting into when you married me."

"I thought we were heading west to get away from you and your brothers finding trouble around every corner," she muttered.

"We've just begun."

Fenna couldn't tell whether he was referring to the journey west or the trouble his brothers had yet to create. Either way, this family was hers now, Will most of all. She leaned into him, ready to traverse the rest of this trail at his side. There were plenty of things to worry over, but tonight she was going to enjoy her man, enjoy being a Bridger by law and enjoy the way she felt in a pretty dress.

She leaned in close to her husband's ear. "Did we ever talk about children?" She watched with delight as his ears turned pink, then she leaned in again. "I want a passel of them."

Dying to know what will happen when stoic, grumpy Ben agrees to a fake marriage with a desperate Ellen? Lasso your copy of *To Bluff a Bride* today to see what's next for the Bridger Brothers.

ALSO BY KATE CONDIE

Aster Ridge Ranch

Ticket to Anywhere

A Winter's Vow

A Cowboy's Vow

A Widow's Vow

A Bandit's Vow

A Secret Brother's Vow

A Christmas Vow

A Soldier's Vow

Want free content and more from Kate Condie? Sign up for her newsletter at

www.subscribepage.com/katecondienewsletter

or follow her on social media @authorkatecondie

ABOUT THE AUTHOR

Kate Condie is a speed talker from Oregon. Reading has been part of her life since childhood, where she devoured everything from mysteries, to classics, to nonfiction—and of course, romance. At first, her writing was purely journal format as she thought writing novels was for the lucky ones. She lives in Utah and spends her days surrounded by mountains with her favorite hunk, their four children and her laptop. In her free time she reads, tries to learn a host of new instruments, binge watches anything by BBC and tries to keep up with Lafayette as she sings the Hamilton soundtrack.

Made in United States
Troutdale, OR
01/03/2025

27553400R00170